THE ANGEL OF MERCY SERIES

THINGS NOT SEEN

BOOK NINE

AL LACY

Multnomah Publishers® *Sisters, Oregon*

THINGS NOT SEEN
© 1999 by ALJO PRODUCTIONS, INC.
published by Multnomah Publishers, Inc.

International Standard Book Number: 1-57673-413-7

Design by David Uttley
Cover illustration by Vittorio Dangelico

Scripture quotations are from *The Holy Bible,* King James Version

Multnomah is a trademark of Multnomah Publishers, Inc.,
and is registered in the U.S. Patent and Trademark Office.
The colophon is a trademark of Multnomah Publishers, Inc.

Printed in the United States of America

For information:
MULTNOMAH PUBLISHERS, INC.
Post Office Box 1720
Sisters, Oregon 97759

Library of Congress Cataloging-in-Publication Data
Lacy, Al.
    Things not seen/by Al Lacy.
        p. cm.—(Angel of mercy series: bk. 9)
    ISBN 1-57673-413-7 (alk. paper)
    I. Title.   II. Series: Lacy, Al. Angel of mercy series: bk. 9.
PS3562.A256T48 1999
813'.54—dc21   99-24570
                                                CIP

05 06 07 08 09 10 — 10 9 8 7 6 5 4 3 2

"Now faith is the substance of things hoped for, the evidence of things not seen."

HEBREWS 11:1

PROLOGUE

AMERICAN HISTORIANS HAVE properly dubbed Florence Nightingale (1820-1910) the "mother of modern nursing." Miss Nightingale made her impact as a loving, compassionate nurse during the Crimean War (1853-56) between Russia and the allied powers of England, France, Turkey, and Sardinia.

As a child in England, Miss Nightingale nursed ill and injured birds, dogs, cats, and other animals. She was known even then as a person of warmth and compassion. These traits became more prominent in her as she matured into adulthood, studied nursing, and went on to make an indelible mark in her chosen field of endeavor.

Florence Nightingale stands out in medical history because she knew the public expected nurses to be warm, caring human beings. When she developed into a trainer of nurses and a reformer of hospitals, she taught student nurses already in the profession that kindness, compassion, and heedfulness for patients and their families were integral parts of being a successful nurse.

In addition to the aforementioned traits, Miss Nightingale believed a nurse should also be well educated in her field to properly carry out her duties. Indeed, she pursued an intelligent and caring mission of service to humanity throughout her lifetime.

The intellectual acumen necessary to successfully practice professional nursing is rarely understood outside the realm of the medical profession.

In the minds of most people, Miss Nightingale's image was solely one of a mother figure bringing comfort to her patients. Few people know that she was also a renowned statistician who used epidemiological data to document the effectiveness of nursing practices. In 1860, the nurse who became a legend in the Crimean War, established a nursing school at St. Thomas's Hospital in London—the first of its kind in the world. In 1907, three years before she died, and by then a blind invalid, Miss Nightingale became the first woman to receive the British Order of Merit.

Since the days of Florence Nightingale, nurses have carried out medically delegated tasks. Successful nursing, however, involves working within a body of knowledge apart from medicine. The nurse, in carrying out her job, also diagnoses and treats human responses to present and potential health problems. With each individual she must make an assessment of how the patient is adapting to the effects of the illness. To do this, the nurse will seek to gain the patient's confidence so she can help relieve any burdens that threaten to impede genuine healing.

The successful nurse's investment in other people's lives is not without price. Often, the patients or their families will reject her well-meaning efforts and even test her mettle by exhibiting hostile behavior. Investment of self sometimes leads to heartache and emotional loss for the nurse. To deny herself this type of relationship so she can properly care for her patients is to miss the essence of nursing. Thus, the best of nurses must make themselves vulnerable to patients and their families.

In our angel of mercy, Breanna Baylor Brockman, we have such a woman. She is warm, compassionate, and intelligent. Breanna has learned that life's investment as a nurse has a price. And as the reader will.soon find out, she will be faced with that fact in *Things Not Seen*. But as always, our heroine is more than willing to pay whatever price she must to be a true angel of mercy.

1

⬆

WHEN DWIGHT MORELAND awakened, early light was seeping through the bedroom windows. He rolled over cautiously and looked at Pamela, trying not to wake her. She had experienced a bad night, and he wanted her to sleep as long as possible.

He picked up his clothes and tiptoed out of the room, quietly closing the door behind him. When he got to the kitchen he pulled on his pants and socks, then built a fire in the stove and put water on to heat. He moved out onto the back porch to get a glimpse of the sunrise.

The eastern sky was alive with pink fire, and a bank of fleecy clouds was turning a brilliant rose. As he watched, the pink of the sky began to fade as the day brightened. Before going back into the kitchen, he glanced to the west. The sky was still relatively dark in that direction, but he could make out the outline of the towering Rockies.

While he waited for the water on the stove to heat for his shave, Dwight went back to the bedroom and peeked in on his young wife. She was still sleeping, for which he was glad.

When he had finished shaving, he added wood to the stove to cook his breakfast, then pulled his boots on and slipped into his shirt. He returned to the back porch and gazed at the majestic Rocky Mountains. Even though it was midsummer, the towering peaks still had their white caps. They loomed before him, standing as they had for thousands of years, silent witnesses to the passing of time.

A year ago, newly wedded Dwight and Pamela Moreland had moved to Denver from the flat plains of Nebraska. They loved their new home and were excited about their soon-to-be-born first child, who was due in about two months. Dwight also enjoyed his job with the Rocky Mountain Construction Company, building roads and bridges.

He moved back inside and went about the kitchen as quietly as possible as he prepared breakfast. He was just finishing the cleanup job when he heard an expected knock at the front door. He hastened to open the door to his next-door neighbor.

Hilda Walz was in her late sixties. She and her husband, Tom, a retired railroad engineer, had been married forty-eight years.

"I hope Pamela had a good night this time," Hilda said as she entered the house.

Tom sighed as he gently closed the door behind her. "No, not really."

"More contractions?"

"Yes. But they're mild, and like yesterday, they're far apart."

"Are they constant?"

"No. She'll have them for about an hour, then not have any for three or four hours. She was awake till about four A.M."

"Probably false labor."

"That's what she says. She remembers her mother doing the same when her sister and brothers were on the way."

Hilda squinted at Dwight. "Is that a black eye you've got there, or are my eyes failing me?"

"Uh…well, yeah." Dwight's features tinted as he placed fingertips to his slightly puffy left eye.

"What happened?"

"Just a little disagreement with one of the guys on the job yesterday."

"I didn't notice it when you came home from work."

"It...uh...it didn't really start showing up till about bedtime."

Hilda shook her head. "Not your quick temper again, was it?"

Dwight rubbed the back of his neck. "Well, I guess if I'd held my temper, there wouldn't have been any blows swung."

The silver-haired woman patted his arm. "Honey, you've got to learn to control that temper."

"I know, I know. Pamela tells me the same thing...just like Mom used to."

"What about Pamela's back pain?"

"That's why she didn't get to sleep until about four. She just can't seem to get relief, no matter what position she tries. It really aggravates her."

Hilda made a clicking noise with her tongue. "Those pains had eased off by the time you got home from work yesterday. I was hoping she wouldn't have any more last night."

"Me, too," said Dwight, turning to pick up his lunch sack. "Well, I've got to go. Thank you again for coming to stay with her. This makes four days in a row. If she isn't better by tomorrow, I'll take her to Dr. Carroll."

"Try not to worry, Dwight, it's probably just false labor. But if it keeps up, she should definitely be checked. The back pain might stay with her all the way until the baby's born, but these mild contractions shouldn't be happening in her seventh month. I'll keep a sharp eye on her."

"Thank you." Dwight gave her a crooked smile. "Till you're better paid, at least."

Hilda chuckled. "You're not paying one red cent for this, young man. Look at all the times you've come over and helped Tom work on the house and the barn. Turn about is fair play."

As Tom took his hat off the hook by the door, Hilda said, "Just in case we should need you, are you still working on that bridge over the South Platte, up by Henderson City?"

"Mm-hmm. See you this evening."

When the door closed, Hilda shook her head and headed for the bedroom, saying in a half-whisper, "Dwight Moreland, you're such a nice young man. But you need to get a handle on that short-fuse temper."

She turned the doorknob quietly and pushed open the bedroom door a couple of inches. Pamela lay on her side, sleeping soundly. Hilda's lips moved in a whisper. "You sleep as long as you can, honey. Hilda's here to watch over you."

Back in the kitchen, Hilda glanced at the table and saw bread crumbs and a small puddle of coffee. "Men!" she huffed. "They're all alike! What they call clean, no self-respecting sow hog would tolerate!"

Moments later, as Hilda was finishing her own cleanup job on the cupboard, she heard a high-pitched wail. She dropped the wet cloth and hurried down the hall.

Pamela was tossing and turning on the bed, gritting her teeth; then she called out her husband's name.

Hilda leaned over her and took hold of her hand. "Honey, Dwight's gone to work. Is it real bad?"

Pamela stiffened, then opened her eyes and managed a slight smile. "Oh. Hi, Hilda." Her breath came in puffs from her exertion. "Yes. It's the contractions. I...I think maybe they're the real thing."

Hilda sat down on the edge of the bed. "Let's not panic, honey. Let's see what they do for a while. Back hurting?"

13

Pamela nodded. "Down low, as usual."

"I know. It's been forty-two years since I bore my last child, but I sure do remember the back pain."

Pamela's face twisted, and tears surfaced. "Oh, Hilda, I hope the baby isn't going to come now. It's too early!"

"Now, now, honey. Let's not borrow trouble. Are you hungry?"

"No."

"Thirsty?"

"Yes."

"I'll get you some water. Be right back."

Hilda returned shortly, and Pamela drained the cup.

"Do you want more?"

"No. Not right now. That's fine. Thank you."

Hilda pulled up a chair beside the bed and sat down. "If you get hungry, you just tell me. You need to eat so you can keep up your strength."

"Maybe in a little while," Pamela said. She groaned through clenched teeth and drew her knees up for a moment.

Hilda watched the young expectant mother carefully. Pamela was right. Most babies who come this early don't make it.

The older woman began to relax when Pamela was quiet for a time, then suddenly a cry escaped Pamela's lips.

Hilda stood up and gripped Pamela's hand. "Is it bad, honey?"

"Y-e-s...bad," Pamela said through gritted teeth. The baby pushed hard against her once more, and Pamela jerked, then stiffened, gasping, "Hurts, Hilda."

She stiffened again, her breaths coming in short, raspy gasps. When the pains finally eased, she said through dry lips, "Water, Hilda, please."

As Hilda helped her drink, she said, "Honey, I'm thinking

we'd better get you to the hospital. I think this labor is real. You hang on, and I'll run over and get Tom. He'll hitch up the horses, and we'll get you to town in a hurry."

At Mile High Hospital, receptionist Madge Landis was in conversation with orderly Dirk Jacobs when her eyes shifted to an elderly man hurrying through the front door. Dirk heard the man's hoarse breathing and pivoted around, then rushed toward him.

"Is there a problem, sir?" he asked.

The silver-haired man sucked hard for air, "My name is Tom Walz. My wife and I live on the west side of town. We have a neighbor lady who's about to give birth to her first baby. She's only in her seventh month. My wife's with her outside in our wagon. Dr. Matthew Carroll is her doctor."

"What's her name, sir?" Dirk asked.

"Pamela Moreland."

Dirk turned and said, "Madge, get Alex. Tell him to bring a cart. See if Dr. Carroll is available. If not, we need a doctor to deliver Mrs. Moreland's baby."

Madge nodded, and headed for the hallway as Tom Walz followed the husky orderly through the door.

Dr. Matthew Carroll's head came up when Madge Landis rushed through the open door of his office and skidded to a halt in front of his desk. "Dr. Carroll, Pamela Moreland was just brought in by a neighbor. She's in labor."

"But she's not due for another two months!"

"I know, Doctor. Dirk and Alex are wheeling her to the delivery room. She's in a lot of pain."

Rounding the desk, he paused. "Do you know where Breanna is?"

"Yes. I saw her go into room seven with Stefanie Langan. They're working on an elderly patient together."

"Please go get her. Breanna's delivered more babies in her traveling work than any nurse in this hospital, and I know she's handled lots of premature births. I want her with me."

"All right, Doctor," Madge said over her shoulder as she took off down the hall.

As Dr. Carroll approached the delivery room, he saw head nurse Mary Donelson holding the door while an orderly moved past her with an empty cart. As Carroll drew near, she said, "I assume you'll want Breanna to assist you."

"Yes, Mary," he said, without breaking stride. "I've already sent for her."

"Good. If you need more help, I'll get another nurse or stay myself."

"I'll let you know if I need more help," he said over his shoulder. "Thank you."

Dirk Jacobs was standing by Pamela Moreland, who lay on the delivery table. She was obviously in a great deal of pain. Carroll immediately took hold of her arm and squeezed it gently as he said to Dirk, "Who brought her in?"

"Neighbors. They've gone after her husband, but he's working several miles away. It'll be a while before he gets here."

Carroll nodded, then looked down at his patient. "Pamela, I have nurse Breanna Brockman on her way. She's the very best and quite experienced in delivering babies. She'll be at my side every minute to help. You try to relax while I get my hands washed."

Dirk leaned over Pamela and said, "You and the baby are in good hands, ma'am."

Pamela nodded, her face distorted by a grimace.

Dirk excused himself and stepped aside as Breanna rushed through the door.

She gave the orderly a quick smile and went to stand beside her brother-in-law. "I came as fast as I could."

"We've got us a seventh-month baby to deliver."

"Yes. Madge told me."

"Let's get washed up."

Breanna leaned over the young woman, whose face was beaded with sweat. "Mrs. Moreland, I'm Breanna Brockman. I'm going to help Dr. Carroll with your baby's delivery. And believe me, you've got the best doctor in the country."

Tension mounted as Dr. Matthew Carroll and nurse Breanna Brockman went to work. It took only minutes to discover they were in a serious struggle to bring about a successful delivery.

When a half hour had passed and the contractions were coming on top of one another, yet the baby had not begun to show signs of coming from the womb, doctor and nurse realized they were in a desperate situation.

It was a warm summer day, and though the windows of the delivery room were open, there was little air stirring. Perspiration poured down the faces of Matt and Breanna as they worked.

Pamela, too, was perspiring heavily. Breanna gave her continual encouragement, telling her what she could do to help them. Suddenly, Pamela stiffened and arched her neck, making a gagging sound. Her body began to jerk and spasm uncontrollably.

Breanna cupped Pamela's face in her hands and said, "Doctor! She's going into convulsion!"

Carroll raised his head and blinked against the sweat in his eyes. "The baby's breech, Breanna. You'll have to take over here. I know you've done these before."

Breanna took the doctor's place, and he went to Pamela's side to keep her from swallowing her tongue.

Dr. Carroll was intent on his task and was unaware that the baby had been brought forth until he heard Breanna emit a tiny whine, and he took a moment to look up. The baby was a deep blue color and lay limply in Breanna's hands. It was a girl.

"Is she all right, Breanna?"

Tears filled Breanna's eyes as she shook her head and said in a low tone, "She... she was breathing at first, but she died in my hands."

Pamela's convulsion was over, and she was semiconscious. The doctor watched Breanna carry the baby to a nearby bassinet and lay down the lifeless little form, covering it with a small blanket.

With tears still rolling down her cheeks, Breanna returned to the table to stand beside Dr. Carroll. Pamela Moreland was unresponsive to anything going on around her.

Matt led Breanna away from the table and said, "We both knew the baby's chances were slim, Breanna...even before we knew she would be breech. You're not blaming yourself, now, are you?"

Breanna shook her head. "No. When I saw how blue she was, I knew her little lungs simply weren't ready to leave her mother's womb. She would have died, even if you had delivered her."

"I'm glad to hear you say it because that is exactly so. Now let's clean Pamela up. I'd like for you to stay until she comes to and I tell her that the baby did not survive."

"Of course," Breanna said, wiping her tears. "You watch her, I'll do the cleaning up."

When Pamela came to and was clear-minded, Breanna stood beside Dr. Carroll as he told the young mother that her baby had died only seconds after birth. As Pamela wept, Breanna bent over her and said all she could to give her comfort. Once the mother's initial shock had subsided, Dr. Carroll explained about her convulsion, and that he was busy trying to save her life while Breanna did the delivery. He made it clear that the baby's premature birth was what brought on her death. She simply had not been ready to leave the womb.

Dr. Carroll took his patient's hand and said, "Pamela, if I had been free to do the delivery, your baby still would have died. Babies in the womb become stronger during those last eight weeks, and they gain a great deal of their birth weight. Those last few weeks in the womb are also essential to build strength in the lungs so the baby can breathe on its own. Your little girl was born too early and didn't have that opportunity."

"I understand, Doctor," Pamela said weakly. She looked up at Breanna. "I know you did all you could, ma'am. Thank you for doing your very best to save her."

Breanna leaned down and kissed Pamela's forehead.

The door opened and Stefanie Langan came in. As she approached the table where Pamela lay, she glanced at the bassinet and saw the blanket that covered the little body.

"It's a girl," said Dr. Carroll. "She didn't make it."

"Oh," Stefanie said softly. "I wanted to see if there was anything I could do to help. I'm so sorry."

Dr. Carroll asked Stefanie to stay with Pamela until he sent the orderlies to take her to her room.

About an hour later, receptionist Madge Landis looked up from her desk to see a man rush through the door. He stopped in front of her and said, "Ma'am, I'm Dwight Moreland. My wife was brought in about three hours ago to deliver our baby. Do you know if the baby's been born?"

Madge swallowed hard. "Mrs. Moreland is in room nineteen, sir. When you reach the hall, turn left."

Dwight ran down the hall, his head swiveling from side to side as he checked the room numbers.

When he came to room nineteen, the door was closed. Without breaking stride, he shoved it open to find Pamela weeping while nurse Stefanie Langan stood over her. Stefanie said to Pamela, "This must be Dwight."

The sight of her husband caused Pamela to break into sobs. Dwight rushed to her side and cupped her face in his hands. "Honey, are you all right? Where's the baby? Is it a boy or a girl?"

"The baby's dead, Dwight. It's a girl, but she's dead."

Dwight turned to Stefanie. "What happened?"

"It couldn't be avoided," said Stefanie. "She was born too early."

Dwight's features reddened. "Was Dr. Carroll in charge of the delivery?"

"Yes."

"I want to talk to him. Where is he?"

"I don't know," said Stefanie. "Go down the hall the other way until you come to the nurses' station. Ask the nurses there. They'll know where he is."

Dwight bent over and held Pamela close for a long moment, telling her he was sorry about the baby. When he released her, he said, "I'll be back after I talk to Dr. Carroll, honey."

The grieving father hurried down the hall. When he

reached the nurses' station, the oldest of the three nurses said, "May I help you, sir?"

"I'm Dwight Moreland. My baby died in delivery. I want to talk to Dr. Carroll."

"Dr. Carroll is doing emergency surgery at the moment, Mr. Moreland. I'm head nurse, Mary Donelson. I'll take you to your wife's room, and—"

"I've already been there, ma'am. I want to know what happened...why my baby died. I know premature babies don't always live, but I'd like to know exactly why my baby died. Do you have any idea how soon I can talk to Dr. Carroll?"

"There's no way to tell. Would it help if you could talk to the nurse who assisted him?"

"Yes, it would."

"All right. Come and sit down in my office, and I'll find nurse Breanna Brockman for you."

Dwight entered Mary's office but could only pace the floor and sleeve away tears while he waited for the nurse.

When Mary came back, there was a blonde woman with her. "Mr. Moreland," Mary said, "this is Mrs. Brockman. She can answer any questions you have."

Breanna moved up to him. "Mr. Moreland, please accept my deepest sympathy in your loss. I know you are hurting, but you must be thankful that Pamela is still with us. We came close to losing her, too."

"What? She didn't tell me that."

"Come, sit down," said Breanna. "I'll explain exactly what happened. If you have questions, I'll try to answer them for you."

A shaky Dwight Moreland sat down on a straight-backed wooden chair, and Breanna sat on an identical one in front of him. Mary circled her desk and sat down behind it, not wanting to leave Breanna alone with the distraught man.

Dwight listened as Breanna carefully told the story, giving every detail. When he heard her say that she had actually delivered the baby while the doctor was laboring over Pamela in the midst of her convulsion, his whole body stiffened.

"The baby was a deep blue color, Mr. Moreland," said Breanna. "She only lived a few seconds after I brought her forth. Her lungs had not developed enough for her to breathe outside the womb. I—"

"Wait a minute!" cut in Dwight, his face flushed. "You're telling me that you delivered my daughter? You're not a doctor! You're only a nurse! Why didn't Dr. Carroll deliver her?"

Flustered by the man's reaction, Breanna said, "I just explained it, sir. Your wife could very well have died while having the convulsion. Dr. Carroll saved her life. He could hardly tend to her and deliver the baby, too."

Dwight's eyes riveted Breanna, the pale hazel contrasting with the flush of his face. "Why wasn't another doctor called in?" he raged. "Nurses aren't qualified to handle what you did! It's your fault my baby died!"

Breanna stood up. Her lips quivered as she said levelly, "Mr. Moreland, I did everything possible to save the baby's life. Even Dr. Carroll said the baby's death was not my fault. He said if he had undertaken to deliver her, she still would have died. And as for calling in another doctor, we didn't have time to leave mother or baby. Every second counted."

Dwight jumped up from the chair and swung a fist through the air. "A lot of good every second did with your blundering! You should never have been entrusted with bringing our baby into the world! Now she's dead, and it's all your fault!"

Breanna's face pinched and she struggled to hold back tears. She was trying to find her voice when Mary Donelson stepped up to him and said, "Mr. Moreland, I know you're upset, understandably so, because your baby died at birth. But you have no cause and no right to speak to Breanna this way. As she told you, Dr. Carroll said the baby would have died even if he had delivered her. Now, you just calm down."

"Calm down?" he blared. "My baby's dead, isn't she? And who was given the job of delivering her? This woman! She is not a doctor and had no business doing it!"

"What's going on here?" came the deep voice of Dirk Jacobs from the doorway.

"This is Mrs. Moreland's husband," spoke up Mary. "He's blaming Breanna for the baby's death."

A scowl captured Dirk's square face. "How can he do that? Everybody on duty in this hospital knows it wasn't Breanna's fault. The baby was simply born too early."

Dwight stomped up to the man who stood a head taller than himself. "Oh yeah? What do you know about it? You're just a cart pusher!"

Dirk saw the lines of inward pain in Breanna's face. Inching closer to the angry man, he said, "You're out of line, mister! Now you get quiet!"

Dwight's jaw jutted and the fire of his temper grew hotter. "Don't tell me what I am, pal! And I don't have to get quiet!" As he spoke, he stabbed Dirk's chest with stiff fingers. "My baby's dead, and this woman is to blame!"

Dirk's powerful right hand caught Dwight's fingers in a grip of steel. Squeezing hard enough to make him suck air through his teeth, Dirk said, "Now, you calm down. Breanna is more experienced at delivering babies than any nurse in this hospital. And we will all speak for her ability."

Dwight winced in pain and said, "But...she...isn't a doctor, and she...shouldn't have been...delivering...my baby."

Dirk squeezed harder. "Just calm down, I said. Why don't you keep your judgment to yourself till you can talk to Dr. Carroll?"

Mary and Breanna saw Matt Carroll angling across the hall from the nurses' station. Two nurses had alerted him as he came out of the surgical ward.

"He can talk to me right now, Dirk," said Carroll, drawing up. "Dwight, the nurses have overheard what's been said in here, and you must lay hold on your temper. I understand you're accusing Nurse Brockman, saying it was her fault your baby died at birth. Is this correct?"

Dirk still held Dwight's fingers in a steel grip. Through gritted teeth, Dwight said, "Would you make this ape let go of me?"

"You gonna settle down and act decent?" Dirk said.

Dwight nodded.

When Dirk released him, Dwight rubbed his fingers.

"Mr. Moreland," Carroll said, "there was absolutely no mishandling of the delivery by Nurse Brockman...and for you to accuse her of it is dead wrong. The baby died because she came too early. Her lungs were not developed enough to live outside the womb. Now, you've got to understand that and act appropriately."

"Okay, okay," said Dwight, still showing temper. "I'm going to Pamela. She needs me." With that, he shoved his way between the doctor and the orderly, paused long enough to give Breanna an accusing look, then hurried down the hall.

Breanna covered her face with her hands and trembled as she wept.

"Don't let him get to you, little sis," Matt said as he laid a tender hand on her shoulder. "He'll get over it when he has time to cool down. Nothing's changed. You are not to blame for the baby's death."

Breanna took her hands from her face and blinked against the tears. "Thank you," she said quietly.

Matt squeezed her shoulder. "You're the best, Breanna. They don't come any better than you."

"We all feel that way, honey," said Mary.

"We sure do," said one of the nurses standing at the office door.

"And if it means anything, coming from a cart pusher," Dirk said with a chuckle, "I believe you're the best, too."

Breanna smiled. "Cart pushers are very important people around here. It means plenty coming from you."

Mary gave her a quick squeeze and said, "Honey, I'm not telling you anything you don't know, but I'll say it anyhow. What you just experienced is one of the prices you have to pay for being a nurse."

Breanna thumbed more tears from her cheeks. "I know. But sometimes it gets pretty tough."

"But it's still worth it, isn't it?" asked her brother-in-law, Dr. Carroll.

"Of course," she said, then drew a deep breath. "Well, we have patients who need us. Let's get back to them."

2

A HOT BREEZE BLEW across the eastern plains of Colorado. Outlaws Nick Thatcher and Fred Dodge slitted their eyes against the white glare of the afternoon sun as they drew near the trading post about a mile west of the small, dusty town called Byers.

The horses snorted as they smelled water and bobbed their heads. Thatcher and Dodge were both slender men and stood just under six feet. Only in their early thirties, they looked ten years older, their faces weathered like saddle leather. The years of robbing, killing, and running from the law had hardened their features and bent their mouths into a permanently sardonic look.

As they drew near the post, they glanced at the sign above the door:

High Plains Trading Post
C. D. Pierce, Prop.

Dodge ran his gaze over the front of the sun-bleached building and said, "Looks like we're showin' up at the right time. No customers at the moment."

"Makes it cleaner," grunted Thatcher. "Let's water the horses first."

There was a large stock tank next to the trading post, and the horses were already straining against the reins, wanting to get to the water.

Moments later, with water dripping from their horses' muzzles, the outlaws wrapped the reins loosely around the hitch rail and headed for the door, which stood open to allow as much breeze as possible to flow through to the open windows on three sides.

Thatcher whispered, "Let's see what kind of a contribution Mr. C. D. Pierce can make to the Thatcher-Dodge fund today."

Dodge snickered, and they stepped inside.

The post was well equipped with food, clothing, hats, boots, belts, ammunition, holsters, gunbelts, saddle gear, and various other items necessary for life in the West.

The proprietor was stocking the ammunition shelf near the counter when he heard the sound of booted feet on the wooden floor. He didn't recognize the men, but that wasn't unusual; about half of Pierce's business was from people passing through the area. At age fifty-five, Pierce had been around long enough to know troublemakers when he saw them. Forcing a smile, he said, "Good afternoon, gentlemen," and made his way behind the counter.

Neither sour-faced man returned his greeting.

"May I help you find something?" Pierce asked, glancing furtively at the butt of the Colt .44 revolver that lay within reach on the shelf under the counter.

Both men whipped their guns out in unison, and Thatcher said gruffly, "Sure can, Pops. Help us to find the money in that cash drawer."

Pierce's heart began pounding. The hair on the back of his neck bristled. "I…I d-don't have m-much in the d-drawer," he stammered. "I…I just m-made a bank d-deposit this m-morning."

Dodge snapped his gun's hammer back, lining the muzzle on Pierce's chest.

"Well, whatever you've got is what we want, Pops. Just stuff it in one of those paper bags over there. And don't try any tricks."

There was a thin thread of ugliness in Thatcher's voice as he said, "That is, if you want to live."

Pierce picked up one of the bags, then opened the cash drawer. Thatcher raised up on his tiptoes to get a look inside the drawer. "He wasn't kidding, Fred. Ain't much there."

"He may be lyin' about that bank deposit, Nick. Might have a safe around here somewhere."

"I have no safe," said Pierce, stuffing the money into the bag. "And I wasn't lying. I made a deposit at the bank this morning."

"All right, all right," grunted Dodge, turning to glance out the door. "Hurry up."

With trembling hands, Pierce folded the top of the paper bag and handed it to Dodge.

A cryptic grin spread across Thatcher's cruel lips. "Thanks, Pops," he said and brought the gun barrel around in a fierce arc, slamming it against the man's head.

Pierce collapsed in a heap behind the counter.

"You hit him hard enough, Nick?" Dodge asked.

Thatcher paused, looked over the counter at the crumpled form, and chuckled. "Yeah. He's out cold."

"Okay. Let's pick up a few things before we go."

C. D. Pierce lay quietly on the floor. He was stunned, but

still conscious. He listened as the two outlaws moved to the food section of the post, laughing as they stuffed their pockets with items. He raised up enough to close his fingers around the butt of the .44 and hold it close to his chest. He eased back the hammer, using their laughter to cover the sound.

"Okay, Fred," said Thatcher, "let's get outta here before somebody shows up."

Pierce heard their rapid footsteps move toward the door. He raised up behind the counter and drew a shaky bead on Dodge then dropped the hammer. The gun roared and Fred Dodge howled as the slug tore through his right thigh. Thatcher wheeled with a curse on his lips and brought his gun to bear on Pierce, who was thumbing his hammer back for a second shot.

The slug slammed Pierce in the chest, the impact of it driving him against the shelves behind the counter. The Colt slipped from his fingers, and he fell to the floor.

Thatcher holstered his gun and picked up the sack of money, then helped his partner up. Dodge gritted his teeth as he looked down at his leg. "The b-bullet went clear through, Nick."

"C'mon," said Thatcher. "Let's get outta here!"

Dodge was breathing in short gasps as his partner helped him toward his horse.

"You can ride, can'tcha?" Thatcher asked.

"I…think so," Dodge said.

"You got to." Thatcher hoisted Dodge into the saddle, steadied him, then went to his own horse. While he was jamming the money sack in a saddlebag, he heard a distant rattle and turned toward the west to see a wagon coming along the road, throwing up small clouds of dust. He vaulted into the saddle and said, "Let's go!"

29

Moments later, farmer Josh Camden watched the two riders head due east as he angled his wagon toward the trading post and pulled rein. He climbed down from the wagon seat and glanced eastward again, saying, "That one fella sure looked like he was hurt." He looked back toward the trading post and saw red spots on the ground.

"It's blood, all right." Camden hurried inside and paused where the blood was pooled just inside the door. He looked around and called out, "C. D.! You in here?"

When no one answered, Camden rushed to the counter and saw Pierce lying on the floor. Rounding the counter, he knelt beside the wounded proprietor.

Pierce was breathing raggedly, his face pallid. Blood covered the front of his shirt and also trickled from the side of his mouth. He looked up at Camden with glazed eyes.

"C. D., was it those two men who left here a few minutes ago?"

"Yeah."

"I'll get you to Doc Grayson."

Pierce moved his head slowly from right to left. "No time, Josh. I'm not…going…to make it. They…called each other Nick…and Fred. Took…money…I—"

Pierce's body went limp and his head fell to the side.

"Aw, C. D.," moaned Camden. "You've been so good to so many people. Why should you have to die at the hands of vile men like that? I hope the wounded one dies, too. And I hope they catch the other one and hang him."

Byers's town marshal, Ned Gonser, was standing in front of his office in conversation with two townsmen when he noticed a wagon veering toward him on the broad street. He recognized Josh Camden, whose face looked drawn and pale.

Pulling rein, Camden brought the wagon to a halt and said, "Marshal, somebody killed C. D. Pierce."

"What? C. D.?"

"Yep. I've got his body here in the wagon."

The marshal and two townsmen moved to the back of the wagon, where Camden had covered the body with a blanket.

Gonser lifted the blanket, set his eyes on the stonelike face of the dead man, then his eyes trailed down to the bullet hole. "Josh," he said grimly, "tell me about it."

After telling the marshal how he saw the two riders leaving the trading post as he drew near, and that one of them was wounded, a man in the crowd stepped up and said, "Excuse me, Marshal…"

Gonser turned from Camden. "Yes, Jim?"

"I was comin' into town from my place, and I met up with two riders. One of 'em was bent over in the saddle, and they weren't movin' very fast. I thought I saw blood on the one bent over."

"Thank you, Jim," said the marshal.

"One more thing, Marshal," said Josh Camden. "Just before C. D. died, he told me the outlaws called each other 'Nick' and 'Fred.'"

Gonser rubbed his chin pensively. "Nick and Fred. I'll see what I can find in my wanted posters."

Deputy U.S. Marshal Billy Martin, who worked the desk at the Denver U.S. Marshal's Office, heard the muffled voices of Chief Brockman and Deputy Stuart Whalen; then Brockman's office door opened, and the two men came out.

Chief Brockman sighed as he said, "I wish I could send another deputy with you, Stu, but as you know, we're still running shorthanded."

"I understand, sir. I assure you, I'll do as you say. When I locate those killers, I'll get help from the local law before I close in on them."

"I appreciate that," said the tall man with the twin jagged scars on his right cheek. "I want you back alive and in one piece."

"I'll do my best," grinned Whalen, as he moved past the desk. "See you later, Billy."

"Take care, Stu," Billy Martin said.

Whalen paused at the open door and looked back. "And I'll do my best to have those killers with me, sir...dead or alive."

Brockman nodded and waved. When the door closed, Martin said, "Chief, a telegram came for you a few minutes ago. I didn't want to disturb you." He handed over the yellow Western Union envelope.

Brockman opened the envelope and read the telegram. Raising his eyebrows, he said, "Nick Thatcher and Fred Dodge."

"Somebody spot those two, Chief?"

"Mm-hmm. Out in Byers. But only after they robbed and murdered the proprietor of the trading post. Marshal Gonser says the proprietor wounded one of them in the leg while they were leaving the post, then he died. But not before he identified them. They were last seen heading east."

"Who are you going to send after them, Chief?"

Brockman shook his head. "Don't know. Unless somebody who's on assignment returns soon, it looks like I'll go after them myself."

✤

At sundown, Thatcher and Dodge drew up to the edge of a thicket-lined gully and looked down its steep slope. "How about down here?" said Thatcher. "Looks like a good place to hide."

Dodge was bent over the saddle horn, clutching his bleeding thigh. Pain, like a red-hot knife, shot down his wounded leg. Without raising his head, he said through clenched teeth, "Whatever…you say. I…just need…to get off of this…horse. We…we've gotta do somethin' to…stop this bleedin', or I'm gonna bleed to death."

Two days after their baby's death, Dwight Moreland was sitting beside Pamela in the hospital room, holding her hand. His face was a mask of emotion.

"Dwight, you mustn't go on this way," Pamela said in a weak voice. "I'm very sorry that our baby died, and having carried her in my womb, I have to say that I miss her even more than you do. But this grudge you're nursing toward Mrs. Brockman is uncalled for, and you know it. You need to face the fact that there was nothing she did, or left undone, that caused our little girl to die."

"Oh yeah? Do you know why Carroll's saying that?"

"Because it's true, that's why."

Neither of them noticed that Dr. Matt Carroll had entered the room.

"No!" Dwight said, shaking his head. "I found out something, Pamela. The Brockman woman is Carroll's sister-in-law. He's just covering for her poor handling of the baby's delivery. It's her fault that our baby died, all right."

Dwight's face flushed when Dr. Carroll moved up to the bed, and he realized the doctor had heard what he'd just said.

Matt Carroll spoke with a definite edge to his voice. "You're wrong, Dwight. Totally wrong. I'm not covering for anybody. I came in to check on Pamela, but I can see there's something else I need to deal with. I'll check her first, then we'll have another talk."

Dwight felt Pamela's eyes on him as he left the chair and stepped back from the bed while the doctor made his examination.

When Carroll was finished, he looked down at Pamela and said, "You are doing quite well for what you've been through, Pamela. I'm thankful for that."

"Me, too," she said with a weak smile.

Stepping closer, Dwight said, "Me, too."

Carroll sighed. "Now, Dwight, I'm going to go over the picture for you again."

Carroll slowly and carefully explained to Dwight that most babies who deliver in the mother's seventh month of pregnancy are not developed sufficiently to live. "Their lungs, Dwight," he said, "are not ready to breathe air yet, and their hearts are not strong enough to function outside the mother's womb. I'm hoping that someday medical science will come up with some kind of apparatus that can duplicate the uniform conditions of temperature and humidity in the womb for babies who are born short of their ninth month. If we had such an invention now, your baby might well have lived."

Dwight stood, hands in pockets, looking at the floor.

"Are you listening to him, honey?" Pamela said.

Dwight looked at his wife and nodded silently, then glanced at Carroll and dropped his eyes to the floor.

"Dwight," Carroll said, "three other doctors on the hospital staff examined your baby girl's body with me. We all agreed that no matter who had delivered her, she could not possibly have lived. If you want to talk to the other doctors, I'll give you their names. You can talk to them out of my presence."

Dwight remained silent. By this time, his head was hanging low. When he raised it, there were tears in his eyes. His lips quivered as he said, "Doctor...I...I'm sorry. I...was very tough on Nurse Brockman. I owe her an apology. I realize now that she did everything she could to save my little girl's life. I...I have a bad temper, and I let it get the best of me just because I was upset over the baby's death. I need to ask Nurse Brockman's forgiveness. Do you think she'll forgive me?"

Matt Carroll nodded, and the severity of his expression lightened as he said, "Breanna is a born-again Christian, Dwight. She knows God's forgiveness for her sins against Him; therefore, I have no doubt she will forgive you."

Both Dwight and Pamela blinked at his statement.

Looking from one to the other, Carroll said, "Am I talking about something that is strange to your ears?"

"I've heard the term 'born again,' Doctor," said Pamela, "but I don't know what it means. I know it has something to do with forgiveness of sins."

Obviously put off balance by Carroll's mention of Breanna being a born-again Christian, Dwight said, "Ever since my childhood, I've heard people speak of how God forgave them for their sins, but I've never known just what they meant."

Carroll stepped closer to Dwight, who stood beside Pamela's bed. "Let me ask you something, Dwight."

"Yes, sir?"

"Are you a sinner?"

Dwight's features tinted. "I believe I've demonstrated that I am by the way I treated Mrs. Brockman."

"Mm-hmm. But what about the way you've treated God? Have you sinned against Him?"

"Countless times, sir."

"What *is* sin, Dwight?"

"Well, it's…ah…disobeying God. Ah…doing the things He has told us in the Bible we shouldn't do."

"Right. And how about refusing to do the things He has told us to do?"

"Yes, sir. I'm guilty on both counts."

Carroll looked at Pamela. "How about you, Pamela?"

"Just as guilty as my husband, Doctor. Maybe in different ways, but I've sinned against God many, many times."

"I appreciate your honesty. Both of you. Dwight, you want to seek out Breanna and ask her forgiveness for how you've treated her. How about God? Have you ever asked His forgiveness for the way you've treated Him?"

Dwight shook his head slowly. "No, sir."

"Are you aware that if you die unforgiven, the Bible says you will go to hell?"

"I've heard that, sir. But I've never felt I did anything bad enough that God wouldn't let me into heaven."

"How about causing God's only begotten Son to be nailed to the cross?"

Dwight looked at him blankly. "What?"

"You stay right here. I'm going to my office to get my Bible. I'll show you right in God's Word what I'm talking about."

While the doctor was out of the room, Dwight said, "This is something my paternal grandparents used to talk about, honey. I remember them bringing it up just about every time we saw them when I was a youngster, but we didn't see them often enough that I could ever make sense of it."

"I've thought a lot about it, myself," said Pamela. "Just never got serious about looking into it."

Carroll came back into the room, pulled up a chair, and sat down next to Dwight. "Let me show you what I was talking about when I intimated that you had caused the Lord Jesus Christ to go to the cross."

Opening the Bible and flipping pages, he stopped in Hebrews, chapter 2. "Listen to this. 'But we see Jesus, who was made a little lower than the angels for the suffering of death, crowned with glory and honour; that he, by the grace of God, should taste death for every man.' Now, Dwight…Pamela…who did Jesus die for?"

"Every human being," said Pamela.

"Yes," agreed Dwight. "He died for everybody."

"That's right. Romans 3:23 says, 'For all have sinned, and come short of the glory of God.' Who does *all* take in?"

"Every human being," came Pamela's reply.

"So far, so good," said Carroll, going to the Old Testament and stopping in Isaiah, chapter 53. "This is prophecy about Jesus dying on the cross. 'But he was wounded for our transgressions, he was bruised for our iniquities…' Whose sins was Jesus wounded and bruised for at Calvary?"

"Ours," said Dwight.

"Correct. My sins, your sins, Pamela's sins. The sins of all mankind."

Both of the Morelands were listening intently.

"Now let me read on. 'All we like sheep have gone astray; we have turned every one to his own way; and the LORD hath laid on him the iniquity of us all.' Tell me what that's saying, Dwight."

Dwight cleared his throat. "Well, Doctor, it's saying that

the whole human race has gone astray. We've turned away from God. And God laid the sins of all of us on Jesus when He was on the cross."

"How about it, Pamela?" asked Carroll. "Is that what it's saying?"

"Yes, Doctor."

"Then every one of us is a guilty sinner who *by our sins* caused Jesus to have to be crucified so we could have a way of salvation and forgiveness."

"I see what you mean now, Doctor," said Dwight. "I caused Jesus to go to the cross because of my sins."

"That's it, Dwight. Forgiveness and salvation come only one way—repentance of sin and faith in Jesus Christ to save you."

Carroll showed them verses on repentance and faith, explaining that true repentance of sin and true faith in Jesus Christ will bring about salvation.

"To sum it up," said Carroll, "the gospel is simply that Jesus died a blood-shedding death on the cross, was buried, and rose again the third day. He is alive, looking down on you from heaven at this moment, and desiring to give you forgiveness and salvation."

"That's what I want," said Dwight. "I sure want Mrs. Brockman's forgiveness, but more than anything, I want God's forgiveness."

"Me, too," said Pamela, brushing tears from her cheeks. "What do we do now?"

"It's quite simple," replied Carroll. "Romans 10:13 says, 'For whosoever shall call upon the name of the Lord shall be saved.'"

"Will you help me?" asked Dwight. "Prayer is something...I...well, that I'm not experienced in."

38

"Neither am I," said Pamela. "Will you help me, Doctor? I want to be saved, too."

3

AT DAWN, NICK THATCHER awakened to find his partner sitting up with his back against a small tree. Fred's eyes were closed and his teeth clenched, giving evidence to the pain he was suffering.

The night before, Thatcher had made a tourniquet with a bandanna. He glanced at his partner's leg and then sat up. "How is it, Fred?" he asked.

"Still hurts like fire, but it ain't bleedin' like it did."

"But can you ride?"

"Not very far, I'm afraid. I'm sure ridin' will start the bleedin' again."

"There's a town called Agate a few miles east. I'm takin' you to the doctor there. You need that leg sewed up."

"I won't argue with that. He can give me somethin' to ease this pain, too."

Dr. William Liddell was bent over the desk in his office, going over a patient's chart with his nurse when the door opened and two rough-looking men came in. Doctor and nurse looked up to see that one man had a leg wound.

"Elsa," whispered Liddell, "it's them! When I take them

40

into the back room, you go get Marshal Dixon!"

Elsa nodded.

"Doc," said Thatcher, "my pal, here, took a bullet through his leg. Accident. I was shootin' at a rabbit for our supper last night and hit him instead. He's losing blood."

"All right," said Liddell. "Come on back to the examining room. We'll get him fixed up."

As they followed the doctor toward the rear door, Thatcher took one look at the fear on the nurse's face and whipped out his gun and snapped back the hammer. "You come back here with us, lady."

"Do what he says, Elsa," said the doctor.

"Good advice, Doc," said Thatcher. "Neither of you give us any trouble, nobody'll get hurt. Let's get my pal taken care of."

"But what if somebody comes in?" Elsa asked.

"You got one of them signs that say the doc ain't here, don'tcha?"

"Yes, but what about the patients who have appointments?"

"They'll just have to come back later. Put the sign up and lock the door."

Doctor and nurse worked together for nearly an hour, stitching up both sides of Fred Dodge's leg. When they were done, the doctor said, "Mister, I'm advising you not to try riding for at least a week."

A menacing look crossed Thatcher's face. "Are you sayin' you didn't stitch him up very good, Doc?"

"Not at all. I did the best I could. What I'm saying is that he needs plenty of rest."

"No time for that. We gotta keep movin'. But before we go, you two have gotta be tied up and gagged."

"I have patients who need me," protested Liddell.

"Well, there's another way to keep you from lettin' your

town marshal know we were here," Thatcher said. "I could fix you up so's you'd both need the undertaker when they find you."

Elsa's face lost color. "Oh, please don't kill us!" she pleaded.

Thatcher looked at Liddell. "How about it, Doc? Bound and gagged or ready for the undertaker?"

Moments later, as the outlaws rode away, Dodge said, "I don't know, Nick. Maybe we should've done 'em in. Somebody's gonna find 'em before the day's out. That means the law will know which way we're headed."

"The law will know that even if they found the doc and his nurse dead. We're east of Byers, ain't we?"

"Well, yeah."

"What we've got to do, ol' pal, is ride real hard. My friends in Kansas will hide us from the law once we get there."

The two outlaws had ridden hard for about a half hour when Dodge passed out and fell from the saddle. Thatcher checked his leg, but the fall had not torn open the wound. When Dodge regained consciousness, Thatcher put him back in the saddle, and they rode slowly till they came to a small brook.

While the horses were drinking and Thatcher was filling their canteens, Dodge stood, favoring his wounded leg, and looked behind them to the west. He squinted against the sun's glare and kept his gaze in that direction.

"Whatcha lookin' at, Fred?" Thatcher said.

Shading his eyes with his hand, Dodge said, "I think there's a lone rider comin' our way. Could be some tin star."

"I'll get my binoculars," said Thatcher, hanging the canteens on the saddle horns.

Thatcher pulled the binoculars from a saddlebag and moved up beside his partner. Squinting into the distance, he said, "Where?"

Dodge pointed due west across the sun-bleached prairie. "There. Near that clump of trees."

Putting the binoculars to his eyes, Thatcher turned the focus wheel, studied the moving object for a moment, and said, "Rider, all right. Looks like he's wearin' black shirt, pants, and hat. Horse is black. And—"

"And what?"

"Just a minute. I think I saw—"

"Saw what?"

"Just hold on. I want to be sure."

"Okay," said Dodge impatiently, "so you saw somethin'. What'd you think you saw?"

"Uh-huh," Thatcher said, still peering through the glasses. "Just as I thought. The sun's reflectin' off a badge on his shirt. We got a lawman on our trail, ol' pard."

"Then we'd better ride."

"Yeah. We gotta shake him. Cut across country."

In the saddle once again, Nick Thatcher and Fred Dodge rode hard, veered away from the road, and finally dropped down into a low spot. Dodge called for Thatcher to stop, saying he needed to rest.

They drew rein, and Thatcher said, "Fred, we can't stay here very long. We gotta keep movin'. That tin star might be a good tracker. When we left the road, we left tracks. We've got to ride on grassy ground so we don't leave no tracks."

"Okay," Dodge said, gasping. He touched his bandaged wound. "I'll just have to bear it. Let's go on."

The two outlaws had stopped several times for Dodge to rest by the time the sun went down. When they dismounted in a deep draw some three or four miles north of the road, Thatcher used his binoculars to scan their back trail. There was no sign of the rider on the black horse. They ate some of the food they had stolen from the trading post at Byers and bedded down for the night.

At sunrise, Thatcher took another look westward through the binoculars and gasped.

"What's the matter?" Dodge said as he limped toward his horse, carrying his bedroll.

"He's still comin', but he's closer than ever. We gotta ride hard, *now!*"

Having to bypass what breakfast they might have eaten, the two outlaws mounted and put their horses to a gallop. They had gone about five miles when Thatcher's horse stepped in a prairie dog hole, threw its rider head over heels, and collapsed with a broken foreleg. Thatcher left the horse in pain and climbed aboard Dodge's horse with him. They galloped due east as fast as the overloaded horse could carry them.

In spite of Dodge's leg and in spite of the labored breathing of the horse, they pushed on without taking time to stop. It was midafternoon when Dodge's horse slowed, though Fred was lashing it with the tips of the reins, and it finally collapsed beneath their weight, hitting the ground hard.

The sudden jolt shot pain through Dodge's wounded leg, and it took a few minutes for Thatcher to get him on his feet. They were on open prairie with no sign of low spots anywhere around and no farms or ranches where they might take refuge.

While the poor animal lay breathing hard, with its eyes rolled back in its head, Thatcher looked westward through his binoculars. After studying the horizon carefully for several minutes, he said, "Don't see him, Fred. Looks like we lost him."

"That's good. So what do we do now? This poor critter's done for, which means we're afoot. And I'm in no shape to walk very far."

Thatcher thought on it for a few seconds. "The road's only a couple miles or so south. We'll flag down the first farmer or rancher who comes by in a wagon and get us a ride into Burlington, which is the next town. Can you make it to the road, you think?"

"Guess I have to. But I'll have to walk slow."

As Thatcher and Dodge made their way toward the road, Thatcher kept looking westward through his binoculars. "Don't see that lawman, Fred," he said. "He must've lost our trail."

"Well," panted Dodge, "that's what we were shootin' for, wasn't it?"

"Guess we outsmarted him. Some of those tin badges are really stupid."

Soon the road came into view. "Tell you what," said Thatcher, "we get that ride into town, we'll steal us a couple of good horses. Even ridin' slow we can make it to Kansas by about noon tomorrow."

"Sounds good to me. Let's go."

By the time they reached the road, Dodge was in a great deal of pain. With Thatcher's help, he eased down on the grass at the side of the road, let out a sigh, and said, "Whew! I'm really hurtin', Nick."

Running his gaze in both directions, Thatcher said, "Burlington's still some thirty miles or so. We need to keep movin' till somebody comes along. I'll help you, but the quicker we get to town, the quicker we can steal some horses and ride. No tellin' when somebody'll show up on this road."

"All right. Just give me a few minutes."

Ten minutes later, the outlaws were making their way along the road, with Thatcher half-carrying his partner. The sun began its descent toward the western horizon, and still no one had come along.

Through clenched teeth, Dodge said, "Don't nobody ever travel this road?"

"Not too often, I guess."

When the sun had dropped from view, Dodge said, "We'll have to find a spot to spend the night, Nick. I can't go on much longer."

"Yeah. Maybe we can make that ravine up there on the right. It's only a couple hundred yards."

"Okay. Let's head for it."

Suddenly there was a sound of pounding hooves and the rattle of a vehicle behind them.

"Hey, Nick, look! A stagecoach!"

The coach was about a half-mile behind them.

"Great!" Thatcher exclaimed. "Now, listen! We'll flag down the stage and tell the driver we were attacked by Indians. The Indians shot you in the leg and took our horses. Got it?"

"Yeah. But what if they notice the blood on my pants is all dried up?"

"They ain't gonna pay that much attention."

"But what if there ain't no room for us on the stage?"

"C'mon, now, Freddie. Who'd turn away a wounded man? Somebody can ride up on the rack if need be."

As the stage drew near, Thatcher held Dodge up with one arm and waved the other to draw the driver's attention. They saw the shotgunner point to them and say something to the driver, who pulled rein. The stage came to a stop just behind them, and Thatcher guided Dodge up to the driver's side.

"Looks like you fellas need a ride," said the driver. "We're bound for Burlington. Will that help?"

"Sure will," said Thatcher. "Indians attacked us back a few miles. Shot my friend, here, and took our horses. Got room for us?"

"Sure do. You hit it good today. Just one passenger back there."

Thatcher snickered. "Guess we did hit it good. C'mon, pal, let's get in."

When he opened the door, a cold spike of fear stabbed through his heart and goose bumps crept across his skin. He was staring into the ominous muzzle of a Colt .45. Behind it was a man in black, with a shiny badge on his chest. The twin, jagged scars on his right cheek lifted as he smiled and said, "Good evening, Misters Thatcher and Dodge. Come on in. I'm John Brockman, chief U.S. marshal out of Denver. And you are under arrest."

Dottie Carroll stood on the platform at Denver's Union Station, waiting for her sister's train to arrive. People were moving past her, hurrying one direction or another. She glanced up at the big clock over the ticket windows. If the Cheyenne City train was on time, it would arrive in six minutes.

From behind, a female voice said, "Hello, Breanna. Waiting for a train to come in?"

Dottie turned and smiled. She recognized Etta Brown, wife of Denver County's assessor.

"Oh!" said Etta, clapping a hand to her cheek. "Dottie, you and your sister look so much alike! I sure thought you were Breanna."

"Lots of people make the same mistake," said Dottie. "Both ways."

"Well, you're both such lovely girls. I'm sure neither of you mind being mistaken for the other."

"Well, I sure don't," said Dottie, "and I've never heard Breanna complain about it."

"Everything all right in the Carroll household?"

"Just fine, thank the Lord."

"I was noticing at church last Sunday how much James and Molly Kate are growing."

Dottie smiled. "Like the proverbial weeds. Especially James."

A train whistle blew, and immediately afterward the big engine chugged into the depot, puffing smoke from its stack.

"I'm meeting my mother-in-law," said Etta. "She lives in Cheyenne City."

"Oh, that's nice," said Dottie. "I'm meeting the lady for whom you mistook me."

"I see. I suppose Breanna's been on another one of her assignments."

"Mm-hmm. In Loveland. She's only been gone a few days on this one. Just filling in at a clinic for a nurse who had to attend a funeral in Montana."

"I see. She stays plenty busy between these travel assignments and working either at the hospital or Dr. Goodwin's office, doesn't she?"

"Yes, but she loves it."

The train rolled to a stop, and Etta smiled as she said, "Oh! There's my mother-in-law in coach number one! She's waving at me. See you on Sunday."

"Sure will," said Dottie as Etta hurried away.

She let her gaze run up and down the line, watching for her sister to appear as the passengers began to alight. Suddenly there she was, coming out of coach number three. Breanna looked surprised to see Dottie, then embraced her sister and said, "John must be out of town."

"How'd you guess?" Dottie said with a chuckle. "Since he's

so shorthanded on deputies, he had to go after a couple of killers himself."

As they started across the depot, Breanna said, "Well, even when his staff of deputies is beefed up, that big lug will still leave his desk in the hands of Chief Duvall periodically. He can only sit behind a desk for so long, then he has to get back in the saddle and on the trail of some bad guys."

"You wouldn't want him any different, Breanna."

"You're right about that."

Breanna recognized the Carroll family buggy as they approached the place where it was hitched. She placed her small pieces of luggage in the back, and as they headed across town, Dottie said, "Everything go all right in Loveland?"

"Mm-hmm. Dr. Grable is a nice man as well as an excellent physician." She paused, then said, "Of course, he's not quite as good as Dr. Goodwin, who is my second favorite physician-surgeon in all the world."

Dottie giggled. "And who might your first favorite be?"

Breanna elbowed her. "You well know it's that man you call your husband!"

As they drew near Mile High Hospital, Dottie said, "Do you need to stop here for any reason?"

"No. I'll let Matt know when I can work at the hospital after I see when Dr. Goodwin wants me. But if you don't mind, I'd like to stop at John's office and see if Chief Duvall has heard anything from him."

"Sure enough. Next stop, the office of the chief United States marshal!"

Dottie waited outside the federal building while Breanna went to talk to Duvall. Five minutes later, Breanna returned, saying, "Chief Duvall isn't in at the moment, but Billy Martin told me a telegram came from John this morning. He sent it from Byers. He caught the killers near Burlington day before yesterday and sent the wire to let Chief Duvall know he would be in late this afternoon."

"Praise the Lord! He kept John safe one more time."

"Amen to that," said Breanna. "Okay, driver. Take me home."

As Dottie guided the buggy south out of town, then took a road that led west, she said, "Breanna…"

"Mm-hmm?"

"You haven't mentioned it since I picked you up, but I'm your sister, okay?"

Breanna set her sky-blues on Dottie. "You mean the Dwight Moreland accusation?"

"Yes."

"Well, honey, it still hurts, but I've tried to keep it out of my mind so it wouldn't affect my work."

"Didn't John say before you left that if you didn't get an apology, he was going to have a talk with Moreland?"

"He did. John wanted to go confront him the day I came home all torn up, but I begged him not to."

Dottie chuckled. "Well, that's all right. Your husband should defend your honor. Moreland was dead wrong and had no right to accuse you like that."

"I know, Dottie, but I had to take into account that he was distraught because he lost his little baby daughter. That's why I asked John to give him some time. Maybe Dwight will think over what Matt told him and realize how wrong he is."

"That's my sister," said Dottie. "Always long-suffering with those who wrong her and always ready to forgive."

"I learned that from my Lord Jesus," said Breanna.

Dottie blinked. "You're so right, honey. I need to learn it

better in my own life. I stand convicted of my own gross short-comings."

"Don't we all, Dottie."

The wide South Platte flowed like a ribbon of silver in the August sunlight as the sisters drew near the Brockman place, which was in the foothills below the majestic Rockies. When they turned into the long driveway leading through rows of cottonwood trees, Breanna focused on a buggy in front of the house. A man was standing beside it.

"Looks like I've got company," mused Breanna.

Soon Dottie's buggy was close enough that Breanna could recognize the man. "Oh, honey. It's Dwight Moreland."

When Dottie didn't comment, Breanna flicked a glance at her, then stared straight ahead as they neared the house. "You knew he was going to be here."

Dottie cleared her throat gently. "You…ah…might say that."

"Well?"

"He's been wanting to talk to you since the second day after the baby died, but as you remember, you headed for Loveland that morning. I told him when you'd be home, and that I'd be driving you from the depot. He's worried that you won't forgive him. I assured him that he had nothing to worry about."

Breanna looked at Dwight as Dottie brought the buggy to a halt and flashed him a smile. "Hello, Dwight. How's Pamela doing?"

He moved toward the buggy. His voice sounded shaky as he said, "She's doing very well, ma'am. Dr. Carroll says she can go home tomorrow."

"Wonderful. I'm glad to hear it."

Extending his trembling hand, he said, "May I help you down, Mrs. Brockman?"

Breanna smiled warmly again. "Thank you."

As soon as her feet touched the ground, Dwight said, "Mrs. Brockman, I should be horsewhipped. I was very wrong to speak to you as I did and to blame you for my baby's death. I'm here to ask your forgiveness."

Breanna touched his arm. "Thank you for relieving my mind, Dwight. I'm so glad you aren't blaming me any more. You're forgiven."

Tears welled up in his eyes. With quivering lips, he said, "Thank you, ma'am. Dr. and Mrs. Carroll both told me that you would forgive me, but I...I was still afraid you might not. I sure don't deserve any mercy from you at all. I—"

"Dwight, let me tell you about forgiveness and mercy. The God of heaven sent His Son into this world to die on Calvary's cross so we could all be forgiven of our sins against Him if we—"

"I know about that, ma'am," Dwight cut in. "You see, when I was so bitter against you, Dr. Carroll told me that three other doctors on the hospital staff had agreed that the baby would have died no matter who had delivered her. He offered to give me their names and let me talk to them without him present. That opened my eyes to the facts, and I knew I had to have your forgiveness.

"Dr. Carroll said there was no question that you would give it because you knew the forgiveness of God. He took the time right there in Pamela's hospital room to show both of us from the Bible about Jesus dying for us, and that as sinners, we needed to be forgiven by God and to be saved. Both of us received Jesus into our hearts."

Now it was Breanna's turn to tremble. Tears welled up in her eyes as she turned to Dottie. "Did you know about them getting saved?"

Dottie grinned and nodded. "Uh-huh. But I wanted to let Dwight tell you."

"Oh, praise the Lord! Welcome to the family of God, dear brother."

After a discreet embrace, Breanna said, "Dwight, it was worth feeling your scorn since it resulted in the salvation of you and your sweet little wife! Praise the Lord!"

THAT NIGHT, JOHN AND BREANNA Brockman sat on the front porch of their large country house, enjoying the night sounds. There was a half-moon midway in the sky, and the aroma of honeysuckle filled the air.

"The crickets are all tuned up tonight, aren't they?" John said, reaching for Breanna's hand.

"In perfect harmony," she replied. Chuckling, she added, "Evolution sure worked that out good, didn't it?"

John laughed. "Yeah. Evolution! To quote Ebenezer Scrooge, 'Bah humbug!'"

The Brockmans laughed together and talked about God's marvelous creation for a while, then Breanna said, "You were going to tell me about those two killers you brought in, but we got sidetracked over supper talking about Dwight and Pamela."

"Oh, sure. Well, those two low-downs are wanted in two states and three territories for robbery and murder. They'll hang."

"I see. Were they hard to catch?"

"Relatively easy. Before they killed him, the proprietor of the trading post at Byers shot Dodge through the leg. That slowed them down quite a bit. Next thing that happened was one of their horses broke a leg. That put both men on one horse. They pushed the horse pretty hard. Wasn't long till he gave out. Once they were on foot, it was quite simple to capture them."

"You said something about using a stagecoach. Why was that?"

"Well, I always carry a pair of binoculars. I stayed out of sight for a while and just watched them. When they were afoot, I saw that Dodge was in pretty bad shape. If I stayed on Ebony when I arrested them, there would be no way to get them to Denver without at least two of us walking, so I left Ebony at the Wells Fargo way station, which is about thirty miles east of Agate. It's the last stop after Agate and before Burlington.

"The Wells Fargo people and their passengers cooperated when I explained that I was trailing a couple of killers who were on foot, and that one of them was wounded in the leg. They kindly waited till we had picked up Dodge and Thatcher and returned to the way station. That stage, its crew, and passengers went on to Burlington some four hours late. A few hours later, my prisoners and I caught the next stage from Burlington and went as far as Byers last night with Ebony tied on behind. There were two other passengers, but they were in no danger since I had Dodge and Thatcher handcuffed. The stage laid over at Byers, and we took the same one for Denver this morning."

Breanna looked at him in the moonlight. "John Brockman, you're a genius."

John raised her hand to his lips and kissed it. "I sure used my extraordinary intellectual power to trick you into falling in love with me so I could be married to the most beautiful and wonderful woman in all the world."

Breanna leaned close and kissed him soundly. "You say the nicest things."

"I simply speak the truth."

She kissed him again.

The next morning, Breanna arrived at Dr. Lyle Goodwin's office just before seven-thirty and found the silver-haired physician turning the key in the lock.

Goodwin smiled at her. "Ah, you're back, Breanna. How was everything in Loveland?"

"All went well, Doctor," She followed him through the door. "Do you want me to work here today?"

"I sure do," he said, opening a window. "I told Dr. Carroll if you were back today, I'd work you here and let him have you at the hospital tomorrow."

"I figured it might turn out like that," she said, opening another window.

Footsteps were heard, and Dr. Goodwin's nurse, Greta Fields, came through the front door.

"Good morning to both of you," said Greta. "Glad to have you back, Breanna."

Goodwin greeted his nurse, and Breanna said, "It's good to be back."

"I assume you're working here today?"

"She is," Goodwin answered for Breanna. "We've got a full schedule of patients. We need her."

"I'll agree with that," said Greta. "Any more and we could use her just about all the time."

"I'd like that," said the doctor, "but that brother-in-law of hers over at the hospital seems to think they need her, too. And then, or course, I still get wires and letters from doctors and clinics all over the West for her visiting nurse services."

Greta laughed. "Breanna, honey, you need to be three people!"

"No, *four!*" corrected Breanna. "My husband seems to think he has some claim on my time, too."

Greta rolled her eyes. "I can't imagine why!"

"Well, ladies," said the doctor, looking through the window onto the street. "We've got some patients pulling up out front. We'd better get ready for them."

It was midmorning when Breanna happened to be at the desk in the waiting room as the front door opened. She glanced at the small, wiry man who entered and saw that it was Zack Miller, one of the Western Union messengers.

"Hello, Zack," she said with a smile.

"And hello to you too, Breanna. Doc in?"

"Yes. He's with a patient at the moment, but he's about through."

Lifting a yellow envelope into view, he said, "I have a telegram for him. If he could look at it—"

The door to the examining room opened, and a mother with a small boy came out saying, "Thank you, Doctor. I'll bring him back in a week."

Dr. Goodwin walked out behind them and smiled when he saw the messenger.

"Zack has a telegram for you, Doctor," Breanna said.

Goodwin reached for the envelope.

"I'll wait till you read it," Zack said, "so's if you need to send a return wire, I can take it and send it for you."

"Fine," said Goodwin. "Just have a seat, and I'll be right back."

Goodwin went into his private office and closed the door. Zack sat down, and Breanna greeted an elderly couple as they came in. She took them to the examining room and closed the door.

Breanna came out of the examining room at exactly the same time Goodwin's office door opened. Holding the telegram, he said, "Breanna, are Mr. and Mrs. Waters here yet?"

"Yes, sir. I have them ready for you."

"All right, but first I need to talk to you in here for a moment." Looking at the messenger, he said, "This wire has to do with Breanna, Zack. As soon as we can talk, I'll have a message for you to send for me."

Zack grinned. "I'll stay right here, Doctor."

Breanna preceded Goodwin into his office, and he closed the door behind them. "I have a request from a doctor over in Redstone for your services. I know Redstone is on the west side of the mountains, but I don't know exactly where it is. Do you?"

"Yes, sir. Do you know where Carbondale is?"

"Mm…no."

"Carbondale is due south of Glenwood Springs about ten miles."

"Oh, yes."

"Redstone is fifteen miles due south of Carbondale. Remember when you sent me to work for Dr. Bradley Allen in Glenwood Springs a couple of years ago?"

"Oh, sure."

"Well, when I finished my job there, I had a couple of days to wait for a train to Denver. Some people in the church there took me all the way down to the marble quarries south of Redstone. It's a beautiful area. Redstone is about 180 miles west of Denver. The town lies at the base of Snowmass

Mountain and sits on the west bank of the Crystal River. It's really something to see. The Crystal's waters come rushing down from the high peaks all year long, and the water is always foamy. So, tell me about this doctor in Redstone."

"His name is McClay Lowry. I've never met him in person, but I do know he is highly respected as a physician and surgeon. I'm told he's quite brilliant. Well, anyway, Dr. Lowry knows about your impeccable reputation as a visiting nurse and is asking me to allow you to come and help him in his office if you are available. His regular nurse left him to take a job in a California medical clinic. Lowry has hired another nurse from somewhere back East, but it will be at least three weeks before she can get there. He needs you to come as soon as possible."

Breanna turned to look at the calendar on the wall next to the door.

"A problem?" asked Goodwin.

"Well, let me see. Mmm…today is Thursday, August 24. My birthday is—"

"September 30."

"Yes. That should work out all right. Dr. Lowry's nurse is to be there in at least three weeks, you said?"

"Right."

"That would actually give me four weeks till I would have to head back to be sure I'm here a few days before my birthday. You see, Doctor, this will be my first birthday since John and I got married, and he's already made special plans for the day. I don't know what they are, but I know he's planning something. I'm sure he would object if I took a job that kept me away at that time. But this will work out fine."

Doc Goodwin nodded agreeably. "So, how soon can you go?"

"I think there are trains to Grand Junction from Denver four times a week. Glenwood Springs, of course, is on the line. And if I remember correctly, one of the trains goes on Saturday. I'll have to check before you send your wire to Dr. Lowry. But I think you can tell him I'll be there on Saturday. I know there's stagecoach service between Glenwood Springs and Redstone every day. I'll run over to Union Station at lunchtime."

"Tell you what," said Goodwin. "I'll ask Zack to do it for you. After all, you have to have a few minutes for lunch amid this busy schedule we have today."

Zack Miller returned to the doctor's office, having made a reservation for Breanna on Saturday's train to Glenwood Springs, and while he was at it, he stopped at the Wells Fargo office and booked her on the afternoon stage to Redstone from Glenwood Springs. Dr. Goodwin then wrote a message to Dr. Lowry for Zack to send as soon as he returned to the Western Union office.

It was late afternoon when Zack returned to Goodwin's office with a reply. In his wire, Dr. Lowry said he was very happy that Breanna was available and would be coming. He assured Goodwin that his new nurse would be there in plenty of time for Breanna to return to Denver as desired, and added that even if not, Breanna would be free to go home whenever she pleased.

That evening, Breanna told John about her assignment in Redstone, and quickly explained that no matter what, she would be home for her birthday. Based on this, John gave his approval.

The next day, Breanna reported in at the hospital and was

instantly given charge of several patients by Mary Donelson. When Breanna met up with Dr. Carroll in the hall an hour later, she explained about her assignment in Redstone, saying she would be leaving the next morning.

It was early afternoon when Breanna came out of a room carrying a tray and saw her sister heading toward her.

"Hi, sweetie," Breanna said. "I didn't expect to see you here."

"I had to come by and talk to Matt for a minute. He told me about your trip tomorrow to Redstone. He said you'd be gone for at least three weeks."

"Yes. John insists, however, that I be back by my birthday. And I very much want to be."

"Of course. Well, I'd like to have you and John come for supper tonight. Do you have other plans, or could you come?"

"We can come," said Breanna. "We always love our times with you and Matt and the children. But I'm starting to worry that John might change his mind about who's the best cook in the world if he eats much more of your food."

Dottie laughed. "That'll be the day!"

"Seven o'clock, as usual?"

"Right."

"Okay. John's picking me up after work, so I'll just steer him to your house instead of ours."

As always, when Uncle John and Aunt Breanna ate at the Carroll household, ten-year-old James and eight-year-old Molly Kate had to sit by them at the table.

The meal was about half-eaten when James looked up at the tall man with the steel gray eyes and said, "Uncle John, you haven't told me a story yet."

"James," spoke up Dottie, "Uncle John may get tired of always having to tell you one of his 'catch-the-bad-guys' stories every time he puts his feet under our table."

"Oh, no, I don't!" said John, after swallowing a mouthful of creamed corn. "This boy says he wants to be a lawman when he grows up, and if he carries through with it, maybe some of the things he's learned from me will be an asset to him."

"I like your stories, too, Uncle John," said Molly Kate, who strongly resembled her mother and her aunt. "I guess girls can't grow up to be lawmen, but I still like to hear about those mean ol' bad guys you put in jail."

James chuckled. "And sometimes Uncle John never gets 'em to jail, Molly Kate. Sometimes he has to shoot 'em."

"Yeah," she said. "I like the stories either way."

"Go ahead, Uncle John," James said. "Tell us another one."

John sipped coffee then set down his cup and said, "Well, let's see…"

"Darling," said Breanna, "why don't you tell them about the latest two bad guys you used a stagecoach to capture?"

"A stagecoach?" James eyes grew wide. "How'd you do that, Uncle John?"

"Yeah, Uncle John," said Matt, "I'd like to hear that one myself!"

The big engine was hissing and the bell atop it clanging as John folded Breanna in his arms. After kissing her three times, he looked down into her sky blue eyes and said, "I'll miss you, sweetheart."

"I'll miss you, too, darling. But we'll both be busy, so the time will pass by quickly. And I promise…I'll be home in time for whatever you've got planned for my birthday."

They kissed again, and John carried her hand luggage onto the train and placed it in the overhead rack. Moments later, he stood on the platform and waved at his lovely wife as the train chugged out of the station.

Breanna dabbed at the tears glistening on her cheeks and whispered, "Take care of him, Lord. You and I both know that badge on his chest is like a target to every outlaw roaming the West."

Soon the train was winding its way through the rugged Rocky Mountains on its regular run to Grand Junction on Colorado's western slope. Breanna had seen the Rockies in all their majesty more times than she could recall, but she never got over being awestruck as her eyes took in their magnificent peaks, shadowed rocky shoulders, and deep canyons.

After making a few stops, the train arrived in the mountain town of Glenwood Springs, just after one o'clock in the afternoon. Breanna took her two pieces of hand luggage down from the rack and followed other passengers off the train. She knew her way around Glenwood Springs and moved down the main street to the Wells Fargo office to check in. The stage would be leaving in about an hour and forty minutes.

Taking a seat in the waiting room, Breanna noted that she was the only passenger. The Fargo agent was in conversation with two men that she soon learned were townsmen who spent a lot of time visiting him.

Her ears pricked up when she heard the agent say, "The first murder was what…a month ago?"

"Yep," said one. "July 22."

"And the second murder was six days ago."

"That's right."

The agent shook his head. "Well, you'd think Redstone's marshal could have caught the dirty killer before the woman had to die."

Murders in Redstone? thought Breanna. Her stomach went sour.

Another townsman came in and joined them, entering the conversation. As the men hashed it over twice more, she learned that the first person murdered was the owner of Redstone's hardware store and gun shop. He had been found strangled to death in the back of his store.

The second victim was a middle-aged woman who had been stabbed to death in her home one night when her husband was across town visiting a friend.

Redstone's town marshal, Mike Halloran, had not been able to come up with any clues, but from what he did find, he knew both murders were by the same person.

The agent commented that it was a shame the killer was still at large. Everyone in Redstone, according to one of the townsmen, was living in terror.

A cold chill slithered down Breanna's spine. She wondered why Dr. Lowry had not told Dr. Goodwin about the murders.

The conversation broke off when other passengers began to arrive and demanded the attention of the agent. Soon they were boarding, and Breanna found herself sitting next to an elderly man, and across from her was a middle-aged couple.

As the stage rolled south out of Glenwood Springs, the man next to Breanna looked at the others and said, "Well, I guess we ought to get acquainted. My name is Will Becker. I live in Carbondale."

The man across from Breanna said, "I'm Lowell Shormann, and this is my wife, Ava. We live in Redstone." His eyes trailed to Breanna "And you, ma'am?"

"I'm Breanna Brockman. My home is in Denver. I'm a visiting nurse on my way to Redstone to work temporarily for Dr. McClay Lowry."

Both their faces brightened. "Well, Mrs. Brockman" said Ava, noting the wedding band on Breanna's finger, "we're very happy to meet you! Ever since Dr. Lowry's nurse told him she was leaving for California, he has been frantic about finding a new one. You say you're temporary. Is this until he finds a new nurse?"

"Yes. He's already hired his new permanent nurse," said Breanna. "She's coming from somewhere back East. She's supposed to arrive in about three weeks. When she comes, I'll be heading back to Denver."

Will Becker leaned forward to get a better look at Breanna.

"Ma'am, that name...Brockman. You say you're from Denver?"

"Yes."

"You wouldn't be related to John Brockman, the chief U.S. marshal, would you?"

"Yes, I am. By marriage. John is my husband."

"Oh! Well isn't that something! I've heard many things about him."

"Me, too!" said Becker.

Ava's brow furrowed. "Didn't he used to be known as 'The Stranger'?"

"That's him, honey," said Lowell.

"Yeah!" put in Decker. "Tell us about him, would you, Mrs. Brockman?"

"How you met and all that," said Ava.

This was nothing new to Breanna. John had become quite famous in the country for his deeds as The Stranger, especially in the West. While the stage rolled along on the bumpy mountain road, she told the story in brief of how she had met John and about their marriage.

When the three passengers were finally satisfied, Breanna said, "What can you folks tell me about the two murders in Redstone?"

The Shormanns had been in Grand Junction for three weeks, but knew about the second murder. Between them and Will Becker, Breanna learned more details about the victims and about the brutal killings.

"There's no doubt in Marshal Halloran's mind," said Becker, "that both killings were done by the same man."

"We heard something while we were in Grand Junction, Will," said Lowell. "Marshal Halloran is saying he believes the killer is a psychopath."

"That's what some folks from your town told me," said Becker. "A crazy, out-of-his-mind psychopathic killer!"

The stage pulled into Carbondale at two-thirty. Will Becker got off, and an elderly woman and a teenage girl boarded. Breanna learned that Hilda Frost and her fifteen-year-old granddaughter Mary Lou were from Redstone and were well acquainted with the Shormanns.

Both Hilda and Mary Lou were glad to learn that Breanna was on her way to work in Dr. Lowry's office until his permanent nurse arrived.

As the stage headed south out of Carbondale, Hilda brought up the murders, and once more they were the main topic of conversation. Breanna let her eyes take in the beauty of the mountain country around her, trying to calm herself. Again she wondered why Dr. Lowry had not at least let her know what she was walking into.

Her attention came back to the conversation when Hilda said, "Mary Lou and I have only been in Carbondale since Thursday. I'll tell you this much…when we left, everybody in town was scared stiff that the killer would strike again."

A cold ball of fear settled in Breanna's stomach.

It was 3:50 when the stage rolled into Redstone. Lowell Shormann stepped out first, helped Breanna alight, then turned to help Hilda, Mary Lou, and his wife.

When Breanna's feet touched ground, she saw a couple in their mid-forties approaching.

"Mrs. Brockman?" said the man, smiling. "I'm Dr. Lowry, and this is my wife, Thelma. Welcome to Redstone."

"Thank you, Doctor," said Breanna. "I'm happy to meet both of you."

"We're so glad you could come, dear," said Thelma, embracing her lightly. "McClay has told me many good things he's heard about you."

"Well, I hope I live up to my reputation," said Breanna, chuckling.

"You have some luggage in the rack or the boot, I assume?" said the doctor, who was nearly six feet tall and well built. Breanna decided he was good-looking in a rugged sort of way…like John, only not nearly so handsome.

"Yes, Doctor. Two small pieces. They're in the rack."

"I'll get them," he said, and went to talk with the shotgunner.

Thelma was dark headed, slightly plump, and a bit shorter than Breanna. Smiling, she said, "I hope you will enjoy working for my husband. He's a good doctor, if I do say so myself, and his patients love him. I think you'll find him easy to get along with."

"I'm sure I will," said Breanna.

While they waited for the doctor to get the luggage, Breanna ran her gaze to the snow-capped peak of Snowmass Mountain, then let her eyes run to the Crystal River as it flowed southward past the town. The afternoon sun danced on its foamy, rippling surface.

"Beautiful, isn't it," said Thelma.

"Sure is."

"Have you ever been here before?"

"Yes. A couple of years ago. Just for a day. I was doing a job for Dr. Bradley Allen in Glenwood Springs. Some folks in town brought me down to the marble quarries. I fell in love with it then, so your husband didn't have to twist my arm very hard to get me to come."

"Well, here we are," said Lowry, drawing up with both bags in hand. "Let's get you to your room at the boardinghouse, Mrs. Brockman."

As they walked toward the buggy, she said, "You can call me Breanna, Doctor."

"All right," he said, releasing a warm smile. "Breanna it is."

It was a short drive through the business section of Redstone. The boardinghouse was at the south edge of town, amid private homes.

The Lowrys introduced Breanna to Frieda Schultz, the landlady, who led them to Breanna's room. Frieda had come from Germany and spoke in a heavy European accent.

Breanna found the room bright and cheery and very clean and comfortable. When Lowry set the luggage on the bed, Breanna said, "Doctor, I'm surprised that neither you nor Mrs. Lowry have mentioned the recent murders here in Redstone. They were the subject at the Wells Fargo office in Glenwood and on the stage all the way here."

Lowry flicked a glance at Thelma, then looked at Breanna without quite meeting her gaze "I…I can tell by your tone that you're upset that I didn't advise you in my telegram."

"Well, yes. You might say that. From what I've been told, the whole town is living in terror."

Lowry sighed. "I'm sorry, Breanna. It's just that I need you so desperately, and…well, I was afraid if I told you about the murders, you wouldn't come. I was wrong not to let you know so you could make your decision based on the present situation. The same stage leaves here at eight o'clock in the morning. I'll put you on it, if you want to go home. Of course, I'll pay you for coming and cover your travel expenses as I told you I would in my wire."

"I can't do that, Doctor," said Breanna. "I came here to help you, and I'll stay and do that as I agreed to do."

Lowry let out a long sigh. "Oh, thank you. Thank you very much."

Thelma embraced her. "Yes, Breanna. Thank you. McClay needs your help as you will see."

5

ON SUNDAY MORNING, Breanna attended Redstone's only church and was pleased to find that Pastor Eldon Severson preached the true gospel of Jesus Christ. She enjoyed getting to meet Severson's wife, Karen, and the rest of the congregation. The people made her feel quite welcome, and when some asked if she was related to the chief U.S. marshal in Denver, they were excited to learn that John Brockman was her husband.

She returned for the evening service, and when it was over, she commended the pastor for his excellent sermon. She asked if the Lowrys ever attended and was disappointed to hear they never had.

Early on Monday morning, Breanna walked from the boardinghouse to the doctor's office, greeting what few people were on the street. Some were folks she had met at church on Sunday.

The mountain air was clear and cool. The Crystal River roared nearby, and Breanna found the peak on Snowmass Mountain a breathtaking sight in the sun's early light.

When she stepped inside the office, Breanna found Dr. Lowry in the examining room, preparing for the day. He greeted her cheerily and told her he needed to give her some pointers on his procedures, show her where the medicines and medical instruments were located in the cabinet, and acquaint her with the files in the front office.

While he was showing her through the medicine cabinet, they heard the front door open and a deep voice call out, "Doc, you here?"

"Marshal Halloran," Lowry whispered to Breanna. "Back here, Marshal!" he called loudly.

Mike Halloran entered the room, cradling an elderly woman in his arms.

Lowry recognized Ethel Phillips, one of the town's widows. Moving toward one of the examining tables, he said, "Put her over here, Marshal. What happened? Is it her hip?"

Ethel groaned when Halloran laid her on the table.

"Could be she hurt it again," said Halloran. "That's why I brought her. She had a bad scare and needs something to settle her nerves, too."

"Marshal Mike Halloran," said Lowry, moving up beside Ethel, "this is my temporary nurse, Breanna Brockman, from Denver."

Halloran gave Breanna a wide smile. "I've already heard much about you from the folks in town, ma'am. Welcome. I'm glad to meet you."

The marshal was well over six feet, broad-shouldered and muscular. His gun hung low on his hip. Breanna was sure he could handle himself with troublemakers, whether it was guns or fists. "I'm glad to meet you, too, Marshal."

"And Breanna, this is Ethel Phillips," said Lowry.

"Hello, Mrs. Phillips. Are you in pain?"

"Hip hurts a little," said Ethel in her quaint, high-pitched voice. "I broke it five years ago, but I don't think I did any real damage when I fell last night."

"Fell?" said Lowry

"You tell him for me, Marshal," Ethel said.

"Ethel collapsed in her kitchen late last night, Doc. She thought she saw a man on her back porch. She—"

"I thought he was the killer, Doctor." Ethel cut in. "I thought he was going to break through the door and kill me like he did Harold Wiggins and Ruby Copeland! I was so frightened, I got dizzy. I...I..."

"She passed out and fell on the floor," Halloran finished for her. "She regained consciousness sometime before dawn, but because of her bad hip, she couldn't get up. You know that her neighbor, Anne Lafferty, checks on her every morning to see if she needs anything. When Anne couldn't get an answer to her knock this morning, she used the key Ethel had given her. Anne found her on the floor and sent her grandson to get me. You know the rest of the story."

Lowry nodded. "Breanna, our first patients by appointment will be coming in soon. I'll go ahead and examine Ethel's hip, and you can be in the front office to greet the patients when they arrive."

"Of course, Doctor."

Halloran followed Breanna into the waiting office.

"It is nice to meet you, Marshal," Breanna said, moving behind the desk to pick up the appointment book. While noting the names of the first few patients, she said, "Is there a Mrs. Halloran?"

"Sure is," he replied with a smile. "Her name's Marcie."

"Any little Mikes and Marcies?"

"Not yet, but we hope to get our family started soon." After a brief pause, he said, "Mrs. Brockman, I was told by some of the church folks yesterday afternoon that you are Chief John Brockman's wife."

"That's right."

"I've long admired your husband, ma'am...since the days when he was known only as 'The Stranger.' I even met him once."

"Oh, really?"

"Yes'm. In Santa Fe, New Mexico. 'Bout eight years ago. John Stranger single-handedly foiled a bank robbery in Santa Fe. I was one of the deputy marshals there at the time. I don't expect him to remember me, ma'am, but when you go home, will you tell him hello from Mike Halloran?"

"I sure will."

"Well," he said, heading for the door, "I've got to get back to duty. I'll check on Ethel later. See you then."

" 'Bye. Tell Marcie I look forward to meeting her."

Even as the marshal opened the door, there was a man about to come in.

"Howdy, Luke," said Halloran.

Looking grumpy, the middle-aged man grunted, "Marshal."

"You not feeling well, Luke?"

"I never feel good when I have a doctor's appointment."

"Oh. Sorry."

Luke came in, and the marshal went on down the street.

"Good morning, sir," said Breanna with a smile. "You must be Mr. Cartman. I see you have the first appointment with Dr. Lowry today."

"I have the first appointment with him every Monday," Cartman said levelly. "You the new nurse from Baltimore?"

"No, sir. I'm filling in temporarily until she arrives. My name is Breanna Brockman. Please, sit down. Dr. Lowry had an emergency this morning. He's with the patient now."

"Well, I haven't got all morning. How long's he gonna be?"

"I really couldn't say, Mr. Cartman, but I don't think it'll be much longer. Please have a seat."

Luke muttered something under his breath and sat down.

"Tell you what, Mr. Cartman," said Breanna, "I'll go back and see how it's going with the other patient. Maybe there's something I can do to help so Dr. Lowry can see you sooner."

"That would be appreciated," said Luke.

Ethel Phillips was sitting up on a chair when Breanna entered. Dr. Lowry was standing over her, saying, "I think that until this killer is caught, Ethel, you should not be alone. How about your friend Gladys; would she let you come and stay with her?"

"I'm sure she would, Doctor," Ethel replied, her voice quivering, "She tried to get me to come and stay with her right after the first murder a month ago."

Lowry sent a glance to Breanna as she came in.

"How's she doing, Doctor?"

"Her hip is fine, I'm glad to say. But I was just telling her she needs to stay with her best friend, Gladys Dimmick, until the killer is caught."

"Good," said Breanna, laying a hand on Ethel's shoulder. "Sounds like you had a pretty good scare. Be best if you're not alone while the killer is on the loose."

"I'm seeing patients with all kinds of nerve problems, Breanna," said Lowry. "Started last month when the first murder was committed. When the second one happened eight days ago, it got a whole lot worse. People in this town—young, old, and in between—are living with jangled nerves, on the edge of panic."

"I sure hope Marshal Halloran catches the killer soon," said Breanna. "Doctor, Luke Cartman is here for his appointment."

"All right, I'll be with him in just a minute." Then to his elderly patient: "Ethel, I'll take care of Luke, then I'll take you over to Gladys's house in one of my wheelchairs."

"Thank you," said Ethel.

Breanna was in the outer office when Luke Cartman came out after his time with the doctor. He left without saying anything to her. Moments later, Lowry left the office to push Ethel home in the wheelchair. His next appointment was in twenty minutes, and he told her he would hurry back.

Hardly had Lowry and his patient passed from view when Breanna looked up to see two women come in. One was about fifty and the other a few years older. She knew these had to be "walk-ins," for the next appointment was a man.

Rising from the desk chair, Breanna said, "Good morning, ladies. I'm Breanna Brockman, Dr. Lowry's temporary nurse. May I help you?"

The older woman said, "My, dear, you are even prettier than I was told. I'm Anne Lafferty, Ethel Phillips's neighbor. This is Isabel Peterson."

Breanna's face tinted at Anne's compliment, but all she said was, "Mrs. Lafferty, you're the neighbor who found Mrs. Phillips?"

"Yes."

"And I suppose you're here to see about her?"

Anne glanced at Isabel, then said, "That's one of the reasons. How is she?"

"Dr. Lowry got her pretty well stabilized, then took her to Gladys Dimmick's house. She's going to stay with Mrs. Dimmick until this killer is caught."

"She didn't hurt her hip when she fell, then?"

"No. Dr. Lowry said her hip is fine."

"Oh, I'm so thankful for that."

Breanna ran her gaze from Isabel to Anne. "You're here for another reason, you said?"

"Yes. Ethel's scare has put Isabel and me on edge. This whole murder thing has kept us upset enough, but after what happened to Ethel last night, we both need a sedative to calm us."

Breanna provided powders for the women and had to do the same for three young mothers who came in just as Anne and Isabel were leaving. Fear was getting a strong grip on the people of Redstone.

A crippled man on crutches was the next patient in the appointment book. When he learned that Dr. Lowry was out, but due back momentarily, he told Breanna he needed to go to a store down the street and would return shortly.

Breanna was studying the patients' files to acquaint herself with the doctor's record system when Marshal Halloran returned.

"I was real close," he said, "so I thought I'd stop and see about Ethel."

Breanna explained that Dr. Lowry had taken her to Gladys Dimmick's house, where she would stay until the killer was caught and the danger was past.

"That's good," said Halloran. "I'm especially glad to know the hip wasn't further damaged. No one will be more pleased than I will when this killer is out of the way."

"I understand he's left no clues at all at the murder scenes," said Breanna.

"None."

"So what can you do to bring this horror to an end?"

"Preventative measures, ma'am. Without clues, I have nothing to go on."

"Preventative measures? Like what?"

"Well, at present, I'm organizing a group of men from in and around town to patrol the streets by shifts at night. Some of the ranchers around are trying to recruit some of their neighbors to help us. I should have it organized within another day. Two, at the most. This maniac must be stopped. By using the patrols, I'm hoping not only to prevent anyone else from being killed, but to catch him when he's about to commit another murder and put an end to this horrible nightmare."

"I hope it works, Marshal," said Breanna. "Dr. Lowry says he's putting more people on sedatives all the time."

Halloran rubbed the back of his neck and said, "Yes, he's got to be stopped. I wish he was dangling from the end of a rope right now."

"Marshal, on my stagecoach ride from Glenwood Springs to Carbondale, I met a man named Will Decker. He said he had been told that you believe the killer is psychopathic."

"That's right."

"Why do you say that?"

"Simple. The two murders have no apparent motive or connection. I dug deep to see if I could find whether either victim had any enemies. In small towns, everybody knows everything about everybody else. The people who knew them stated that they had no known enemies. Their mates concurred."

Breanna thought on it for a moment. "I guess there have to be exceptions to every rule, Marshal."

"What do you mean?"

"I agree that in small towns everybody knows everything about everybody else, but you've got an exception in Redstone. Someone among you is a killer, but nobody knows he's a killer."

"Yes. That's an exception staring me right in the face."

"So because there were no known enemies of the victims, you assume the killer is a psychopath."

"Right. The victims seemed to be chosen at random as though the murderer simply had an urge to kill and picked whoever was available at the moment. I don't know a lot about psychopaths, but I do know this is typical. Dr. Lowry agrees with me."

A sound from the boardwalk met their ears. Dr. Lowry appeared at the door with the man on crutches behind him. As they came in, Lowry greeted the marshal, placed the wheelchair next to the wall, and said, "I assume Breanna told you Ethel's hip is all right."

"Yes, sir. Hello, Gunther."

Gunther Peabody spoke to Halloran, then said to Breanna, "I found Dr. Lowry coming down the street when I was on my way back."

"So I gathered, sir."

Peabody set his gaze on Halloran. "How goes the search for the killer, Marshal?"

"The search? Not so good, Gunther," replied Halloran, "but preparations to stop him are in the works."

"The patrols, eh?"

"Yes, sir."

"Well, that's a great idea. I hope it scares that bloody rat enough to make him leave these parts, or he's so brave that he'll try to kill somebody in spite of the patrols and get himself caught. *Killed* would be best. Then we'd be rid of him for sure."

"He's got to be stopped," said the doctor. "Everybody in Redstone is walking a tightwire."

"Doctor," said Breanna, "Marshal Halloran says he believes the killer is a psychopath and that you agree."

"Sure do. The typical pattern is there. The killer had no

apparent motive in either case, except the urge to take a human life. His mind has to be off balance."

"Sounds like it," said Breanna. "Had there been any killings like this in or around Redstone prior to July?"

"None," said Halloran. "There hasn't been a murder here since a bartender was killed on his way home one night by a man he'd made angry earlier in the evening. The man was hanged. That was over ten years ago, and I wasn't marshal then."

"Did someone move into town or into the area a short time before the first murder was committed a month ago?" Breanna asked.

"Nobody," said Lowry. "There haven't been any new people move to our town or area for what, Mike…two years?"

"At least two years," Halloran said.

"More likely three years," put in Peabody. "The Vernon Pace family are the newest folks around, and they've been here nigh onto three years."

"Just wondered," said Breanna. "So we just might have us a psychopathic killer, after all. I've studied a little about it, but my knowledge of the subject is quite limited. Have you studied the subject, Doctor?"

"I have. I minored in psychiatry in medical school and learned a great deal about psychopaths."

"I understand they're not necessarily born with the mental disorder that makes them psychopathic. Am I correct?"

"Yes, you are, Breanna. Some are born with the disorder, yes. But a perfectly normal person can become a psychopathic killer overnight. This usually comes, of course, as the result of some injury to the head that affects the brain. Suddenly, nice people become killers. Amazingly enough, nine out of ten of them are men."

"I would have guessed that," said Breanna. "And don't some people become psychopathic because they're subjected to some kind of prolonged mental pressure that is more than their minds can handle?"

"Did you say you don't know much about this subject?" Lowry said with a chuckle. "I'd say you know quite a bit."

"Not as much as I'd like to, Doctor."

Lowry smiled. "Sometimes when a perfectly normal person comes under extended torturous mental pressure, it will become so unbearable that the mind snaps. When a person slips into this condition, it's almost impossible to bring him back."

"Don't psychopaths usually have severe headaches, Doctor?" asked Breanna.

"Absolutely. I would say almost without exception. The psychopath will suffer extremely painful headaches, which will cause him to react with violence against innocent people. With some, this is the only time they kill. Studies have shown that the headaches actually do subside after they have done something violent, especially if they've killed someone."

Mr. Peabody shuddered. "Gives me the creeps to think there's somebody like this running around our town. We probably see him every day and have no idea we're looking at the killer."

"Right, Gunther," Lowry said. "The worst part about the sickness is that a psychopath may appear absolutely normal to everyone around him in public, then in private he can turn into a killer. When he's done his vile deed, he can revert to normal again. If no one has seen him in this deranged state, the public is none the wiser. And like you just brought up, apparently this horrid mental sickness has overtaken someone who lives in or around Redstone."

"Tell you what bothers me," said Halloran. "I not only fear that the killer will strike again, but in the frightened state the people find themselves, I'm afraid some innocent person is going to be mistaken for the killer and get shot. When people are jittery and on edge like the citizens of Redstone are right now, they're liable to shoot at anybody, especially at night."

"You're right, Mike," said Lowry. "If there had been only one person murdered, it might be reasonable to assume it was someone passing through. But when the second murder took place, that idea was ruled out. Especially because you're certain the killings were done by the same man."

"Exactly why is that, Marshal?" Breanna asked.

"Well, ma'am, the killer inflicted damage to the heads of both victims, after they were dead, in exactly the same way. This was never revealed to the public, so it had to have been the same man."

"I just hate to see everyone so frightened," said Peabody. "It's a terrible thing."

"Yes," agreed the doctor. "No one in this town doubts that the killer is still lurking about, and this stimulates everyone's imagination. The credible is always a greater menace to us than the incredible. This is because we know it *can* happen—and even worse—it can happen to *us*. Our deepest fears lay buried in our imaginations and are summoned forth when we're living in a state of fear and see strange shadows or hear curious sounds."

That evening, Clyde and Earline Drummond stepped out onto their front porch on the river side of Redstone to sit together and enjoy the sweet smells and soft sounds of the night, including the rumble of the Crystal as its waters flowed south to join the flow of other streams and eventually, hundreds of miles away, to flow into the sea.

Clyde was a teller at Redstone's only bank and had stubbornly refused to allow the presence of a killer in town to keep him and his wife from enjoying their summer custom of spending their evenings together on the front porch.

The Drummonds had two sons—Bobby and Billy—who were nine and seven years of age. The boys were upstairs in their room playing. Their room was directly above the porch, and the windows were open to let in the cool night breeze.

Since the first murder took place, Clyde had tucked a revolver under his belt when he and Earline sat on the porch at night.

This night, they were unaware of a man moving, wraith-like, among the shadows in the dark yard directly across the street. Keeping himself behind a heavy clump of bushes, he observed the Drummonds by the pale glow of light coming through the parlor window. From time to time, he glanced up at the open windows on the second floor when one of the boys would laugh or say something loudly.

The observer was breathing hard and periodically rubbing his temples with the tips of his fingers.

Suddenly there was an outburst from the room above the Drummond porch. The boys were yelling and banging something on the floor. The man in the shadows ran his gaze to Earline as she shouted from the swing, "Bobby! Billy! Quiet down up there!"

The noise persisted. Earline left the swing, stepped to the edge of the porch, and shouted in a loud, piercing voice, "Hey! Boys!"

The room abruptly went quiet, and the boys appeared at one of the windows. "What did you say, Mom?" called one of them.

"I said quiet down up there! There's no need for you to be so noisy!"

"All right," came Bobby's reply.

Across the street, the man in the shadows scowled while pressing his fingertips to his temples and hissed angrily in a low whisper, "You don't have to shout at them like that, Earline! Stop it!"

Earline took her place on the swing next to Clyde and said, "I wonder what it would be like to have girls."

"Well, since I had three sisters, honey, I can tell you. Instead of yelling and banging, there would be incessant giggling. Besides, you ought to know. You're a girl."

Earline laughed. "Yes, I am. But I don't remember how noisy I was. It just seems to me that girls are much quieter than b—"

A loud wail came from upstairs. It was little brother, for he shouted at Bobby at the top of his lungs, telling him to stop whatever he was doing. When Bobby shouted back, Clyde started to get out of the swing, but Earline beat him to it.

"I'm going to warn them one more time, dear, and if it doesn't work, they're all yours."

With that, she bounded from the swing, stomped off the porch, and stood on the grass, looking up at the open window of the boys' room. Her voice pierced the night air, grating on the skulker's ears. "Bobby! Billy! You two get quiet this instant! If we hear one more peep out of you, your father is coming up there, and he'll whip you good! You hear me?"

The man in the shadows was shaking from head to foot. His eyes were wild as he hissed again in a low whisper, "Earline, stop it! When you scream like that, you sound just like *her!* Stop it! Stop it! Stop it!"

"Do you hear me?" Earline's voice increased in pitch. *"Answer me!"*

Saliva dripped from the corners of the man's mouth. He was now pressing his hands to the sides of his head, his face wrenching from the pain that stabbed like hot knives through his head.

The man in the shadows wanted to shut her up. It was as if the knife blades inside his head were twisting and turning, adding to his agony. He wanted to shout out at her to shut her mouth, but now he didn't have the breath to form the words.

While Earline stared up at the window, one of the boys said something that hit Clyde Drummond the wrong way. He was off the swing and through the front door of the house instantly. Even the man across the street could hear his feet pounding up the stairs.

Earline shook her head and returned to the swing, dropping into it with a sigh. While the sounds of Bobby's spanking came from the house, the man in the shadows crept across the street and hid behind the bushes at the end of the Drummond porch.

Soon, Bobby was wailing while the spanking went on, promising his father he would be good. The spanking stopped, and Billy began wailing even louder than his brother, knowing that his spanking was yet to come.

While Billy was getting his spanking, the fierce-eyed man ducked under the bushes and approached the porch railing.

Earline sat in the swing, muttering something under her breath as a dark form stealthily climbed onto the porch behind her.

MARCIE HALLORAN STRETCHED a cloth measuring tape across her husband's shoulders as he stood before her with his arms hanging loosely at his sides.

"But, honey," he said, "why do you have to measure me again? I love that shirt you made for me before."

"As I told you, I didn't get it quite large enough across the shoulders, and the sleeves were a tad short. I want to get this one just right. You're a darling not to tell me how it *really* fits."

There was a rapid knock at the front door, followed by an excited voice calling, "Marshal! Marshal!"

"Sounds like Doug Pollock," said Mike. "May be trouble." Even as he spoke, he wheeled about and rushed toward the front of the house.

"Marshal!" Pollock said, when the door opened. "The killer has struck again! Earline Drummond was strangled to death a few minutes ago!"

Marcie watched her husband vanish into the night with Doug Pollock, who lived next door to the Drummonds. Then she shut the door and locked it.

When Halloran and Pollock reached the scene, neighbors were gathered in the Drummonds' front yard, gazing in disbelief at a blanket covering Earline's lifeless form.

A weeping Clyde Drummond stood over her body and held onto his two sons, who wept with him.

As Halloran hurried toward the porch, one neighbor said, "We tried to get Clyde and the boys to go inside the house, Marshal, but Clyde won't move."

Halloran nodded and patted Clyde's shoulder, then knelt down beside the body to block the view of Earline's head from the group in the yard. He lifted the blanket just enough to expose her face and neck. Halloran felt his blood heat up when he saw the red marks on her throat. His stomach lurched when he saw the usual damage done by the killer after his victim was dead.

He dropped the blanket in place and fought to bring his emotions under control as he stood up and placed a hand on Clyde's shoulder. "I'm so sorry, Clyde," he said softly. "I'll need to know the details as soon as you feel like talking."

Clyde hugged his sons closer and nodded. "A couple of men went after Doc Lowry…" he said, his voice trailing off.

Halloran nodded. Dr. McClay Lowry also served as the town's undertaker.

"I'll have Doc give Bobby and Billy sedatives, Marshal," said Clyde. "After…after Doc takes the body away, I'll talk to you."

"If you're not up to it tonight, we can talk in the morning."

"I'd rather tell you tonight. The beast has to be caught, Marshal."

The group that had gathered in the yard turned at the sound of rattling wheels. It was Dr. Lowry, arriving in the funeral wagon with two men on the seat beside him.

Lowry went directly to Clyde and the boys and uttered some words of comfort, then turned to the body. After he had examined the face and neck, he covered her up and asked two of the men in the group to carry the body to the wagon and to be careful that the blanket stayed over her.

Lowry looked at Halloran. In a hushed voice, he said, "Did you look at her?"

Halloran nodded.

"Then you saw the eyes. Same thing as the others."

Halloran nodded again.

Lowry was kind and gentle to Clyde and the boys as he took them inside the house. Before following, Halloran told the people to go home and lock their doors and windows.

The doctor gave sedatives to the boys and tried to administer the same to Clyde, but he refused. Clyde let the boys lie down together on a couch in the parlor, and after Dr. Lowry had gone, he told the marshal the story. He explained about the boys' rowdiness up in their room while he and Earline sat on the porch. He had gone upstairs to discipline them. When he came back down, he found Earline lying dead on the porch. The red marks on her throat told him she had been strangled. The vile damage done to her eyes made him doubly angry at the heartless killer.

Halloran told him he would get someone to stay there through the night, but Clyde said he wanted to be alone. The marshal then said he would come back in the morning and look for clues in the daylight.

The next morning, Halloran was at the Drummond home at sunrise, but the only clues he could find were boot prints between the bushes and the end of the porch where the killer had apparently climbed up to get at Earline. It appeared that the man had purposely twisted his feet as he made his way past the bushes to the porch in order to leave no sharp imprint in the dirt. The prints were so vague they offered no help regarding the size of the killer's feet. Not only was the killer a vicious psychopath, he was very clever.

Word of Earline Drummond's murder spread through Redstone as the morning progressed. Intense fear spread with it. It was the subject of everyone's conversation on the streets, in the stores, and at Dr. Lowry's office. The doctor and his temporary nurse had more jangled nerves to deal with, along with the normal physical problems.

Marcie Halloran went to her husband's office at midmorning to serve coffee to the large collection of townsmen and ranchers who filled the room. All were eager to help the marshal protect the people of Redstone and bring the killer to justice.

As Halloran laid out his plan for the night patrols, a crowd was gathering in the street in front of his office.

Marcie, who was facing the street as she poured more coffee into the tin cups the men held in their hands, said, "Mike, you're getting quite a crowd outside. I think you'd better go out and talk to them. Looks like mostly women and older men. Of course, you have a large number of the younger men packed in here at the moment. I think they're trying to choose a leader who will speak for them."

Halloran turned to look out the window. "Oh! Guess I'd better. I'm sure they're wanting a report about what I'm doing to catch the killer."

The men in the office followed the marshal as he stepped out onto the boardwalk. There was a hubbub among the crowd, but it died down quickly when the marshal appeared.

Running his gaze over their frightened faces, Halloran lifted his voice and said, "Folks, I'm sure you're here concerning Earline Drummond's death last night."

"We sure are, Marshal!" called out Clem Farris, a man in his sixties, who seemed to be the chosen spokesman. "We're wantin' to know when you're gonna have these patrols operatin' like you been tellin' us."

"As you can see," said Halloran, "we're working on it right now. We'll be ready to patrol the streets from dusk till dawn starting this evening. Some of our rancher friends are here to help us. I've set up groups of four men each to patrol in shifts, so there'll be men moving about town all through each night till the killer is caught. If any of you see or hear the slightest thing out of the ordinary, a loud shout through a window or a door will be heard by whatever patrol band is near you."

Another older man stepped forward, raising a hand to gain the marshal's attention.

"Yes, Ralph?" said Halloran.

"Marshal, I don't mean to offend you, understand, but have you considered the possibility that one of these patrolmen could be the killer?"

"No offense taken, Ralph. I have indeed considered that possibility. I discussed it with these men, and they all agreed that I was correct in assigning them to work in groups of four, as I mentioned a moment ago, just in case one of them is the killer. It would be quite difficult for him to overcome three men. I've taken every precaution I can think of. If the killer is amongst the patrolmen, or if he is not, we're going to stop him one way or another."

There was a rousing cheer, punctuated by applause.

Looking around at the crowd, Halloran said, "Any more questions?"

"Looks like you told us what we need to know, Marshal," said Clem Farris.

"All right. All of you stay alert, and call for help if you need it. I know you have guns, but I caution you to be very careful. I don't want some innocent person getting shot by a frightened citizen. Now, if you'll excuse us, we'll get back to our meeting."

✦

At the doctor's office, Lowry and Breanna were working on a small boy who had fallen out of a tree and broken his arm. They were just finishing with the cast when they heard a male voice in the outer office asking the boy's mother if Dr. Lowry was in.

"Go ahead, Doctor," said Breanna, "I'll take care of this."

Stepping into the office, Lowry found Carl Stubbins, a local rancher whose wife was nearing delivery of their fourth child. He could tell by Stubbins' face that his wife was in labor. "Baby coming, Carl?"

"Yes, Doctor. Laura made me wait till her pains were fifteen minutes apart. That was thirty minutes ago. We've got thirty minutes to get back to the ranch. Her mother's with her, but she needs you. Can you come right now?"

"Sure," said Lowry, turning back toward the examining room door. "I'll be right with you."

The doctor told Breanna he was going to a ranch outside town to deliver a baby. She would have to handle the appointments as best she could and the "walk-ins," too. Then he grabbed his medical bag and dashed out the door with Carl Stubbins.

Breanna finished wrapping the cast and returned the boy to his mother, who thanked her and moved outside, talking about last night's murder.

Two people came in for appointments, and Breanna took care of them efficiently. An older couple entered, requesting sedatives.

Things had quieted down by midmorning, and there wasn't another appointment until one o'clock. With her mind on the murder of Earline Drummond, Breanna was doing some filing

90

when she heard the door open. She turned to face a tall, muscular man in his mid-forties who held a bloody bandanna over his right eye.

"Good morning, sir," she said. "I'm Dr. Lowry's temporary nurse, Breanna Brockman. Dr. Lowry is delivering a baby at a ranch. I'll do what I can for you. What happened?"

Keeping the bandanna over his eye, he said, "I was chopping wood for my cookstove. The ax hit a knot in the log and sent splinters flying every direction. Some of them hit my face. A sharp splinter stuck in my eye. I was afraid to try taking it out myself."

"Let's go to the examining room, Mr.—Oh! I don't know your name."

"Bart Gibson."

"All right, Mr. Gibson, follow me."

As directed by the nurse, Gibson lay down on one of the examining tables, still keeping the blood-soaked bandanna to his eye.

Standing over him, Breanna said, "All right, Mr. Gibson, take the bandanna away from the eye now."

Breanna leaned close, touched the eyelid, and studied the damaged area. The eye was naturally shedding tears, and blood was flowing from where the splinter had penetrated the eyeball. Going to the cabinet, she returned with a magnifying glass and looked at the eye again.

Taking a square of gauze from a small cart next to the table, she said, "Hold as still as you can. I've got to soak up the blood and tears so I can see the splinter better."

After dabbing at it carefully for a moment, she said, "Mr. Gibson, I know it's hard to keep your eyelid from wanting to close, so I'll have to hold it open. Tell me, can you see with the eye?"

"Not real clearly, but I can see. So what are you going to do?"

She bent down and examined the eye again through the magnifying glass. While doing so, she said, "Let me explain what we have here. The splinter is embedded in the eyeball, as best as I can tell, about a quarter of an inch. We have a serious problem. The splinter is 'winged.'"

"What does that mean?"

"Well, it's shaped something like an Indian arrowhead, so that to remove it means it will do severe damage as it's being extracted. It's stuck at the edge of the iris. Removing the splinter will do more damage to the iris and possibly the pupil. The cornea is damaged, too. The real problem here is if the splinter is not removed properly, you could lose sight in the eye. We'll have to wait till Dr. Lowry gets back. He will need to remove the splinter. I will make you as comfortable as possible until he returns."

Gibson's mouth pulled into a thin line. "But if he's delivering a baby, it could be hours before he's back."

"I know, but there's nothing else to do but wait till Dr. Lowry returns. He must remove the splinter."

"Lady," Gibson said petulantly, "I'm in a lot of pain. I can't lie here for hours, hurting like this. Since you know so much about eyes, certainly you can remove the splinter."

"I know what every nurse should know about eyes, Mr. Gibson," Breanna said evenly, "but I'm not a doctor. I can give you something to ease the pain, but I'm not qualified to remove the splinter."

Gibson sighed in disgust. "Can you deaden the pain altogether?"

"Only by putting you completely out with chloroform, but I couldn't keep you under for hours. The best I can do is give you some powders that will take the edge off the pain."

Gibson's voice had steel in it. "I don't want the edge taken off the pain, lady! I want that splinter out of my eye *now!* I want the pain gone altogether! I came to this office to get the splinter out. If you can't handle it, you shouldn't be working here at all! Now, what's it going to be? You going to do it or not?"

The man's insolence brought life to Breanna's temper. Struggling to subdue it, she held her voice steady. "Mr. Gibson, I am a nurse, but I am not a doctor. I am not qualified to take out the splinter. I don't want you to lose the sight in your eye."

Gibson's lips pulled over his teeth in anger. The cords in his throat stood out as he said, "If you can't take care of it, lady, get me somebody who can! Right now!"

Breanna recoiled from his violent response. She drew the back of her hand across her forehead and found it clammy with cold sweat. Suddenly she remembered what Dr. Lowry had said about psychopaths—how quickly they can become violent.

She jumped with a start as Gibson said loudly, "You're a nurse, lady! You should care that I'm hurting! I want this splinter out, and I want it out right now!"

"B-but, I'm not qu-qualified. I—"

Suddenly he had her wrist in a hard grip. She tried to pull free, but his strength was too much.

"I said *now*, lady!"

Afraid to cross him, Breanna bit down on her lower lip and said, "All right. If you insist."

"I insist."

Looking at the strong fingers that were clamped on her wrist, she said, "I can't remove the splinter unless you let go of me."

With trembling hands, Breanna went to the cabinet and brought the instruments she would need to extract the sliver. As she sterilized them with wood alcohol, she said, "I'll put you under with chloroform, Mr. Gibson. I should have it out in a few minutes, and—"

"No chloroform!" he rasped. "I don't want to be unconscious."

"But the pain, you—"

"I'll endure the pain for a few minutes. No chloroform."

"All right. Whatever you say."

Breanna forced her hands to cease their trembling as she positioned herself over the man she now feared, and took up the finely honed instrument she would use to pull out the sliver. Her hands were steady as she began the extraction.

Bart Gibson amazed Breanna at how well he handled the pain when she finally was able to get the splinter out. As she had feared, the winged little piece of wood tore pupil, iris, and cornea. The eyeball bled profusely. She worked furiously to get the bleeding stopped while Gibson endured the pain, his only response a stiffening in his body and the set of his jaw.

When the bleeding ceased, Breanna cleared the damaged eye and said, "All right, Mr. Gibson. Tell me what you can see with the eye."

Gibson strained, brow furrowed, and closed his good eye. "I can't see a thing."

"Not even light?"

"No," he said in a bitter tone. "Only darkness. You've blinded my eye."

A shiver went down Breanna's backbone. "Now, don't give up so quickly, Mr. Gibson. Hopefully, it's only temporary blindness. When the swelling goes down and the eye clears up from the strain I put on it in extracting the splinter, you'll be able to see again."

"*Hopefully.* Is that all you can say? *Hopefully?*"

Breanna did not like the look he gave her. "Mr. Gibson, I did the best I could. I told you I wasn't qualified to work on your eye. The splinter did further damage as I was taking it out. I told you it would. You insisted I do the job, and as I said, I did the best I could. We won't know the actual results for several days."

Breanna felt Gibson's intense displeasure as he stared coldly at her with his good eye. The other eye remained closed.

"I need to bandage the eye," she said, turning to the cart for the materials she needed.

Gibson stared at her while she bandaged him. When she was finished, she said, "I can give you something to ease your pain if you wish. You need to lie right here and rest until Dr. Lowry returns. He will want to examine the eye."

The muscular man sat up, a scowl framing his face, and said, "I'm not waiting for Doc to come back. I've got work to do."

Breanna knew it would do no good to argue with him. As he started toward the front office on shaky legs, she said, "When Dr. Lowry returns, I'll tell him about the splinter, Mr. Gibson. I'm sure he'll want to take a look at the eye."

She followed him into the office, her stomach feeling like something was clawing at it. When he took hold of the knob to the outside door, he paused and said, "I better be able to see when the swelling goes down and the eye clears up."

A chill washed over Breanna as he stood there glaring at her, then moved out and headed down the boardwalk, leaving the door open.

Breanna's hand rose to the base of her throat as if to stop

the cry rising there. Bart Gibson was being totally unreasonable, and he frightened her.

She moved to the door and watched the man walk unsteadily down the street. When he vanished from view, she was about to turn from the door when she saw Marshal Halloran trotting his horse up the street in her direction. She hurried out onto the boardwalk and called to him.

He veered the horse to the hitch rail in front of the doctor's office. "Yes, ma'am?"

"Marshal, would you have a few minutes to talk to me?"

There was fear plainly etched on her face. Halloran frowned as he dismounted. "Of course. What's wrong, ma'am?"

"I...I just had a frightening experience. I'd like to talk to you about it."

"Has this anything to do with the killer?"

"It might. Dr. Lowry's delivering a baby at a ranch at the moment. I was alone when it happened, and I'm alone now. Please come into the office."

The marshal took a seat in front of the desk where Breanna sat down. She told him about Bart Gibson and how he demanded that she remove the splinter. She explained that his eye had no sight before she bandaged it and quoted Gibson's threatening remark as he left.

The marshal eased back on the seat, rubbing his chin thoughtfully.

"The man's violence made me wonder if he's the psychopathic killer," Breanna said.

"I can see why, ma'am."

"What do you think?"

"Well, to tell you the truth, Bart has crossed my mind many times since these killings started. He's known for his hair-trigger temper and periodic sour mood swings. But I can't arrest him on supposition."

"I understand, but I thought I should tell you about this frightening experience I just had with him."

Halloran nodded. "I need to tell you something about him, ma'am. It's no secret here in town, so I'm not telling tales out of school. Bart was recently released from the Colorado Territorial Prison at Canon City."

Her eyebrows arched. "Oh?"

"Mm-hmm. He served eight years on a manslaughter charge."

Breanna listened breathlessly as Halloran said, "One day, eight years ago, Bart took a trip to Denver. He was supposed to be gone a week but returned to Redstone in five days. He found his wife with another man. In a jealous rage, Bart beat both of them severely. The man left town in a hurry and never came back, but Bart's wife died two days later from the beating."

Breanna's hand went to her mouth.

"Bart was convicted of manslaughter and given a fourteen-year sentence. He got out in eight on good behavior. It was this incident and the display of temper that I've seen in Bart that has made me suspicious of him. But until I have enough to go on, I can't arrest him."

"Of course, Marshal Halloran. But what should I do if his eye turns out to be permanently blind? There was a definite threatening tone in his voice to go with his choice of words."

Mike's jaw jutted. "When Dr. Lowry returns and you tell him about this incident, I want to be with him whenever he examines Bart's eye. I'll tell the man in no uncertain terms that no matter how it turns out, he had better not bother you about it. When he seized your wrist and insisted you take out the splinter in spite of the fact that you said you weren't qualified like Dr. Lowry is, he forfeited any recourse against you if the eye was damaged more by removing it."

"That's how I look at it, Marshal. He gave me no choice. The way he was acting, I was afraid to refuse."

A wagon rolled to a stop outside. Breanna looked out the window, past Halloran. "It's Dr. Lowry."

Carl Stubbins pulled away as Dr. Lowry came toward the office, carrying his black medical bag.

"Howdy, Marshal," said Lowry, moving past him into the office.

"How did it go, Doctor?" Breanna asked. "You're back so soon."

Lowry chuckled as he set his medical bag on the desk. "Pretty simple. By the time we got to the ranch, Laura's mother had already delivered the baby. All I had to do was check mother and baby and tell Carl to bring me back to town."

"Well, I'm glad it went well."

Lowry frowned as he looked straight into Breanna's face. "Are you all right? You look a little peaked."

"You're quite observant, Doctor," said Mike. "Breanna just had a good scare."

"Hmm?" said Lowry, looking at the marshal, then back at Breanna.

When Lowry heard the story, he said, "Bart is probably home. Let's go. I want to examine the eye, but I also want to talk to him about the way he treated Breanna, and I want you there to back me up, Mike."

"Tell you what, Doc," said Halloran. "No doubt you can examine the eye better here at the office, right?"

"Yes."

"Then you and Mrs. Brockman sit tight, and I'll be back with Bart shortly."

⚘

Some twenty minutes had passed when Marshal Halloran returned with Bart Gibson. A mother and her teenage daughter were just leaving the office when they came in.

Bart ignored Breanna, and there was a sour look on his face as he said to Lowry, "Mike said you wanted to take a look at the eye, Doc."

"Yes." Then to Halloran, "Did you explain that I wanted to see him about something else, too?"

"Mm-hmm. I didn't elaborate, but he's smart enough to know what it's about."

Gibson flicked a glance at Breanna. Another cold chill washed over her.

"Let's go in the back room so I can get a good look at the eye, Bart," said the doctor. "Breanna…Mike…come along."

Breanna stood opposite the doctor, and Halloran moved up beside her. They watched as Lowry removed the bandage, then used the magnifying glass and a light reflector to do a careful examination of the damaged eye.

When he finished, he laid both instruments aside and said, "Bart, do you want it straight from the shoulder?"

"Are you going to tell me I'll never see out of the eye again?"

"Precisely."

Gibson's jaw snapped shut, and he looked at Breanna.

"Listen to me, Bart," said the doctor. "Don't go blaming this dear lady. She did the best she could. Before you got here, she showed me the splinter. It's over here in the cabinet. I'm telling you right now, no matter who removed it, the splinter would still have done the same damage when it was extracted. You understand what I'm saying?"

Gibson glanced at Breanna again, then looked at Lowry. "Yeah."

"You're not very convincing, Bart," said Halloran. "Looks to me like you're still blaming Mrs. Brockman for your blind eye."

Bart didn't reply.

"Now, look, pal," said the marshal. "Mrs. Brockman told both Dr. Lowry and me that you forced her to remove the splinter, even when she told you she wanted you to wait and let Doc do it."

Still, Gibson did not reply.

Halloran's features went crimson. "Did she lie to us, Bart?"

Gibson rolled his single eye and looked up at the marshal, a scowl framing his face.

"Well, did she?" pressed Lowry.

Gibson cleared his throat. "No. She didn't lie."

Halloran leaned down close. "So you forced her to do it, right?"

Gibson cleared his throat again. "I guess you could say I strongly insisted on it."

"Strongly insisted? She said you grabbed her wrist and clamped down so hard it hurt her. Did you?"

"Well..."

"Did you?"

"Okay. I did."

"All right, now listen closely, Bart. I want you to apologize to her for that. And I want you to understand me when I say you had better never give this dear lady any trouble over this incident again. Understand?"

Bart nodded.

"Say the words, Bart."

"I understand."

"And?"

"I won't give her any trouble over it."

"Fine. Now, the apology."

Bart worked his jaw, looked up at Breanna, and said, "I'm sorry. I shouldn't have made you take out the splinter."

7

AS DARKNESS FELL OVER REDSTONE, the people of the town rested a little easier with Marshal Halloran's four-man teams walking the streets from dark to daylight.

In her room at the boardinghouse, Breanna sat on a chair by a window overlooking the street. Periodically she saw four-man patrols pass by.

When bedtime came, she slipped between the covers after reading her Bible and praying. Lying there in the darkness, she thought over the Bart Gibson situation. Bart had apologized, but to Breanna it seemed hollow. She was sure he was still blaming her for the loss of sight in the damaged eye.

She thought of Mary Donelson's words in reference to the death of the Moreland baby and that being blamed was one of the prices she had to pay for being a nurse.

She had just paid the price again.

Morning came to Redstone, clear and cool, bringing with it the fragrance of pine and spruce in the air. The rising sun reddened the canyon walls in the high country to the north, where the Crystal River made its sinuous journey to the lower elevations.

Breanna emerged from the boardinghouse, took a deep breath, and relished the mixed spicy fragrance in the air. She cast an appreciative glance at majestic Snowmass Mountain and headed down Main Street toward the doctor's office.

People were milling about, and traffic was moderate on the broad, dusty street.

As she crossed at the first intersection and stepped up onto the boardwalk, she saw a man leaning against the front of the hardware store and gun shop on the corner. When she drew near him, he caught her eye and smiled. She smiled back and kept her pace. She noticed that his gaze remained fixed on her as she passed him.

She had seen him standing outside the door of the general store the previous afternoon when she came out carrying a small sack of goods. He had smiled and stared at her then, too. He was a big, muscular man, and looked to be in his mid-thirties. This second incident unnerved her.

As Breanna moved on, she shook her head and told herself she was just jumpy because there was a killer on the loose and because of her experience yesterday with Bart Gibson.

Dr. Lowry smiled at Breanna and greeted her as she entered the office.

"Good morning, Doctor," she replied.

"You sleep all right last night, Breanna?"

"Not real well."

"Your episode with Bart?"

"Mm-hmm."

"Bart is a hothead, Breanna, but I think Mike put some fear into him about his attitude toward you. There won't be any more trouble from him."

"I hope not."

"Well," Lowry said, picking up his medical bag, "I've got a

103

couple of elderly ladies to make house calls on, so I'll see you later. I shouldn't be gone more than half an hour."

"I'll hold down the fort," she said cheerfully.

"Atta girl," he said, patting her shoulder.

When the doctor was gone, Breanna picked up the appointment book, noting that the first patient scheduled was at nine o'clock. The doctor would be back by then.

She took the appointment book with her and went to the file drawer to pull the folders for each patient coming in that day. When she turned to the desk and laid them down, her eyes strayed to the front of the general store across the street. She felt an icy prickling on the back of her neck as she focused on the same man who had stared at her this morning and yesterday.

He was looking her direction. She wasn't sure if he could see through the window, but her stomach went queasy.

Abruptly the door came open and a small, wiry gray-haired man entered, his left hand wrapped in a white cloth. Breanna recalled having seen him at church on Sunday. He had spoken to her but had not told her his name.

She shook off the feeling of dread caused by the man across the street and smiled at her walk-in patient, saying, "Good morning, sir. I'd say something has happened to your hand."

"Yes, ma'am. My name's Woody Jones. I'm the Western Union telegraph operator here in town. We met at church Sunday."

"Yes, I remember."

He looked at his wrapped hand and said, "I'm a widower, Mrs. Brockman, so I have to do my own cookin'. I cut my finger this mornin' when I was slicin' some bacon for breakfast. I'd like for Doc to take a look at it."

"Dr. Lowry is making house calls right now, Mr. Jones.

Would you like for me to look at it?"

"Sure."

"Let's go to the back room."

Breanna had Woody sit on one of the examining tables, then she carefully removed the cloth wrapping. Studying the cut on his forefinger, she said, "It won't need stitches. It's not that deep."

"Well, praise the Lord for that," said Woody.

While Breanna cleaned the cut, soaked it with iodine, and bandaged it, she and Woody had a wonderful conversation because of their shared faith. Woody also wanted to know how she had met the famous John Stranger. The story amazed him, and he was glad to hear they had a happy marriage.

When they returned to the front office, Breanna glanced across the street. The big man was still there in front of the general store, and he was looking her direction.

As Woody headed toward the door, she said, "Ah...Mr. Jones—"

"You can call me Woody, ma'am," he said, grinning.

"All right. Woody. I need to ask you something."

"Sure."

"Take a look across the street. Right there by the door of the general store."

The little man moved up to the window. "Mm-hmm?"

Two men had stopped to talk to the man in question, and he was occupied with them.

"See the big man who's leaning by the door?" said Breanna. "He's facing this way and talking to those two well-dressed men."

"Yes'm. The one in the plaid shirt?"

"Yes. Who is he?"

"His name's Biff Matthews. Why?"

"Well…ah…he's sort of been staring at me, and he makes me nervous. What do you know about him?"

"He's a carpenter and cabinet maker."

"Is he married?"

"Not now, ma'am. You see, Biff fought in the Civil War on the Confederate side. When the War was over and he went home to Georgia, he found that his wife had been killed when Sherman marched on Atlanta. Brokenhearted, he left Georgia and came west to start a new life."

"Oh. I'm sorry to hear about his wife. Did they have any children?"

"Guess not. He's never mentioned any children." Woody looked at Matthews again and chuckled. "I know Biff has been lookin' for a new wife. Maybe he doesn't know you're married and has been starin' at you, tryin' to work up enough courage to introduce himself."

"Well, I hope he finds his new wife very soon," she said drily.

"Women are a bit scarce in these parts, but I'm sure one of these days he'll find one."

Breanna nodded. "I'm going to come to your office at lunchtime and send a telegram to my husband. When I'm away from home, John likes to hear from me every few days."

"Well, tell you what, ma'am. If you'd like to write the message down for me, I'll send it for you as soon as I get back to the office. Save you a trip over there."

"That's nice of you, Mr. Jones. I'll—"

"Woody."

"Oh, yes. Woody. I'll write it down for you."

Pulling a piece of paper from a desk drawer, Breanna dipped the desk pen into the inkwell and quickly wrote a message. She made it brief, telling John that she was fine and included a few words about the work at the office and the church services. She didn't mention the murders nor the killer.

Using a blotter, she said, "There you are, Woody. Take a look at it and tell me what I owe you."

Woody counted the words and said, "It'll be thirty-five cents, ma'am."

Breanna paid him, plus some extra for his kindness, and Woody left, assuring her the message would be sent to Denver immediately.

On Breanna's fifth day in Redstone, Thelma Lowry was in the front office learning what she could from Breanna about John 'The Stranger' Brockman. Dr. Lowry was examining a little girl with tonsil problems while her mother stood at her side.

The conversation between the two women was interrupted when they heard a commotion at the front door, and four men wearing the clothing and boots of lumbermen came in, carrying a lumberman who was unconscious and soaked with blood.

Breanna hurried to them, took one look at the bloody man and said, "Dr. Lowry is in the examining room with a patient, but let's take him on back." Breanna surmised that he had been mauled by a wild animal. There were deep scratches on his face and hands, and his blood-soaked shirt was torn to shreds. His chest and midsection had been mauled, too.

As Breanna led them toward the examining room door, Thelma said, "Breanna, we'll take up our conversation another time. I need to get home now."

Breanna nodded at Thelma and opened the door. When Lowry looked up from his examination, she said, "We have an emergency, Doctor."

She led the men to the other examining table.

Lowry set his gaze on the victim. "What happened?"

"We were cutting trees in the forest a couple of miles west of here, Doctor," said one of them. "Our friend, here, is Will Clancy. He was working by himself about a hundred yards from the rest of us. It was Half-Paw that got him."

"Half-Paw!" exclaimed Lowry, leaving the mother and child to hurry to the other table. "Are you sure? As far as we know, he's never attacked humans before."

"No question it was a cougar, Doctor, but the prints left in the soft ground around Will and the claw marks on his body leave no doubt it was Half-Paw. We heard the beast roaring and Will screaming, but by the time we could get to him, the beast was gone."

Lowry noted that Breanna was already cutting away what was left of the victim's shirt. Hurrying back to the mother and child, he gave the mother a bottle of medicine, told her how to use it, then rushed back to the unconscious lumberman and sent his comrades to the waiting room.

As doctor and nurse began working on Clancy, Breanna said, "Doctor, who is this Half-Paw?"

"A killer mountain lion," responded Lowry, assessing the damage as he went over the man's upper body. "Half-Paw's a huge cat, Breanna. He has half of his right forepaw missing. We assume that he must have stepped into a woodsman's bear trap and had to tear off part of his paw to get free.

"For the past year, Half-Paw has killed horses, cattle, and sheep in these parts. Ranchers have banded together to track him down and destroy him, but he's highly intelligent and has managed to evade them." The doctor took a deep breath and sighed, then added, "And now it appears he's going after humans."

Breanna didn't comment, but she thought to herself, *Isn't this something? Not only do we have a killer psychopath on the loose, but we also have a vicious mountain lion to fear.*

They labored together to save Will Clancy's life. They were able to stop his bleeding and to sew up the lacerations where the cougar's claws had ripped through the skin. When the bandaging was done, Lowry left Breanna to clean up the table and went to the front office.

The four lumbermen rose to their feet as the doctor came in, their eyes searching his face.

"Your friend was mauled very seriously, gentlemen, but I can tell you he's out of immediate danger. He's still unconscious, but things look positive."

All four were about to ask questions when the door behind Lowry opened and Breanna said, "Doctor, he's coming around."

"You men take a seat," said Lowry. "I'll let you know more when I see how he is."

Moments later, Dr. Lowry returned and said, "He's awake, men, but awfully weak. He did confirm that it was Half-Paw who attacked him. The beast leaped on him from a high rock, and there was no way to avoid him."

"It's a wonder Half-Paw didn't kill him," said one of the men as Breanna came into the office.

"Must've been something that scared him off before he could claw Will to death," said another.

Breanna smiled and said, "Praise the Lord for that!"

Two of the lumbermen looked at each other, then one of them said, "Well, amen to that, ma'am. The Lord kept Will from being killed by Half-Paw!" Turning to Lowry, he said, "Right, Doctor?"

Lowry appeared a bit off balance at the question, but

replied, "Ah…well, yes. God did something that caused the cougar to run before he killed your friend."

"Doctor," said Breanna, noting Lowry's awkwardness at the mention of the Lord, "Will asked if his friends could come in and see him."

"It'll have to be short, but I can allow it."

As the men filed through the door behind the doctor, Breanna's heart was heavy for him. Neither the doctor nor Thelma gave any indication that they were Christians. She wanted to see them saved before she went home.

Late that afternoon, Woody Jones entered the doctor's office to find Breanna and Lowry in conversation at the desk. Both turned and looked at him as he said, "Have a telegram for you, Mrs. Brockman. From your husband."

"Oh, thank you." Breanna read the message silently. John told her how lonely he was without her, and that he was looking forward to her return. He added that he still had big plans for her birthday.

As she folded the paper, Woody said, "Chief Brockman sure wants you home for your birthday, ma'am. Do you mind if I ask when that is?"

"September 30," Dr. Lowry answered for her. "How well I know. I promised her she would be home before that day, even if my new nurse, Martha Waverly, hasn't arrived yet." Then to Breanna: "I sure am hoping Martha will make it in time."

"Me, too," said Breanna. "But I appreciate your understanding my situation."

Lowry chuckled. "Well, the last thing I want to do is get on the bad side of the chief U.S. marshal!"

Late that afternoon, after a hard day's work, Breanna was making her way along Main Street, looking forward to an evening of rest and relaxation. Her mind was on John as she neared the corner where she would take a side street to the boardinghouse. Suddenly she was aware of a man leaning against the front of the store on the corner.

Biff Matthews!

Breanna instinctively broke her stride for a second, then forced herself to keep walking at her normal pace. When she drew up to the spot where Matthews stood, she couldn't help but meet his gaze. He smiled and nodded. This time, she did not smile, but made a weak nod and kept walking. As before, she saw his eyes remain on her as she passed and could feel them on her until she turned the corner.

Her skin prickled and her heart thudded in her chest. She wanted to run but feared that he might be looking at her from the corner of the building. The sensation of being watched was on her again, but she forced her legs to carry her at a normal pace and did not look back.

As the days passed, Breanna got to know many of the people in Redstone. It bothered her that not a day went by but she found Biff Matthews along her path, idly leaning against a building or standing briefly in front of the general store looking in her direction when she was in the doctor's office.

Could Matthews be the Redstone killer? Or was it Bart Gibson? Bart had been back to the doctor's office twice to have his bandage changed and both times was cool toward her. On the second occasion, she saw what appeared to be hatred in his good eye when he looked at her. It made her blood run cold, but she didn't say anything to Dr. Lowry about it, nor did she tell Marshal Halloran.

One evening, Pastor Eldon Severson and Karen took Breanna to supper at one of Redstone's three cafés. They both had heard much of The Stranger and were interested in learning all about him from Breanna.

When Breanna had satisfied their curiosity about John, she said, "Pastor, you told me when I first came that the Lowrys have never attended a church service. I'm sure you've invited them."

"Oh, yes. Many times. Karen and I have visited them in their home at least a dozen times. We've witnessed to them, given them the gospel on every occasion, but they will not respond at all. They're always kind and cordial, but they show no concern for their eternal destiny. They simply are not interested in the Lord, nor do they want to have anything to do with Him."

"We haven't given up on them, Breanna," said Karen. "We pray for them every day, asking God to bring about something in their lives that will cause them to turn to Him."

"Me, too," said Breanna. "I have brought the Lord into conversations at the office with Dr. Lowry, but he simply passes it off. I've had very little opportunity to be with Thelma, but I'm going to try to find ways to spend some time alone with her so I can talk to her about the Lord."

"Bless you for that," said the pastor. "We'll be praying that the Lord will give you wisdom as you deal with her."

"We sure will," Karen assured her.

Severson took out his pocket watch, glanced at it, and said, "Well, Karen, it's getting late. We'd better take Breanna home."

The Seversons escorted Breanna to the boardinghouse. As they pulled up in front of it, two lanterns glowed brightly on the porch.

Across the street, an unseen observer stood behind a tree in the darkness. The pastor hopped out of the buggy and helped both ladies down, and the Seversons walked Breanna up the porch steps. The three of them stood talking in the glow of the lanterns.

Across the street, the man behind the tree focused on Breanna's blonde hair as it caught the light. His breathing quickly became uneven, and his blood heated up. "Yes!" he hissed in a low whisper. "You have the same color of hair that *she* had! And you look so much like her, it's unbelievable*! I hate you! I hate you! I hate you!* Why did it have to be a woman who looks so much like my evil mother to fill in for that nurse who's coming?"

The killer watched until Breanna went inside and the Seversons drove away, then faded back into the shadows. As he headed toward home, memories were burning into his brain— horrid memories of his vile mother. Each atrocity committed against him by his mother seemed to multiply a thousand times in his tortured mind, and he cursed her over and over in a hateful whisper. Suddenly he was aware of a buggy coming down the dark street. Gasping for breath, he dashed into a yard and ducked behind some bushes. When the buggy had passed, he started toward the street again, but the pain in his head caused him to stumble.

The pain. The pain was coming back. Stabbing lances of excruciating pain.

Suddenly, in the dark chambers of his mind, it was a cold January day. She was dragging him out of the house with that iron grip on his wrist, swearing at him for spilling his milk at the table. He went flying off the porch and landed in a snow bank. As she gripped his wrist again, he wailed, begging her not to beat him.

The raw, icy wind cut through his thin shirt as she dragged him through the snow, facedown, using her free hand to sink strong fingers in his hair, pulling at the roots.

When they reached the shed, she let go of his hair and threw the latch. She was swearing at him when the shed door came open hard and swift and connected with his head. He saw lights flash like meteors against a black sky, then seemed to be swallowed into a dark whirlpool.

He had no idea how long he had been unconscious when he came to, but he was in the shed.

Alone.

In the dark.

The wind beat against the boards, driving cold, thin blasts through the cracks in the walls, around the windows, and around the door. His head hurt something fierce. Glowing lights flashed in the corners of his eyes. He could feel pressure building as if black water were being pumped into his head....

From that time on he had suffered periodically with the headaches, the flashing lights in the corners of his eyes, and the sensation of black pressure. Just like now, as he stood swaying in the darkness on one of Redstone's streets, pressing fingers against his throbbing temples.

His entire body trembled. He thought of that horrible night spent in the cold shed. He was only ten or eleven years old, but he was so angry at his mother that he wanted to kill her.

But she was much stronger than he was, and he feared her. When she came to take him out of the shed the next morning, thoughts of killing her raced through his mind, but he knew she was too strong. He would never be able to do it.

On the way home from school that afternoon, the hatred he felt toward his mother began to fester. His head was beginning to hurt like the night before, and the lights were flashing in the corners of his eyes. He ran to the nearby forest, found a small, furry animal, and killed it, pretending it was his mother.

It had brought great relief to his pain.

As the years passed, each time he had the horrible headaches and the flashing lights, he would kill an animal, and the pain would go away…for a while. Now the relief only came when he killed humans.

And now, having seen Breanna Brockman's blond hair in the light of the lantern, and having studied her face again, it was like his mother had come back to torture him some more.

Kill! Yes, he needed to kill in order to relieve the pressure inside his head. No way to get to the Brockman woman now. He would find a way to get her later.

The killer took a deep breath and moved on down the street, holding the tips of his fingers against his temples. Suddenly, by the street lamps at the next corner, he saw the forms of four men coming his way. It was one of the four-man patrols who were out to get *him.*

He dashed into the nearest yard and flattened himself on the ground behind a clump of bushes. He lay there, covering his mouth to stifle the sound of his hard breathing until they had passed and he could no longer hear their footsteps.

Still fighting the pain inside his head, he hurried down the street, keeping to the shadows. His pain was becoming unbearable. Abruptly, he stopped in front of a house where the blinds were down on the windows, but he could see a woman's shadow as she moved about inside.

She dies tonight!

Inside the house, Thelma Lowry was waiting for her husband to return from seeing a patient across town. She had decided to rearrange some of the pictures on the walls.

Humming to herself as she carried a painting from the parlor to the dining room, Thelma laid it down, then took one off the wall next to the china cabinet. Setting it on a chair, she picked up the other one and hung it in its place. Backing away from it, she cocked her head to one side, trying to decide if she was satisfied with it there.

She jumped when the back door crashed open. Her heart leaped in her breast. It could only mean one thing...*the killer!*

McClay kept a loaded revolver in the desk in his den, which was across the hall. She had to get to the gun!

She darted for the hall but found herself suddenly standing face to face with a wild-eyed man...a man she knew well.

8

AT FIRST, MARCIE HALLORAN thought the thunderous noise was part of her dream, but she came awake as it continued, and opened her eyes to darkness.

Suddenly it came again. Someone was pounding on the front door.

Mike was sleeping deeply next to her and hadn't stirred.

"Mike! Mike!" She rolled over and shook his shoulder.

He groaned and then settled back into slumber.

"Mike! Honey, wake up!"

He sat up with a start, and the pounding began again. "Wha—What is it, Marcie?"

"The door. Somebody's pounding on the door."

Mike rolled out of bed and groped for his pants while Marcie lit a lantern. He yanked his gun out of its holster, took the lantern from her, and said to stay put.

The pounding thundered through the house again as Mike hurried to the front door. "Who is it?"

"Doc Lowry!"

Mike swung open the door and held up the lantern light to see an anguished look on Lowry's face.

"What is it, Doc?"

"It's...it's Thelma! Sh-she's been murdered! I was visiting

117

Florence Roberts. Y—you know she's been quite ill."

"Yes."

"I got home a few minutes ago, and…and…I found Thelma on the floor of the hall. She was strangled, Mike! It's the killer! He strangled my Thelma!"

"Oh, Doc, I'm so sorry!" Marcie said as she drew up behind her husband.

The marshal made sure Marcie was locked safely in the house with one of his revolvers in hand, then went with the grieving doctor to his house. On the way, they encountered one of the patrol teams and informed them what had happened. The team had seen nothing out of the ordinary but assured Doc and the marshal they would alert the other teams immediately.

The doctor led Mike into his house and to the body of his wife. He lifted the blanket he had covered her with and said, "I didn't touch her, or anything around, Mike. I wanted you to see her just as I found her."

Halloran nodded, then knelt down and looked at the red marks on Thelma's throat. "Doc, I hate to ask you to do this, but will you examine her throat for me? I think I'm right, just by looking, but I need to know if the throat cartilage is crushed like Ruby Copeland's and Earline Drummond's."

Lowry knelt down beside him and with trembling fingers pressed on Thelma's throat, probing for the telltale signs. He quickly pulled his hands away and choked on a sob as he nodded.

"I thought so," said Halloran. He looked at her neck again and said, "The man has to be strong as an ox to crush the neck cartilage, wouldn't you say, Doc?"

"Yes. It's the same man who strangled Ruby and Earline, I'm sure."

"Has to be, but this time he didn't ram the eyes into the skull."

"I...I noticed that."

"Probably because he knows we won't question that it's him, now that he's murdered four people in this town."

"I'm sure you're right. He doesn't have to leave his calling card anymore."

Halloran cleared his throat gently. "Doc, what about...well, you're the undertaker in this town. Would you like for me to wire Stan Lockwood up in Glenwood Springs and have him come down and prepare her for burial?"

Lowry's lower lip quivered and fresh tears filled his eyes. "If you wouldn't mind."

"Of course not. I'll send the wire in the morning. How about I carry her somewhere now?"

"The spare bedroom," said Lowry. "But I'll carry her."

"All right, Doc."

When the doctor bent down to pick up his wife's body, a sob burst from his throat and he wept without restraint.

"I'm sorry, Doc," Halloran said as he laid a hand on Lowry's shoulder.

It took the doctor several minutes to bring his emotions under control; then he carried his wife into the spare bedroom and covered her with the blanket.

When he came out of the room, the marshal said, "How did the killer get in, Doc?"

"Oh, I'm sorry. I haven't even thought to tell you that. Come. I'll show you."

Lowry led him to the kitchen and showed him the back door. It had been hit hard. The lock was shattered, and there were slivers of wood on the floor from the door frame.

Mike looked around, checked the outside of the door by

the light of the kitchen lantern, then checked the inside. There was nothing to tell him a thing about the killer, except that he was quite strong.

Glancing at the clock on the kitchen wall, Doc Lowry said, "Mike, it's almost two o'clock. You need to go home and get your sleep."

"No, Doc. You've been through a horrible experience, and I'm not leaving you."

Lowry's fingers trembled as he ran them through his hair. "I can't ask you to stay with me, Mike."

"You didn't. I volunteered. Why don't you fix yourself a sedative? Wouldn't it help to settle your nerves?"

"Yes. I guess it would."

After the doctor had taken the sedative, the two men sat down in the parlor and talked.

When dawn came, the marshal got up from his chair and stretched. "Well, Doc, I guess I'd better be going. Come to think of it, would you like to have breakfast at our house? I'm sure Marcie would be glad to add an extra plate to the table."

"Thanks, Mike," said Lowry, "but I'm really not hungry. I'll eat something later, maybe. Would you do me a favor?"

"Name it."

"After you send the wire to Stan Lockwood, I need you to stop by my office and tell Breanna about...about Thelma. Tell her I'm just too torn up to work today. She should handle the patients as best she can. If there's an emergency, of course, she can send for me."

After the men on patrol had learned of Thelma Lowry's murder, word spread quickly through the town. Breanna's heart was heavy as she walked toward the doctor's office. Her opportunity to reach Thelma for the Lord was gone forever.

As she drew near the office, she saw Mike Halloran waiting for her.

"Good morning, Marshal," she said in a soft tone. "I know you've been with Dr. Lowry. He isn't coming to the office today, is he?"

"No. That's why I'm here. He wanted me to tell you he's not up to it, but you should send for him if you have an emergency."

Taking the key from her purse, she said, "I think you need to go home and get some rest, too. You look worn out. Were you up all night with him?"

"I was. But I'll be all right."

"Any clues on this one?"

"None, other than we know it was the same man who killed the others."

"Can we talk for a moment?" she asked, opening the door.

"Sure."

Mike followed Breanna inside. She laid her purse on the desk, turned to face him, and said, "I haven't told you or Dr. Lowry about Biff Matthews, but I'm wondering if he could be the killer."

"What do you mean, you haven't told us about Biff? Has he done something?"

Breanna explained about Matthews crossing her path at least once a day and about seeing him across the street, looking toward the office so often. She told him that Matthews had never spoken to her when eyeing her, but only smiled.

Mike scratched the back of his neck. "Well, to tell you the truth, ma'am, Biff has passed through my mind as a possible suspect, for a couple of reasons. One, he's big and strong. The other, he's a loner. Doc told me that oftentimes psychopaths are loners. But, like with Bart Gibson, I have no evidence against him."

Breanna nodded silently.

"Speaking of Bart," said Halloran, "have you seen him much lately?"

"A few times, and he always gives me a hard stare. He never speaks, just stares."

"Maybe I need to have another talk with him."

"I think he'd just deny his hostility. I guess as long as he keeps his distance from me, there's no use talking to him."

"I do want you to know, Breanna, that other people have come to me, speaking their suspicions of both Bart and Biff being the killer, so you're not alone in this." He drew a short breath and said, "Of course, it might not be either one. There are lots of men in Redstone who are strong enough to do what the killer has done. And, like Doc said, a psychopath can appear absolutely normal unless he's in his killing mood. It could be any one of a hundred men, for that matter."

"I wouldn't want your job," Breanna said.

"Well, somebody's got to do it. Right now, I feel like I'm failing. Four people have been murdered, and I'm no closer to capturing the killer than I was when Harold Wiggins was murdered."

"Stay with it, Marshal. Your break will come."

"Yes. That's what I keep telling myself. Every killer, psychopath or otherwise, makes a mistake sooner or later. I just wish this one would hurry up and make his before someone else is killed."

"I'm praying that way, Marshal."

Halloran's brow furrowed. "You really feel that God would step in here and help us to stop these killings?"

"Absolutely. He doesn't always do things in the way we think He should and exactly *when* we think He should, but prayer definitely moves His hand. Of course to have power with Him in prayer, you have to know Him."

"Know Him? I believe He exists and that He created the universe."

"Marshal, there's a difference in knowing God and merely knowing about Him. You can only come to God and become acquainted with Him through His only begotten Son, the Lord Jesus Christ. I have a small Bible here in my purse; I'd be glad to show you all about it."

Halloran stiffened. "Oh, ah, well I have to get going. Maybe some other time."

"All right. Some other time. It'll have to be soon, though. I won't be here very long."

"Sure. Soon. See you later, Breanna."

With that, the marshal was out the door and heading down the street toward his office.

Watching him, Breanna said, "Lord, I'd sure like to see the Hallorans saved before I leave this town."

By the time the news of Thelma Lowry's murder had spread through the town, the people of Redstone were on the verge of panic. Even though the patrol teams were on the streets at night, adults and children alike had a hard time sleeping. The slightest bump in the night had them thinking the killer had gotten into the house.

On the third day after Thelma's death, Pastor Eldon Severson preached the funeral service, which was held in the church auditorium. There was standing room only, even after extra chairs were set up on both sides of the aisle. Severson gave a clear-cut gospel presentation, urging those who didn't know Christ to turn to Him.

At the graveside service, when the pastor was finished, everyone walked by Dr. McClay Lowry to extend their condolences.

When Breanna came to him, she spoke tender words, doing what she could to give him comfort. He thanked her for taking care of the office so well while he had been at home, and her heart went out to him.

The next day at the office, Breanna watched Dr. Lowry as he worked with his patients. He seemed so grieved over Thelma that his concentration was affected. Twice she had to pull him aside and point out an error he had made with his patients. He thanked her and quickly made corrections.

A lull came at eleven o'clock, and with no one else in the office, Breanna joined him in the back room. "Doctor, maybe you shouldn't try to work a full day yet. I'm pretty sure I can take care of the patients who have appointments this afternoon. Why don't you go home and get some rest?"

"Oh, no, Breanna. I'll be all right. It's just that, well, I miss Thelma so much. I know the grief will ease with the passing of time, but it sure is overwhelming right now."

"Doctor," Breanna said with compassion in her voice, "I'd like to help you. There is one who can ease your grief like no other. I've known the precious Lord Jesus Christ since I was a girl, and I can testify that He has a way of helping His children bear the pain of grief like no other. Both of my parents were taken from me—"

The doctor raised a palm toward her. "Breanna, I appreciate what you're trying to do, but I just have different beliefs than you and your fellow Christians. I don't mean to offend you, but I'm simply not interested."

Breanna's countenance fell. "I'm not offended, Doctor. It's just that I know what the Lord Jesus can do to ease grief and to give salvation. I only want you to know Him as I do."

"Like I said...I appreciate what you're trying to do, but I have my own beliefs."

The sounds of someone in the front office met their ears. Breanna excused herself and headed for the front office.

Dusk fell in Redstone, and the men on the patrol teams who worked the first shift were leaving their homes to join their groups and begin the first shift.

Ray Slone, a forty-year-old veteran of the Civil War, put on his hat, strapped on his gunbelt, and then folded his wife of twenty years in his arms. He kissed her and said, "See you later, honey. You be sure to keep that gun in your hand wherever you go in the house. I checked all the windows and the back door. You lock the front door behind me when I go out."

"All right, darling. And you be careful. That maniac is out there somewhere."

They kissed again, and Betty watched her husband join his group as they waited for him in the street.

She closed the door and locked it, then went to her sewing room, which was at the back of the house, opposite from the kitchen. Two lanterns burned in the room, and she had already pulled the shade. She laid the .44 caliber revolver on the table and looked at it as she sat down. Ray had worn the Navy Colt as an officer in the Union Army.

As the evening progressed, Betty worked on the dress she

was making, but from time to time when there was a squeak or a bumping sound, she stiffened and laid her hand on the gun. After a few seconds, if there was no repeat of the sound, she went back to sewing.

Next door to the Slones, Ben and Ellen Murray sat in their parlor, reading. Ben had the family pet, a cat named Napoleon, lying in his lap.

At one point, Ellen looked up from her book and said, "I don't know about you, but I'm having a problem concentrating."

"Me, too," said Ben with a sigh. "I just read page forty-seven for the third time, and I still don't know what's going on. I can't get my mind off the killer."

Ellen glanced at the clock on the mantel. "It's time for Napoleon to go outside, Ben."

"Oh, it sure is," he said, noting that the it was almost nine o'clock. The Murrays were getting along in years, and were always in bed by nine-thirty.

Stroking the cat's head, Ben said, "Well, Napoleon, let's take you out for a few minutes."

Ellen headed for the bedroom while Ben carried Napoleon to the kitchen and out the back door. When he reached the back porch, he let the cat down, and as usual, Napoleon dashed off into the darkness.

Ben waited patiently, noting the light in the Slones's sewing room next door. He knew that Ray was on the first patrol shift, and Betty spent a great deal of time sewing whenever Ray wasn't in the house in the evenings.

As Ben stood there, he suddenly remembered that Marshal

Halloran had warned the citizens of Redstone not to be out at night unless they had to, but when they did, to carry a gun. Ben's revolver lay on the table beside the chair in the parlor, where he had been reading.

Oh, well, he thought. *Napoleon will be back in a few seconds.*

When minutes had elapsed, Ben called in a low whisper, "Napoleon? Come on, Napoleon! You should be through by now! Here, kitty, kitty, kitty!"

He waited, but Napoleon did not appear.

Still keeping his voice to a whisper, he called the cat again. This time he heard a "meow" over by the rear of the Slone house.

There was a little light from the windows of the Slone house, and from his own windows Ben could barely make out the shape of Napoleon on the Slones' back porch. He called again, but only got another "meow."

His sibilant whisper showed irritation as he said. "Come here, you stubborn cat!"

Ben stepped up on the porch, trying to see the cat, who now had retreated into deep shadows. "C'mon, Napoleon," he whispered and took a step toward what he thought was the cat.

Suddenly he stumbled over something and fell.

Betty Slone's heart leaped in her chest as she heard a rumbling sound on her back porch.

She picked up the revolver with shaky fingers and thumbed back the hammer, determined that if the killer was going to break down the door like he did Thelma Lowry's, he would find a bullet to greet him.

Her mouth went dry as she moved silently into the kitchen.

↑

Ben Murray felt around to see what he had fallen over and realized it was a small stool. He set it aside with a slight thump and used the knob on the door to help pull himself to his feet.

Napoleon brushed against his legs and dashed off the porch, but the sudden touch of the cat against him threw him off balance, and he fell against the door with a heavy thump.

Betty's nerves were strung tight. Her pulse pounded violently, and cold sweat beaded her brow. The killer was twisting the doorknob!

She raised the gun, holding it with both trembling hands and lined the muzzle at what would be chest level on an average man.

When the loud thump against the door came again, Betty set her teeth in a tight clench and squeezed the trigger. The gun bucked in her hands as it roared.

When the preacher finished the brief graveside service, the mourners filed by Ellen Murray, who was supported on either side by Karen Severson and another of her close friends.

Ray Slone leaned close to Marshal Halloran and said, "Mike, I just can't bring myself to say anything to Ellen. I'm going back to Doc's office to see how Betty's doing."

"Sure," said Halloran. "You want me to speak to Ellen on your behalf?"

"That would be all right. Please tell her how bad I feel and make sure she knows that Betty is about out of her mind over it."

When Ray reached the doctor's office, he found Dr. Lowry and Breanna Brockman standing over Betty, who lay on an examining table.

"What to you think, Doc?" Ben asked.

"I've given her a heavy sedative," said Lowry. "She'll be totally under in a few minutes."

"I'll stay with her, Doctor," said Breanna, "so you can take Ray to your office and talk to him."

When both men were seated, Lowry said, "Betty's in bad shape. This thing has affected her deeply, and her mind is almost unhinged. She needs psychiatric care, and she needs it *now*. I highly recommend Dr. Clayton Burgess in Denver. He's the best in his field this side of the Missouri."

"I'll take her tomorrow, Doc," Ray said.

The next morning, a crowd of people were at the Wells Fargo office to watch Ray Slone help his glassy-eyed wife board the stage. He thanked them for coming, then climbed in beside her. People wept as the stage rolled away, and their hatred for the killer in their midst grew even more intense. He was the guilty party in Ben Murray's death, not Betty Slone.

During the day, Marshal Halloran put out word that he was calling a meeting of the townspeople at the church house. By permission of Pastor Severson, the church often served as the town meeting hall.

At seven o'clock that evening, the people gathered, their faces etched with fear. Halloran told them he understood their fear but strongly cautioned them to be extremely careful with their guns. They must not allow anyone else to become an innocent victim.

He answered their questions as best he could and admitted

there were no clues to the killer's identity. However, sooner or later the killer would make a mistake and get caught.

A week passed without incident, but the people of Redstone knew better than to relax. The killer was still in their midst and no doubt would strike again.

Several people had left town to stay with friends or relatives.

The patrols continued night after night, and the people clung to the hope that the killer's inevitable mistake would happen soon.

At noon one day, Woody Jones looked up from his desk in the Western Union office to see Breanna Brockman enter.

"Howdy, ma'am." He stepped up to the counter. "Another wire to your husband?"

"You guessed it, Woody," she said with a smile.

Breanna wrote that she was fine and assured John she would board the stagecoach out of Redstone on September 23 even if Dr. Lowry's new nurse had not arrived by that time. She did not tell him anything about the murders.

Breanna pushed the written message across the counter to Woody and paid him.

As the days passed, patients who came into the doctor's office mentioned they had learned that her birthday was September 30, and she would be leaving for Denver a few days ahead of that date.

Breanna realized that since she had made no secret of her birthday, or that she planned to go home in time to celebrate it with her husband, Woody had not violated the Western Union telegrapher's code in sharing the information.

ON THE NIGHT OF SEPTEMBER 17, one of the four-man patrol teams paused under a street lamp in a residential section.

An unseen figure observed them from the deep shadows of a yard across the street. He knew every man in the group and listened intently to their conversation. His head was hurting and tiny lights were beginning to appear in the corners of his eyes, contrasting with the darkness around him.

Len Drazek, a lumberman, said, "Tell you what, fellas, the more I think of it, the more I believe the maniac is a man we all know and trust, and I believe he's serving in one of these patrol teams. What better way to disguise his identity than to make it appear he's one of us? Which shift he's working is anybody's guess, but mark my word, when we finally catch him, he'll be a man we all respected, admired, and trusted."

"If you only knew," the killer said, smiling to himself in spite of the pain in his head.

The four men moved on, and the man in the shadows pressed shaky fingers to his temples, feeling the urge to kill come over him. His mind went back to his thirteenth birthday and how angry his mother had been when he asked if he could invite some friends over for a party.

His mother had beaten him over the head with a broomstick

until he went unconscious. When he woke up, he promised himself that someday he would kill her.

Another small animal in the forest had to die that day as he vented his hatred for his abusive mother.

The killer rubbed his temples and told himself he must kill again to be rid of the pain. But not Breanna Brockman; not yet. He had special plans for her. Len Drazek thought he was so smart. It was his turn to die!

The killer left the shadows and headed down the street in the direction of the Drazek house. Len Drazek had the respect of everyone in Redstone. The people would be horrified when they found out he had been murdered.

Alta Drazek tucked her two-year-old daughter back in bed after giving her the requested drink of water. She glanced at her other daughter who lay in the bed beside her sister. The four-year-old was fast asleep.

Alta picked up the Colt .45 that Len had insisted she keep within reach at all times and returned to the kitchen. While putting away the silverware she had just polished, she glanced at the wall clock. Five minutes after ten. The shift change came at ten. Len would be home any minute.

Her husband always came in the back door, so Alta left a lantern burning in the kitchen and headed for the bedroom with the .45 in hand. While she was changing into her night clothes, she heard voices out front. The men on the second shift were walking the men of the first shift home, one by one.

Alta hurriedly slipped into her robe, picked up the gun, and headed for the kitchen to greet Len when he came in.

✦

The killer waited in the adjoining yard and watched Len Drazek tell his fellow patrolmen goodnight.

Len rounded the corner of the house noting the glow from the kitchen windows. Alta would be there to welcome him home with a hug and a kiss.

He was about to step up on the porch when he heard a husky voice call his name. He turned, squinted into the darkness, and said, "Who is it?"

Len was not a big man, but was quite strong. The vague light from the kitchen window showed him the dull flash of a knife blade as a dark figure came at him.

From inside the kitchen, Alta heard Len's voice and wondered who he could be talking to. She opened the door and heard struggling sounds and hard breathing. She moved onto the porch and could make out two dark figures wrestling on the ground.

She pivoted and stopped just inside the door to grab the lantern, then dashed back to the porch. At the same moment, she heard Len cry, "Alta, get back in the house!" The words were followed by a grunt of pain, and the lantern light showed her that Len was on the ground. His assailant's back was toward her, but she could see the man raising a knife.

Terrified, Alta brought the gun up with a shaky hand and fired. Suddenly the figure sprang to his feet and ran. Alta fired another shot at the man, but he kept running and quickly disappeared.

Alta rushed to her husband's side and saw that his left arm had sustained a deep cut.

At the same time, lantern lights came on in the windows of

neighboring houses, and the four-man team who had said goodnight to Len only moments before came on the scene.

Patrolmen Randy Frazer and Walt Robinson were standing on the porch with Len Drazek between them when Dr. Lowry opened his door, holding a lantern. Lowry could see two more patrolmen behind them. Frazer and Robinson were steadying Drazek, whose left arm was wrapped in a towel.

"What happened?" Lowry asked, opening the door wide.

"The killer attacked Len when he went home after his shift, Doc," said Frazer. "Cut his arm up pretty bad."

Lowry sat Len down in his parlor, examined the cut, and said, "We'll have to go to my office. You'll need several stitches, Len, but you'll be all right."

"A couple of Len's neighbors have gone after Marshal Halloran, Doc," said Robinson. "They'll take him to talk with Alta first, so she can tell him what she saw."

When Halloran arrived at the doctor's office, Dr. Lowry was almost finished with Len. It had taken twelve stitches to close the wound. After bandaging it, the marshal told Len that Alta had not been able to give him a description of the assailant. She had seen no more than the flash of the knife and the killer's dark form.

Drazek wasn't able to provide Halloran a description either. The attack had come in almost total darkness, and when the killer called his name, it was done in a hoarse whispering sound to disguise the voice.

By midmorning the next day, everyone in Redstone knew about Len Drazek's encounter with the killer.

Pastor Severson called for special prayer meetings at the church, saying that he and his people must unite in fervent prayer and ask God to bring the killer to justice. The meetings would be held for an hour every weekday evening between seven and eight o'clock.

Marshal Halloran was all for it and provided the four-man teams to escort the people to and from the church.

At first it was only the members of the church who attended the prayer meetings, but each night more and more of the town's frightened citizens began crowding into the building.

On September 19, a tall, slender man in his early thirties rode into Denver under a clear sky and reined in at the hitch rail in front of the federal building on Tremont Street.

Across the broad street, two greenhorn would-be gunfighters, who had only been in town a few hours, were leaning against a storefront, talking to a couple of drifters.

"Well, if you're such great gunfighters," said drifter Jake Clubb, "why don't the names Rick Denison and Virgil Mills ring any bells with us?"

"Yeah," put in his traveling companion, Rufus Dodd. "How come?"

"Well, we ain't hit the big-time gunfighters' roster yet," said Mills, "but give us time. We will. We're both gettin' faster all the time, and we're beginnin' to take out some well-knowns."

Clubb chuckled. "Well, how about namin' some of the well-known gunfighters you've braced and left dead in the street."

"Ever heard of Vince Lanyard?" Mills said.

The drifters exchanged quick glances.

"Yeah," Clubb replied. "We both have. Ain't he out of Nebraska?"

"Mm-hmm. But he's buried in Wyoming. My pal Rick,

135

here, took Lanyard out last week up in Cheyenne City."

The drifters eyed each other again. Clubb said, "I think he's joshin' us, Rufe."

"No, I'm not," said Virgil Mills. "I saw it with my own two eyes. Rick spotted him and told me Lanyard was his. He issued the challenge in the Bullmoose Saloon. Lanyard took it. They went outside with a bunch of us followin'. Rick clean outdrew him. We rode away with hotshot Lanyard lyin' dead in the street."

Mills felt his friend's elbow stab his ribs.

"Hey, Virg. Take a look over there."

They all looked across the street and saw a tall, slender rider dismount in front of the federal building.

Mills gasped. "Well, lookee there! If it ain't Rusty Atwood!"

"Rusty Atwood?" the drifters said in unison.

"Yep, that's him all right. In the flesh. I ain't heard nothin' about him for a couple of years. Wonder where he's been keepin' himself. Last time we saw him was down in New Mexico. Where was it, Virg? Santa Fe?"

"Yeah," Mills said with a nod. "Santa Fe, when he took out that loudmouth, Ruben Escobar."

"I'll never forget it. Escobar shoulda known he wasn't fast enough to take out Atwood."

"Well, he found out, didn't he?"

"Yeah! He found out all right."

"Tell you what, guys," said Jake Clubb, "ain't neither one of you can outdraw Rusty Atwood!"

"That's for sure," agreed Dodd. "Talk about a big-name gunfighter! Atwood's big-time! You don't wanna mess with him."

While they watched the tall man enter the federal building, Denison said, "That's where you're wrong, Jake. I can take him."

"I can, too," spoke up Mills. "In fact, after I took out Chet Callison over in Tucson, I knew I was ready for Atwood. I told myself if I ever saw him, he'd get the challenge."

"Chet Callison?" said Dodd. "He was a pretty big name. So you took him out, eh?"

"That I did. And now I'm takin' out Rusty Atwood."

"But I've been dreamin' of the day I would put Atwood down," said Denison. "He's mine."

"Sorry, pal. You got Vince Lanyard. I get Rusty Atwood."

"Look," said Denison, "I'll flip you for him. Fair enough?"

Virgil's mouth started to form a pout, but he grinned instead and said, "All right, but only because you're my best pal."

Rick pulled a silver dollar from his pocket. "Okay, I'll toss it, you choose."

"Okay," said Mills, his eyes dancing. "Heads."

The drifters watched with interest as Rick tossed the coin in the air. It flipped several times on its way down. He caught it in midair and slapped it on his wrist. When he took his hand away, the backside of the coin was facing up.

Mills snapped his fingers in frustration, swore, and said, "Okay, Rick. He's all yours."

Denison laughed and pocketed the coin.

"Wait a minute, Rick," said Jake. "How do you know you can outdraw Atwood?"

Denison snickered. "I just know it. You'd have to be a gunfighter to understand, Jake. There's just somethin' down inside that tells you you're better than the other guy. A little voice says the big name can be taken down. When you brace the big name and leave him lyin' in the dust, suddenly your name is on everybody's lips. Then you move on and challenge someone even bigger. Pretty soon, you're famous."

Denison pulled his revolver from its holster, broke it open, and spun the cylinder. Satisfied the weapon was loaded, he eased it into the holster. "Okay, Virg. Let's go. He'll be comin' out sooner or later. And when he does, he gets two things…the challenge and a bullet in his heart."

Deputy Billy Martin looked up from his desk and saw a tall, slender man come through the door of the Chief U.S. Marshal's Office. "May I help you, sir?"

"Believe so. My name's Rusty Atwood, Deputy. Is Chief Brockman in?"

Billy Martin felt the impact of the name—a gunfighter known all over the West.

"Yes, he is," replied Martin, noting that Atwood's holster, which he wore on his left side, was not low-slung and tied to his thigh. All gunfighters wore their guns low on the hip, which made for a quick draw.

"May I see him?"

"Is Chief Brockman acquainted with you, Mr. Atwood?" Martin asked, observing the man's right arm. It seemed to hang from his shoulder lifelessly, like a piece of rope.

"He is. We're good friends."

"Be right back," Martin said, heading for Brockman's office door.

"Yes, Billy?" came the familiar voice from inside.

Martin opened the door and said, "Chief I have a man out here who wants to see you. He says you're good friends. His name is Rusty Atwood."

"Rusty Atwood! Well, by all means, Billy, bring him in here!"

Martin turned and said, "He'll see you now, Mr. Atwood."

The tall, lanky man thanked Martin and moved past him.

"Rusty! It's good to see you!"

Martin noted that the handshake was left-handed. Indeed, Atwood's right arm was useless.

"Billy," said Brockman, smiling broadly, "you've heard this man's name before."

"That I have, sir," said Martin. "For that matter, who hasn't, if they live west of the Missouri River?"

"But his gunfighting days are a thing of the past, aren't they, Rusty?"

"They are, sir."

"I hadn't heard that," Billy said. "As of when?"

John looked at Rusty. "Well, let's see. It's been over two years, right?"

"Yes, sir. It was May of '69."

"What happened, Chief?" Billy asked.

"It was in Los Alamos, New Mexico," John replied. "I was riding through town. It was just about noon, so I decided to grab a quick lunch at one of the cafés. About the time I rounded the hitch rail, I heard this sharp voice say, 'Hey, Stranger! John Stranger!' I turned around and here was this ugly dude staring at me, a wild look in his eyes."

Atwood chuckled.

"Go ahead, Rusty," said John. "Tell Billy what was going through your mind at that moment."

"Well, it's like this, Deputy. I'd heard an awful lot about this John Stranger. How he'd been braced by some of the West's best and put them down. I was pretty cocky, and I figured I could outdraw any man on earth. I'd seen this Stranger guy on a couple other occasions, so I knew what he looked like.

"I decided this was my day to put a monstrous feather in

139

my gunfighter's hat. Take out the famous man-in-black, and the world would fall at my feet. You know…that kind of thing."

Billy nodded. "There've been a lot of them think the same thing. I suppose just about every Boot Hill in the West has one or two graves where those fools were planted because they thought they could outdraw the Stranger."

Rusty chuckled. "Well, had it not been for some mercy on the Stranger's part, this body would he lying six feet underground in Los Alamos's Boot Hill right now."

"Go on," said Billy.

"Well, the man-in-black tried to talk me out of bracing him. But my foolish mind was made up. I was bent on making a name for myself by outdrawing and killing John Stranger."

John spoke up. "I tried desperately to talk him out of it, but he went for his gun."

"And you beat him to the draw, of course," said Billy.

"Mm-hmm. I knew his reputation for being lightning fast, but behind the gunfighter's tough mask, I saw what I thought was a young man who could be a blessing to society if he was turned the right way. Instead of putting a bullet in his heart, I put it through the bone of his right arm where it joins the shoulder."

"And this was designed to end his gunfighting career," said Martin.

"Exactly," said Brockman. "And it did."

"I lost the use of my arm, Deputy," said Atwood, "but if this man hadn't shown some compassion on me, I would have lost my life."

"So what I did, Billy," said John, "was stick around Los Alamos while this guy was recuperating. I had something else I wanted to do."

Billy grinned. "I know what that was. The same thing you did to me shortly after you became the chief U.S. marshal. Preached the gospel to me."

John nodded. "You got it."

"He's some kind of preacher, I'll say that," put in Atwood. "He had me cornered in a sick bed so I couldn't get away from him. It didn't take very long for the Holy Spirit to use the Word to tear away my humanistic philosophy and put me under conviction. I repented of my sin and asked Jesus to save me."

"He got into a good church there in Los Alamos," said John, "and the last I knew, he was proprietor of the local stable. Something he could handle with one hand. Still have the stable, Rusty?"

"Yes, sir. I have a hired man who helps me, and I guess I should tell you…I'm also mayor of the town now."

John looked at Billy Martin. "See what I meant about his potential to be a blessing to society, Billy?"

"Sure do," said Martin, grinning at Atwood. "I'm glad for you, Rusty." He paused, then said, "I see you wear your gun on your waist."

"Mm-hmm. For protection, as most men in the West. Of course, it's on my left side, but I've learned to fire the gun with my left hand. Not as accurately as I did with my right hand, but enough to get by. And even if I wore it slung low and tried to fast-draw, it wouldn't be anything like I once did.

"And now that I'm a Christian, even if I had my right arm, I wouldn't want to be a gunfighter anymore. Either way you want to look at it, thanks to my friend John here, my gunfighting days are over."

"Praise the Lord for that," said Billy. "So where're you from originally?"

"Coffeyville, Kansas. Born and raised there. Broke my parents' hearts when I turned eighteen. Got the fool notion that I wanted to become a gunfighter, so I ran away from home, leaving my parents and siblings behind. I fell in with a bad bunch who encouraged me to sharpen my fast-draw and accuracy and make a name for myself. I never went home again."

"Must've been rough on your family," commented Billy.

"Yeah. Had to have been. Well, after John led me to Christ and I got into church, my entire outlook on life changed."

"Jesus will do that for you," Billy said, grinning.

"Amen to that! Anyway, I decided to go home to Coffeyville and see my family. When I got there, I learned that both of my parents had died. My brother, Jim, had moved to Wichita, and my sister, Marcie, had married a lawman, but no one in Coffeyville knew the man's name or where they had gone.

"I went to Wichita and found Jim. He told me Marcie had married a man named Mike Halloran. He had been deputy marshal in Fort Hays, Kansas. However, Jim informed me that some three years ago, Halloran became the town marshal in Redstone, Colorado. I'm on my way now to see Marcie and her husband in Redstone. Then I found out that The Stranger had become chief deputy U.S. marshal, and since you were on the way, John, I decided to stop and see you before going to Redstone."

Brockman chuckled. "Well, what do you know? The world is getting smaller all the time."

"What do you mean?"

"Well, my friend, I got married just this past June, and—"

"You got married? Really?"

"Sure did."

"Tell me about it."

"I'll make it short," said John. "I met the most beautiful

142

and wonderful woman in the world, so I married her. In fact, I met her in your home state. She's a visiting nurse, and at this very moment she's in Redstone, working for the town's doctor, McClay Lowry. He has a new permanent nurse coming from back East shortly. Breanna's filling in."

"Breanna," said Rusty. "Is she as pretty as her name?"

"Words can't describe her beauty," sighed John. "You'll see her in Redstone if you're going up there right away."

"I'm planning to leave tomorrow morning. Rode my horse this far, but I'm going to leave him with a hostler and take the Grand Junction train. I'll get off at Glenwood Springs and take a stage to Redstone."

John smiled. "You go introduce yourself to Breanna. And tell her I'm sure looking forward to having her home."

"Will do."

"Does your sister know you're coming?"

Rusty released a crooked grin "No. I want to surprise her."

"She'll be surprised, all right," said Billy.

"I'll say. Marcie probably thinks I'm lying in a cold grave somewhere. Well, I'd better get out of here so you men can get back to whatever you were doing. Can you tell me of a hostler close to the railroad station? And how about a hotel?"

"Tell you what, Rusty, how about my treating you to dinner this evening? As to a hotel, I recommend the Westerner, which is close to the station on Champa Street. We can eat dinner there too. You'll find a hostler right across the street from the hotel. How about it?"

"Sounds good to me."

"All right. I'll meet you in the hotel restaurant at six-thirty."

"How about letting me treat *you* to supper?"

"You're too late. It's already settled that John Brockman is buying Rusty Atwood's supper."

"No sense arguing with my boss, Rusty," said Billy. "It'll just end up like when you drew against him. You'll lose."

Rusty laughed. "Okay. I'll see you at six-thirty, John. Nice to have met you, Deputy."

"Same here" Billy said.

Brockman stood at his office door and watched as Rusty moved past Billy's desk toward the outside door. Just before stepping outside, he looked back and smiled at John.

10

RUSTY ATWOOD STEPPED OFF the boardwalk in front of the federal building and headed toward his horse. Suddenly a loud voice cut the air.

"Hey, Atwood!"

The owner of the voice stood spread-legged, his hand hovering over the butt of the revolver in his low-slung holster. There was a mean glint in his eye.

At the edge of the crowd that was gathering stood Virgil Mills, Jake Clubb, and Rufus Dodd.

"My name's Rick Denison, Atwood!" said the gunslinger. "Ever heard of me?"

Meeting his harsh gaze head-on, Rusty said, "No, can't say that I have."

"Well, I'm challengin' you right now! Let's square off lengthwise in the street so's none of these nice people who now know my name will get hurt."

"Forget it—What did you say your name is?"

"Rick Denison. D-E-N-I-S-O-N!"

"Well, forget it, Rick Denison. I'm not a gunfighter anymore."

Denison's face flushed. "Whattya mean you ain't a gunfighter no more? You're wearin' a gun, ain'tcha?"

"You ever see a gunfighter wear his weapon on his waist like this?"

"No."

"That proves I'm not a gunfighter. Besides, I always wore my gun on my right hip. Notice it's on the left?"

"Yeah."

"That's because I've lost the use of my right arm. I can't even move it. What kind of glory are you going to get by gunnin' me down, when all of these people are witnesses to what I just told you? Why don't you just get on your horse and ride?"

"Don't tell me what to do!" spat Denison. "I'm challengin' you!"

Squinting at him, Rusty said, "You deaf? I said I'm not a gunfighter anymore. Why do you want to kill me?"

"Because you're Rusty Atwood, that's why! Big name gun-fighter!"

"You're two years too late, Rick. Now get on your horse and ride." As he spoke, Rusty moved toward his horse.

"You ain't walkin' away from me, Atwood!" Denison said. "Draw, or I'll cut you down like a dog for bein' a coward!"

Rusty turned toward him and with slitted eyes, said, "You don't listen good, do you?"

Inside the federal building, Billy Martin knocked on John Brockman's door as he called, "Chief! Chief! We've got a problem out here!"

"What is it?"

"Some gunslick's trying to press Rusty Atwood into a gun-fight out there on the street!"

John's angular features blanched. "If he lets him do it, he'll get killed!"

Even as he spoke, he rushed to the outside door.

"You're not thinking, Rick," said Atwood. "If we draw against each other, and you kill me, it won't help your reputation as a gunfighter at all. These people are witnesses to the fact that my gun arm is useless. If you force this, and kill me, you'll hang. Go find yourself somebody else to badger into killing you."

"I say you're a lowdown coward if you don't draw against me!" Denison shouted. "You're wearin' a gun! Go for it!"

Virgil Mills took a step into the street. "Go ahead, Rick! Make him draw! When people all over the West hear that you outdrew Rusty Atwood, they ain't gonna know but what he was still usin' his gun arm! And you ain't gonna hang if you kill him. He's armed. Do it!"

"Hold it right there!" boomed the voice of John Brockman as he threaded his way through the crowd. Pointing to Mills, he said, "You get quiet, quick!" Then to Denison. "Back off, mister!"

Denison eyed Brockman with contempt. "*You* do the backin' off, lawman!" Baring his teeth in a sneer, he said, "There ain't no law against two men squarin' off, so there ain't nothin' you can do about it."

"Oh, but I can," John retorted. "Just because Rusty is wearing a gun doesn't mean he has to take your challenge. There's a law forbidding you to shoot him unless he agrees to square off with you. If he doesn't agree to it and you kill him, you'll hang. Now, like I said, back off."

"Guess I was wrong, Rick," Virgil Mills said. "Forget it. Takin' Atwood out ain't gonna gain you nothin' if you're six feet under."

Denison spit in the dust, then stepped up to Atwood. "Tell me somethin'."

"What's that?"

"How'd you lose the use of your arm?"

"I was foolish enough to go up against a man who was faster than me. He chose not to kill me. Just made it so I couldn't be a gunfighter anymore."

"And just who was this softhearted gunslinger?"

"Ever hear of John Stranger?"

"Yeah. Who hasn't? Are you tellin' me it was Stranger who crippled your arm instead of killin' you?"

"That's right."

Denison grinned wickedly. "I've always wanted to meet up with him. Personally, I think he's overrated. I could take him."

"Well, now's your chance."

"Huh?"

"The man in black there…with the chief U.S. marshal's badge on his chest. That's him."

Denison's head whipped around. Eyeing Brockman, he said, "You? You're Stranger?"

"Yep. All these people can testify to that."

"We sure can, Chief Brockman!" shouted a young man.

The crowd spoke their agreement.

Virgil Mills's eyes widened as he took in the legendary Stranger.

"John Stranger's real name is Brockman, and he's a chief U.S. marshal, eh?" said Rick Denison.

John pointed to his chest. "You can read my badge, can't you?"

"Yeah. And if you weren't wearin' it, I'd challenge you. I still say you're overrated. Ain't nobody can be as fast as they say you are."

"Let me tell you something, Denison," said Atwood. "Many a man has tried to outdraw John Brockman, but none ever has. The best thing for you to do is take your friend over here, mount up, and ride."

A stubborn look etched itself on Denison's hard features. Looking Brockman in the eye, he said, "Take off the badge and meet me in the middle of the street."

There was a murmur among the crowd. One man called out, "You square off with John Brockman, Denison, they'll bury you before sundown!"

Denison's jaw jutted, and he snarled the words, "Take off the badge, Brockman! I can't challenge you as a federal marshal, but I'm challengin' you as a man!"

Brockman's cool gray eyes settled on Denison. "You really want to die today?"

"I'm not worried about it. I think it's *you* who is afraid to die."

"I can take you, Denison. You can't outdraw me. And I don't want to kill you. So let me suggest something."

"What's that?"

"Let's empty our guns right here in front of all these people, then draw against each other. Let me show you that you can't beat me to the draw. But this way, you'll still be alive when it's over."

Denison started to object, but Brockman cut in and said, "If you won't agree to this, I'm going to arrest you and your partner for being nuisances. That will carry at least a three-month sentence in the Denver County Jail. Choice is yours."

The greenhorns looked at each other.

"Be best if you go along with him, Rick," said Mills.

Denison licked his lips and turned to Brockman. "Okay. Let's empty our guns and square off."

While the crowd looked on, both men emptied their guns and handed six cartridges each to Deputy U.S. Marshal Billy Martin.

Brockman and Denison squared off, standing some thirty feet apart.

"Okay, Denison," Brockman said. "Go for your gun."

Denison's hand darted downward. Before he could clear leather, Brockman's gun was out, cocked, and lined on him.

Denison froze with his revolver halfway out of the holster, blinking in amazement.

"Bang!" said Brockman.

A man on the boardwalk shouted, "Overrated, is he?"

Laughter rippled through the crowd.

Another man shouted, "If there'd been bullets in the chief's gun, you'd have been buried before sundown, Denison!"

Denison's face was crimson as he went to Martin and took his cartridges in hand.

"Now, I want you two out of town immediately," Brockman said.

Without a word, both would-be gunslingers walked across the street and mounted their horses while the crowd booed and hissed. They rode away without a backward glance.

When Denison and Mills had ridden a few blocks, Denison said, "I still want to kill Atwood."

Rusty stepped up to John Brockman and said, "Chief, I owe you my life. If you hadn't interfered, I'm afraid Denison would have prodded me till I went for my gun."

"That's what I was concerned about. Anyway, the episode is over. I'll meet you in the hotel restaurant at six-thirty."

"Looking forward to it," Rusty said. He mounted his horse, then gave a little wave and rode away.

Rick Denison and Virgil Mills had doubled back and were sitting their saddles between two buildings. They watched Atwood as he rode down Tremont Street, then followed him at a safe distance. When he turned onto Champa Street, they noted that he dismounted in front of the livery stable across the street from the Westerner Hotel.

Rusty paid no attention to what was going on around him as he crossed the street to the hotel. He was thinking about what the next day would bring, and that he would get to see his sister. He hoped Marcie would forgive him for deserting the family so many years ago.

When he reached the front of the hotel, he found men working on the double doors. One of them explained that hotel and restaurant guests were using the rear entrance in the alley while the front doors were being repaired.

Rusty walked the length of the hotel and was just reaching the back corner of the building when shots rang out and he went down.

Billy Martin was in conversation with a deputy who had just returned from tracking down an outlaw gang when the front door burst open. Billy recognized orderly Dirk Jacobs from Mile High Hospital.

"Billy!" Dirk said. "A friend of Chief Brockman's has just been shot! His name's Rusty Atwood. Is the chief in?"

"Yes. I'll take you to him. C'mon."

As they headed for the door to Brockman's office, Billy said, "Is…is Rusty—"

"He's still alive."

"Yes, Billy?" came Brockman's response to the knock on his door.

Billy opened the door. "Chief, Dirk Jacobs is here to see you. Rusty Atwood's been shot."

Brockman was standing behind his desk as Dirk said, "Your friend is still alive, Chief. He's in surgery at the hospital right now. Two men shot him in the back when he was going into the Westerner Hotel at the rear entrance. A couple of hotel employees saw them from a second-story window. They got a good look at them. Sheriff Langan is at the hospital right now and is talking to the witnesses."

"Let's go," said Brockman, rounding the desk. "What do the doctors say?"

"Well, sir, your friend has two bullets in his back. When I left, Dr. Carroll and Dr. Hollingsworth were just starting to put him under. He was conscious when another orderly and I picked him up. He told us his name, said he was a friend of yours, and asked that we notify you."

"Let's go," said Brockman. "Billy, you know where to find me."

"Yes, sir. I sure hope Rusty's going to be all right."

"Me, too."

"Denison and his pal, don't you think?" Billy said.

"Yes, but I need to see what the witnesses say."

"Chief," Dirk said, "I used one of the ambulances to get over here. You want to ride with me?"

While Dirk was driving the ambulance, urging the horses as fast as he dared in the thick traffic, Brockman said, "Two bullets in his back, huh?"

"Yes, sir. Both of them hit him high in the back near the right shoulder. They're about an inch apart. If they'd hit him much lower, his lung would have been pierced. Or a few inches to the left and they'd have plowed into his heart."

"Do you have any idea about his chances for surviving?"

"Not really. As soon as we got him to the emergency room, I left to come after you. I do know he's lost a lot of blood. He certainly could bleed to death if they don't get it stopped before they remove the slugs. He's been shot up pretty bad, but he's got Dr. Carroll heading up the surgery team. Not to take anything away from Dr. Hollingsworth…he's very good. But Dr. Carroll is the best surgeon I know of."

Dirk guided the ambulance around a milk wagon that had overturned in the intersection. There was a crowd looking on, partially blocking traffic. Milk cans lay scattered in the inter-section, and the normally dusty street was awash in milk.

When they had passed the scene, John said, "You did say the bullets were on Rusty's right side, didn't you?"

"Yes."

"Well, if it had to happen, it's best that it was his right side."

"Why do you say that, Chief?"

"Because his right arm's already impaired."

"Really?"

"That's right. He can't move it."

"Seems like I've heard his name before, Chief," said Dirk, "but I can't place him."

"Used to be a gunfighter."

"Oh, yeah! That's it! Rusty Atwood. Pretty fast, wasn't he?"

"Mm-hmm. Until he lost the use of his gun arm."

"How'd that happen?"

"He challenged the wrong man a couple of years ago down in New Mexico."

"I see. It's a wonder he's still alive. Every quick-draw

shoot-out I ever heard of, the loser lies dead in the dust. Seems to be the rule of the game."

"That's usually the way it is," commented Brockman. "I guess every rule has an exception."

"Guess so," agreed Dirk.

The hospital was in sight.

"I wanted to ask about Mrs. Brockman, sir," said Dirk. "Have you heard from her since she went to that town in the mountains...what is it?"

"Redstone."

"Oh, yeah. Redstone. On the west side of the Rockies, isn't it?"

"Yes. Near Snowmass Mountain. And I have heard from her by wire. She's doing fine."

They turned off the street into the circle drive that led to the front door of the hospital.

"I'll let you out at the door, Chief," said Dirk. "You'll find Sheriff Langan in Mrs. Donelson's office or in the surgery waiting room. When I left to come after you, he was talking to the witnesses inside Mrs. Donelson's office."

John thanked the orderly and hopped off the wagon seat, then dashed into the hospital.

There was no one at the receptionist's desk as John hurried through the lobby. Making a right turn when he reached the hall, he met up with a nurse carrying a tray. "Hello, Louise. Do you happen to know if Sheriff Langan is in Mrs. Donelson's office?"

"No, sir, he's not. I just walked past there. I know Mrs. Donelson is with Drs. Carroll and Hollingsworth in surgery. They're working on that ex-gunfighter who was shot over at the Westerner Hotel."

"Thanks, Louise. I think I may find Sheriff Langan in the surgery waiting room."

"Probably. What do you hear from Breanna? She doing all right?"

"Yes. She's fine. We're keeping in touch by way of Western Union."

John hurried down the hall the opposite direction and stepped into the waiting room.

Sheriff Langan was there, reading the morning edition of the *Rocky Mountain News*. When he saw Brockman, he laid the paper aside and stood up. "I was hoping you'd be in when Dirk came with the news."

Brockman grinned. "Well, I'm in the office once in a while. Any word on Rusty?"

"Not yet. From what Mary said just before she went in to help with the surgery, he's lost a lot of blood."

"That's what Dirk said."

"She also said it could take a while. I guess both slugs are buried deep."

John sighed. "I sure hope he'll be all right. I understand you talked to the two hotel employees who saw the men shoot Rusty."

"I did. They got a good look at them."

"And gave you descriptions?"

"Mm-hmm." Curt reached into his vest pocket and drew out a folded slip of paper. "Wrote them down."

John read the descriptions. Nodding, he said, "Denison and his pal, all right."

"So you know them?"

"Yes."

John explained about the incident in front of the federal building.

"So that's what brought it on," said Curt. "Dirty skunks couldn't leave him alone. Had to gun him down."

"Yes. I'm going after them myself once I know about Rusty's condition."

There was a moment of silence, then Langan said, "Dirk said Rusty told him you and him are friends."

"That's right."

"Did you know him when he was a gunfighter?"

"Yes, but he quit that foolishness a couple of years ago."

"Do you know what made him quit?"

"Yes. He got shot in his gun arm. Couldn't draw anymore."

"What a blessing for him, eh?"

"It sure put the brakes on his gunfighting career."

"I can see why," said Curt.

"You ever hear of a gunfighter living to be an old man?"

"No. Most of them don't live past twenty-five."

"That's right," said John. "But even if Rusty hadn't been shot up so he couldn't use his gun arm anymore, he'd have quit anyhow."

"Oh? Why?"

"He got saved. The guy who shot him ended up leading him to the Lord."

Curt's face looked quizzical. "The guy that shot him was a Christian?"

"Yep."

"And I suppose you even know who this guy was."

"Sure do."

"Who?"

The door to the surgical ward opened, and Mary Donelson appeared. "Oh, John!" she said. "I'm glad you're here. Mr. Atwood talked some before we put him under. He thinks the world of you. Said you led him to the Lord two years ago."

"So it was you who shot him, John!" said Langan.

Brockman cleared his throat. "Um…yes."

"Then he must have challenged you."

"Mm-hmm."

"And you crippled his gun arm so he'd have to give up gunfighting."

"You might say that."

"Sounds just like you."

John gave an impish grin, and looked at Mary. "So what can you tell your son-in-law and me about Rusty?"

"The slugs have been removed. We've got some complications, but Dr. Carroll and Dr. Hollingsworth are confident Mr. Atwood will live."

"Praise the Lord!" John said. "What kind of complications, Mary?"

"Well, the bullets did some damage to the nerves in his shoulder and in his neck."

"What does this mean?"

"Maybe nothing...and maybe some problems using the shoulder and turning his head. It depends on the extent of the damage and how well he heals."

"But he won't be crippled in any way because of it?"

"No. At the worst, he'll be stiff in the shoulder and the neck."

"So it's the peripheral nervous system that may be damaged," said John.

Mary raised an eyebrow. "Exactly. You know about the peripheral nervous system?"

"A little. The peripheral nervous system comprises cranial nerves, controlling face and neck; spinal nerves, radiating to other parts of the body; and autonomic nerves, which form a subsidiary system regulating the iris of the eye and muscles of the heart, glands, lungs, stomach, and other visceral organs."

Curt Langan's mouth hung open.

"Excuse me, John," Mary said, "but as far as I know, you never took any medical training."

"No. Never have."

"Well, how did you learn this?"

"Breanna talks in her sleep."

The three of them had a good laugh, then Mary said, "I've got to get back to the doctors and the patient."

"Will you tell Rusty something for me when he wakes up, Mary?" asked John.

"Of course."

"Tell him that I'm going after those two lowdowns who shot him. It was Rick Denison and his pal. He'll understand."

"Will do," said Mary. "You're leaving right away then?"

"Yes."

"I'm sure Mr. Atwood will still be in the hospital when you get back. See you then."

With that, she was gone.

"John, I'll go with you," said Curt. "Steve can look after things here."

"Thanks, Curt, but I prefer to do my tracking alone. You stay with your deputy and keep this town safe."

Moments later, John entered the U.S. Marshal's Office and told Billy Martin that he was going after the men who'd shot Rusty. He asked Billy to get hold of ex-Chief U.S. Marshal Solomon Duvall and tell him he needed him to take over as usual. It might take several days to pick up their trail and hunt them down, but he would be back when he'd caught them.

11

LATE IN THE DAY ON SEPTEMBER 19, a lone figure stood near the bank of the roaring Crystal River, high in the Rockies. The sun had gone down over the jagged peaks to the west, but its pale gold sun-shafts painted the broken clouds a metallic hue.

A cool wind moaned through the darkening trees, and in the distant east, ominous thunderheads gathered. There were towering mountains on every side. Their looming crags and spires, like huge pipe organs, stood against the sky, growing dim in the fading light of the dying day.

At his feet lay the body of a hunter who had been mauled by a wild beast. As he knelt beside the lifeless form, he noted the telltale claw marks on the face and chest and muttered, "Half-Paw." The hunter's shirt was ripped to shreds. "Hasn't been more than a couple of hours since you died, mister. Blood's still moist."

He rose to his feet and looked searchingly into the dark forest. "You're in there somewhere, Half-Paw. Maybe you and I have a kindred bond. Seems to me, the way you kill so savagely, you must have the same kind of headaches I have. Did your mother treat you mean, too?"

He glanced at the tempestuous river that seemed to boil with rage. The Crystal was fed by many streams that flowed from the peaks above timberline. By the time it reached the ten-thousand-foot level where the Redstone killer stood, it was swift and dangerous. He felt a kinship with it, too.

"Wherever you are, Half-Paw, when your headaches return, you'll kill again. I understand." He took a deep breath and let it out slowly. "Half-Paw, I think you killed your mean mother like I killed mine. Your mother's gone forever and won't hurt you anymore. I thought mine was gone forever, too. But she's back to torment me. She came back inside Breanna Brockman."

His head was beginning to ache, and his breathing grew labored. He leaned over, took hold of the dead man's shirt collar, and began dragging him toward the river bank. The collar suddenly tore loose from the tattered shirt, and the corpse fell from his grasp. Muttering to himself, he reached down and bunched up the shreds of shirt in his fists and finished dragging the body to the edge of the river.

His head was pounding now, and lights were flashing in the corners of his eyes. He stood for a moment, swaying on the edge of the bank, then rolled the dead man into the turbulent river.

He watched the body sink into the foamy waters and bob to the surface a few seconds later. It whirled and turned in the rapid current, then disappeared where the Crystal bent out of sight.

The killer turned and looked at the cabin near the riverbank upstream. There was relief for his pain inside the cabin. He felt wetness on his hands and looked down and saw blood. He turned back to the river and dropped to his knees on the edge of the bank, dipping his hands in the cold water. When he had washed the blood away, he remembered putting his fingertips to his temples and now scooped water onto his face, scrubbing till he was sure he had removed the blood. The cold water dulled the pain in his head momentarily, but as he headed toward the cabin, the spots of light in the corners of his eyes became horizontal streamers across his vision.

He staggered past the privy up to the back door of the cabin, which overlooked the river some thirty feet from the bank, and moved inside. It was still light enough to see without a lantern. He shuffled to the kitchen cupboard and took out a paper envelope containing salicyclic acid powders. *Not much left.* He looked for another envelope, but the shelf offered no more.

Blinking against the streamers of light shooting across his vision, he dipped water from the bucket on the cupboard and poured the contents of the envelope into the dipper, mixing it with his forefinger. He gulped the liquid and forced himself to relax, saying, "It will ease off, now…. Soon it will ease off."

The kitchen window faced the river, and his attention was drawn to the dark thunderheads filling the eastern sky. A storm was brewing. He should head back to town, but he had to wait till the pain lessened and hope he could make it home before the storm hit.

He lay down on the bed in the larger bedroom and drew up his knees in a fetal position.

Nearly an hour had passed and the lights in his eyes no longer tormented him. He sat up and rubbed his temples for a moment, then picked up the lantern. Yes, he felt much better now.

He carried the lantern from room to room, and said, "Mother, you haven't fooled me at all. I know you've come back from the dead. You're in that blonde nurse. Uh-huh. Two-in-one now. You will die again, Mother. Right here in this cabin. On your birthday, like when I killed you before. Strange, isn't it, Mother? The Brockman woman's birthday is the same day as yours."

161

He laughed fiendishly. "I killed you on your birthday, Mother! September 30! Now, I'll kill you again! This time you won't come back to haunt me and look at me through her eyes!"

He doused the lantern and set it on the kitchen cupboard. Lightning flashed through the window against a black sky, and immediately there was a deep growl of thunder. The wind was blowing hard when he went out the front door of the cabin.

Breanna Brockman lay in her bed at the boarding house and watched the lightning flash through the window. It lit up the whole room and was immediately followed by the booming of thunder and the spattering of rain on the window.

"John, darling," she said aloud, "the rain, lightning, and thunder take me back to the day we met on the Kansas plains. You saved me from getting trampled by those stampeding cattle. The Lord sent you along just when I needed you so desperately."

Time slid back and she remembered the events of that day...

Breanna was doing her visiting nurse work in Kansas under the authority of Dr. Myron Hunter in Wichita. She had finished a weeklong assignment, nursing farmer Will Scott through a serious illness. When Scott was out of danger, she told her patient and his wife good-bye and climbed into her buggy. She waved at Althea Scott, who had come out onto the porch to see her off; then she put Nellie to a trot across the plains toward Wichita.

In the distance to the northwest, dark thunderheads were gathering, but Breanna felt sure she could make it to town before the storm hit. The sky was still clear above, all the way to the eastern horizon, and the sun was shining brightly.

However, as Breanna guided Nellie along the road, the wind came up, driving the storm toward her. She had been on the narrow, rutted road for an hour when she topped a gentle rise and spotted a huge herd of cattle about a mile ahead of her. The herd was headed south toward the railhead at Wichita, and was being driven by a crew of shouting, whistling drovers who rode back and forth on long-legged ponies.

The angry storm began closing in on her, and the sun had vanished just moments before behind dark, rolling clouds. Lightning crackled in the north, followed by the rumble of thunder.

It had rained good the day before and there was not the usual cloud of dust behind the herd. Breanna had no way of estimating how many head there were, but they covered the road and spread out on each side of it, a span of at least seventy yards. She was looking for a ranch or farm where she could go for shelter, but there was nothing in sight. She remembered a small community maybe three or four miles ahead. If she could get the drovers to clear a path for her, she could probably beat the heavy part of the storm to shelter.

Thunder boomed, and the wind was getting stronger as it swept over the rolling plains. Breanna snapped the reins and put Nellie to a gallop. Soon, she drew up to the rear of the noisy herd. A pair of young cowpokes saw the buggy and rode up to her. "Howdy, ma'am," one of them said. "Were you needin' to get through the herd?"

"Yes! That storm looks plenty mean. I need to get through as fast as possible."

"All right, follow us! We'll guide you."

Nellie whinnied nervously as she pulled the buggy amid the

milling, bawling cattle. Breanna noted the long, sharp horns that clattered as the steers jostled each other. It took some ten minutes to bring the buggy out in front of the herd. She thanked the drovers and put Nellie to a steady trot.

The entire sky was a black, swirling mass, and the wind was getting even stronger. Breanna had gone another mile or so when lightning split the sky above her. Nellie whinnied at the fearsome sound and tossed her head, slowing down.

"No, Nellie!" shouted Breanna, snapping the reins. "Go, girl, go!"

Deafening thunder clapped like a thousand cannons all around, and the frightened horse bolted, heading straight south on the road. The buggy bounced and fishtailed. Terrified, Breanna screamed at Nellie to slow down and pulled back on the reins with all her might.

Suddenly the spooked animal veered off the road and plunged down a grassy slope. There was a two-foot ditch some eight feet wide at the bottom of the slope. Breanna braced herself for the impact. The buggy hit the ditch full force and came to a sudden stop against the far bank, sending Breanna headlong into a patch of long, thick grass. When she stopped rolling, thunder was shaking the earth, and Nellie was bounding across the field dragging reins, harness, and singletree behind. The buggy was dug into the bank with both front wheels broken.

Breanna scrambled to her feet, her heart pounding and her breath coming in short gasps. She was a bit dizzy and bruised, but the soft bed of grass had saved her from serious injury.

She made her way back to the road as the rain began to fall, driven by the fierce wind. All she could do was keep going south and hope to find shelter.

As Breanna stumbled along the road, she heard something

different than wind, lightning, and thunder. It took her a few seconds to place its source, but when she looked behind her, she realized it was the sound of rushing hooves. The lightning had frightened the cattle, and they were stampeding straight toward her. There was nowhere to run. An overpowering sense of helplessness took possession of her, a foreboding of death.

The herd was no more than two hundred yards away now. Breanna thought of the ditch beside the road, but the solid wall of wild-eyed cattle told her they were in the ditch, too. It could offer no protection.

Frozen with terror, Breanna steeled herself for what was coming. Then something out of the corner of her eye caught her attention. It looked at first like some kind of apparition speeding toward her, but it quickly crystallized into a horse and rider. The horse was jet black, and the man in the saddle was dressed in black. He was risking himself and his horse to rescue her!

The cattle and the rider were closing in fast. The front line of steers was so close, Breanna could see the whites of their bulging eyes. Horror and panic stabbed at her heart. She could scarcely breathe.

The herd was no more than fifty yards away when the rider leaned from the saddle and snatched her off the ground, holding her tight against him as they veered to the right and headed south.

The black gelding quickly put space between himself and the deathly horns and hooves. Breanna watched the space widen as the gallant horse carried his master and her on a beeline south, outrunning the pending danger...

Tears flowed down Breanna's cheeks as the rain beat against the window and the storm unleashed its fury over Redstone. She used the corner of the sheet to wipe her tears and said with quivering voice, "Thank you, Lord, for bringing John to my rescue that day and using my peril to bring us together. You have been so good to me. What a wonderful husband you have given me! Thank you!"

Weary from a hard day at the doctor's office, Breanna finally fell asleep in spite of the storm. Her last thought was of John and how good it would be when she was in his strong arms once again.

In the deep of the night, he suddenly sat bolt upright in his bed, gasping. Sweat beaded his brow and he was trembling all over.

Rain pounded the roof of the house, and lightning flashed in the dark sky. He looked at the rain-spattered window and saw a face in the glass. He scrubbed palms over both eyes and looked again at the wet window.

"No, Mother!" he cried. "Leave me alone!"

It was dark for a few seconds, then came another lightning flash. This time the face in the window was Breanna Brockman!

The room went dark again and thunder shook the house.

When the next lightning bolt slashed the sky, the face was still there. It was Breanna— No, it was his mother! He closed his eyes, wishing her gone. When he opened them, the face was still there, glaring at him, as he had seen so many times.

"No, Mother, no! Please don't beat me!"

Suddenly the nightmare that had awakened him came back to his mind. His mother was giving him one of his regular thrashings, beating him with a stick.

He screamed, bounded out of the bed, and staggered to the

dresser, leaning on it with both hands. There was a long flash of lightning. He looked at his reflection in the mirror. His face was ashen. Suddenly, behind him in the reflection, he saw a woman.

It was—Mother? No, the Brockman woman! No, it was Mother *inside* Breanna, staring at him furiously through Breanna's eyes!

He forced himself to turn around and look.

The woman was gone.

Thunder shook the house, and he stumbled back to bed and pulled the covers up over his head. Soon the storm began to wane. When it finally passed, he went back to sleep.

The streets of Redstone were a sea of mire and puddles glistening in the sunlight from a clear morning sky as Dr. McClay Lowry unlocked the office door and pushed it open for Breanna and the two elderly widows waiting on the boardwalk.

The subject of discussion was the heavy rain during the night; then the widows explained that they were there for something to calm their nerves.

Breanna was at the desk in the front office when the widows came out of the back room, thanking Dr. Lowry for the sedatives he had given them.

The first patient in the appointment book for the day was Bart Gibson. Dr. Lowry was keeping a close watch on the eye socket of the blind eye. It had been red and swollen for the past few days, and Lowry wanted to check it regularly. Gibson was now wearing a "pirate patch" over the eye.

When Gibson arrived, he had barely spoken to Breanna.

Lowry took Gibson's folder from the rack by the door and said, "Come in, Bart."

Gibson let the widows pass, then followed the doctor into the examining room.

When the widows were almost to the door, it opened, and a beefy man held it open for them. They both said in unison, "Thank you, Mr. Bentley," and went on their way.

Breanna knew Clark Bentley, whom she had met on several occasions in the general store and on the street. In his late forties, he was a bachelor and made his living as a lumberjack. He had told her that he was a patient of Dr. Lowry's, and she had seen his folder in the file.

"Good morning, Mr. Bentley," she said with a smile, noting that he looked peaked.

"Good morning, Breanna," he said, rubbing his temples. "I don't have an appointment, but I need to see Doc if I can."

"You don't look like you feel well," she said. "Is your head hurting?"

"Yes. I've had problems with headaches off and on for some time. Doc keeps me supplied with salicyclic acid powders, but I'm out. I know he won't give me another supply without seeing me."

"That's how doctors are," she said, rising from the desk. "Please sit down. I'll get your file." Moving toward the file cabinet, she spoke over her shoulder. "Dr. Lowry is with a patient at the moment. The next patient with an appointment isn't due in till nine o'clock, so I'm sure he'll have time to see you."

Bentley eased onto a chair and watched Breanna open one of the file drawers and pull out his folder. She sat down at the desk again, opened the folder, and scanned the records. "Mm-hmm. Looks like you've suffered with these headaches for some time."

"Too long," he said, a trace of bitterness in his voice.

Breanna placed the folder in the rack beside the examining room door and went to work quietly on records from other files on her desk. Some twenty minutes had passed when Bart Gibson came out, spoke to Bentley, and left the office without a word or a nod to Breanna.

Dr. Lowry appeared at the examining room doorway, took the folder from the rack, and said, "Come in, Clark. Head hurting again?"

"Yeah. I ran out of the salicyclic powders."

As Bentley walked toward him, Lowry looked at his pant legs. "Is it just your head, or have you cut yourself?"

The lumberjack looked at the dark red stains and said, "Oh, that. I...ah...shot me a couple squirrels yesterday afternoon while working up in the mountains. Got some blood on me. My head was hurting so hard when I got up this morning, I plumb forgot to change pants."

Lowry smiled. "Well, let's take a look at you, and we'll get you some more powders."

After a few minutes, Clark Bentley came out, carrying several envelopes of salicyclic acid. He nodded at Breanna as he passed the desk. She was in conversation with the patient who was to see the doctor at nine o'clock.

The morning was a busy one until about eleven-thirty, then things quieted down. Dr. Lowry laid the files of the patients he had seen thus far on Breanna's desk.

She heard him sigh and looked up, commenting, "Doctor, you look like you don't feel too well. Is there anything I can do?"

He met her tender gaze, then closed his eyes for a couple of seconds and said, "Nothing physical, Breanna. I...I'm just having an awful time."

"Thelma?"

Tears filled his eyes. He nodded silently. "I miss her so much."

"I'm sure you do, Doctor," she said in a compassionate tone. "I can't say I know how you feel since I haven't lost my mate, but I can imagine what it must be like. I'm so sorry."

Lowry pressed a handkerchief to his face briefly, dabbed at his tears, and took a deep breath. "It's just so hard."

"Dr. Lowry," Breanna said tentatively, "I don't mean to be overbearing about my faith in the Lord, but if you would let Jesus come into your heart and life, and—"

The front door opened, and a young couple came in. The man had his arm around his wife, who was obviously in pain. Her right hand was wrapped in a white cloth, and she was holding her wrist with the other hand.

"Melinda burned her hand on a hot skillet, Doc," said the husband.

Dr. Lowry told Breanna to bring Melinda Farley's file and come help him with the burn.

While Breanna was pulling the folder, the man said, "Can I come in while you work on her, Doc?"

"Sure, Don. Come on back."

Don Farley sat down and watched as Dr. Lowry examined the burn on Melinda's hand. Lowry eased their minds by telling them it was a first-degree burn and should leave no scar.

While doctor and nurse worked together on Melinda's hand, Don said, "Mrs. Brockman, we've heard much about your work here with Dr. Lowry. People are saying they wish you could stay and be his permanent nurse."

"It's nice to know they feel that way," said Breanna.

"Don and I learned that you're leaving Redstone in time to be home for your birthday on the thirtieth," said Melinda.

"Yes."

Farley looked at Doc Lowry and said, "Do you know when your new nurse is coming?"

"Haven't had a definite date yet," said Lowry. "Should be soon, though. However, I promised Breanna that even if Martha isn't here, she could leave whenever she wanted to."

"When do you plan to leave, Mrs. Brockman?" Melinda asked.

"On this coming Saturday, the twenty-third. The reason this birthday is so important is because it's my first one since John and I got married last June."

"Oh, how sweet," said Melinda. "Of course you should be home with him."

Melinda's hand was soon bandaged, and after paying the doctor for his services, the Farleys left the office. They had been gone only a few minutes when Breanna looked up to see Woody Jones carrying a yellow envelope in his hand.

"Howdy, Mrs. Brockman," he said. "I have a telegram for Dr. Lowry from Martha Waverly."

Breanna's face brightened. "Oh, yes! Just a minute. I'll get him."

"I heard, Breanna!" called Lowry from the back room and came through the open door. "Let me see it, Woody!"

Breanna waited with interest as Lowry opened the envelope and took out the telegram. "Well, good!" he said with a chuckle. "Martha will be here this coming Sunday on the afternoon stage!"

"Dr. Lowry," said Breanna, "I was just thinking. It would help you immensely if I was here for Martha's first day to sort of break her in, wouldn't it?"

"Of course, but I don't want you to run it too close on your return home."

"If I go on Tuesday, I'll still have three days at home before my birthday. I know there's a train to Denver on Tuesday."

Lowry's features brightened. "I'd really appreciate that, Breanna, if you don't mind waiting till Tuesday."

"I'll have to see if there's room on Tuesday's stage," she said. "May I go over to the Wells Fargo office right now and find out?"

"Certainly."

Breanna and Woody started out the door together. "Breanna," said Lowry.

She stopped and turned around. "Yes, Doctor?"

"Thank you."

"Glad to do it. I'll be back in a little while." As nurse and telegrapher walked along the boardwalk together, Breanna said, "Woody, if I'm able to get on Tuesday's stage, I'll be over to your office and send a wire to John so he'll know there's been a schedule change."

"That'll be fine, ma'am," said the little man. "It always pretties up my office when you come in!"

Breanna laughed. "Woody Jones, you are a flatterer."

"No flattery to it, ma'am," he said with a chuckle. "It's a plain fact!"

12

AFTER WASHING UP THE DISHES from lunch, Woody Jones left his apartment above the Western Union office. He waved to a couple of elderly women as he descended the stairs and entered the office by the back door.

A glance through the large window on the street side showed him two men standing at the door, awaiting his return. He removed the "gone to lunch sign" in the window and unlocked the door. "Howdy, Frank...Biff."

Both men returned his greeting, then Frank Bowman said, "I need to send a wire to my son in Kansas City, Woody."

"Come on over here to the counter," Woody placed a sheet of paper in front of Bowman, along with pen and inkwell. "Write it out for me, and I'll get it on the wire right away." He looked at Matthews. "You needin' to send a wire, too, Biff?"

"No, I'm with Frank. We've been working together this morning. We'll have lunch together, then go separate ways for the afternoon."

Woody nodded and returned his attention to Frank Bowman while Frank wrote out a message.

Light footsteps were heard on the boardwalk. Woody looked past the two men and saw Breanna Brockman enter.

He noticed her slight hesitation when she saw Biff Matthews and he turned to look at her.

"Get that reservation set up for Tuesday, Mrs. Brockman?" Woody said.

"Yes." Breanna moved up to the counter beside Frank Bowman. She kept her gaze on Woody, but she could feel Biff's eyes on her.

Woody slid a sheet of paper in front of her and produced another pen and inkwell. "Put it down like you want it, ma'am, and I'll get it on the wire as soon as I'm through with Frank here. Oh, forgive me. Have you met these gentlemen?"

"Well, I've seen them around town," said Breanna, "but I've not met them formally."

"Mrs. Brockman is Dr. Lowry's temporary nurse, fellas. Ma'am, this is Frank Bowman, and this is Biff Matthews."

Bowman smiled at her, touched his hat brim, and said, "Glad to meet you, ma'am."

Biff said, "We've crossed each other's paths several times, ma'am. I'm very happy to actually be introduced to you."

Breanna manufactured a smile while a queasy feeling settled in her stomach. "Yes, we have seen each other several times," she said. *"Crossing paths" was not the way it happened*, she thought to herself. He had deliberately stationed himself where she had to walk past him, and he certainly was not crossing paths with her when he stood across the street in front of the general store and stared at her through the office window.

While Breanna was writing the message to let John know she would be arriving in Denver on Tuesday instead of Saturday, Frank finished his message, paid Woody, and he and Biff headed for the door.

"Nice to have met you, ma'am," Frank Bowman said, as he paused at the door.

Breanna looked up and smiled, saying, "You, too."

Biff gave her the same inscrutable smile she had seen on several occasions, and said, "Wish you could stay longer in Redstone, ma'am."

A sour taste rose up in Breanna's throat. She forced another smile, then put her attention back on what she was writing.

Dr. Lowry was at the file cabinet when Breanna returned to the office. He closed the file drawer and turned toward her, saying, "Get a seat on the stage?"

Still jittery from her awkward encounter with Biff Matthews, Breanna nodded absentmindedly.

"Breanna, I really appreciate your willingness to stay and break Martha in for me."

"I'm glad to do it, Doctor," she said, at last noticing that his medical bag was sitting on the desk. "Are you leaving?"

"Mm-hmm. I've got an elderly woman to see down near the marble quarries. She's an invalid and can't leave her bed. Should be back in two to three hours. I feel so at ease with you minding the office. You seem to be able to handle more than the average nurse."

"Probably because of my experience, Doctor."

Lowry picked up his bag and was out the door. Breanna heard his buggy pull away as she went back to her paperwork at the desk.

Moments later, a mother came in with a sick child. Breanna lovingly comforted the little girl while administering the proper medicine, and with warm words of thanks, the mother left with the child in her arms.

Breanna was making notes in patients' records at the desk when she looked up to see Bart Gibson fill the door frame. She felt her pulse quicken. His single penetrating eye was fixed on her as he moved toward the desk. Reflex made her rise to her feet.

"Something I can do for you, Mr. Gibson?" she asked with a dry mouth.

"Doc in?" he queried, halting a few feet from her.

"Ah…no. He…he'll be back later."

"Oh. I saw him leave a while ago but thought he might be back by now. Just needed to talk to him for a minute." He took another step. "How long, do you think?"

"Oh, ah…well, not very long."

His eye seemed to grow stern and cold as he moved toward her slowly.

She took a step back, her throat constricting.

Suddenly there were excited voices at the door behind him. He stopped and looked over his shoulder.

A man preceded four others who were carrying two wounded men. The first man brushed past Gibson and said, "Ma'am, is Dr. Lowry in?"

Breanna breathed a silent sigh of relief and replied, "Not at the moment, sir, but I'll do everything I can. What has happened to these two?"

"I'm Leonard Rogers, ma'am. A local rancher. These other men are ranchers, too. We're neighbors to J. T. Yeager and his son, Curtis, here. Apparently they are victims of Half-Paw, ma'am…the cougar who's attacking people in this area."

"Yes, I know about Half-Paw," said Breanna.

She rounded the desk and came within arm's reach of Bart Gibson, then headed for the door of the examining room. "Bring them back here," she said, opening the door.

While the ranchers were putting the injured man and his

son on examining tables, Breanna heard Bart Gibson go out the front door. She had a passing thought that if these men had not shown up when they did, he might have done something to harm her.

Father and son were both conscious and watched Breanna as she made a quick appraisal of their condition. To the men who had brought them in, she said, "Gentlemen, I'm going to be very busy here. If you will take seats out in the office, I'll let you know what I think about their condition as soon as I can."

Leonard Rogers nodded. "Thank you, Miss—"

"Breanna Brockman, Mr. Rogers. Mrs. Breanna Brockman."

"Thank you, Mrs. Brockman. We'll wait out front."

When the door had closed, Breanna stood over the father and said, "Mr. Yeager, your son is in worse condition than you. I'll go to work on him first."

"Thank you, ma'am," said Yeager.

Moving to the boy, she said, "Your name's Curtis, right?"

"Yes, ma'am."

She took scissors from the cart by the table and said, "I've got to cut your shirt in order to do what's needed here. Okay?"

"Yes, ma'am," said the boy. She could tell he was frightened but was trying to be brave.

"You and your father are going to be all right, Curtis," she said in a confident tone. "I'll have to clean these claw marks before I can stitch you up. It's going to burn some, but I'll try not to hurt you any more than I have to. There'll be some pain when I use the needle to stitch you up, too. Just want you to know ahead of time."

Curtis swallowed hard and nodded without comment.

Breanna excused herself, saying that she needed to let their friends know they were in no danger of dying. When she returned, she looked at the boy and said, "All right, Curtis, let's get you taken care of."

As she started to work on Curtis's wounds, Breanna said, "Do you have any brothers or sisters?"

"Yes," said the boy through clenched teeth. "Two sisters. Mom took them with her and another rancher's wife to Carbondale early this morning."

"I see. So your mother doesn't know what's happened."

"No, ma'am."

To the father, she said, "How did this happen, Mr. Yeager?"

"Curtis and I were repairing a stretch of fence on the ranch by the road, about a half-mile from the house. We had several new posts to set. I should've taken a rifle along but didn't think about it. It's been a while since Half-Paw has invaded our area. My mind was on the work and not on the killer cougar."

The boy winced when Breanna touched an open claw mark with wood alcohol, but he didn't cry out.

"You all right?" she said, pausing in her ministrations.

He nodded. "I know you have to do it, ma'am. Go ahead."

J. T. went on with his explanation. "So while we were repairing the fence, we had no idea the cougar was anywhere near. He came like a streak of lightning from behind some trees and brush on the other side of the road and hit Curtis, knocking him down. All I had to use on the beast was a tamping bar. Half-Paw was ripping and tearing at Curtis when I swung the bar at him. I was a bit off balance, and it was only a glancing blow.

"It was enough to divert his attention from Curtis, though, and he turned on me. I tried to hit him with the bar again, but he had me on the ground before I knew it. He would have ripped me to shreds if Leonard Rogers hadn't come along at that moment on horseback and fired his revolver at him. The bullet barely grazed Half-Paw's ear, but it was enough to send him running away. Leonard fired a couple more shots at him but missed. By that time, he'd disappeared."

"Well, you both need to thank the Lord that Mr. Rogers came along when he did."

"That's for sure," said J. T.

When Breanna reached a certain point in her delicate work on Curtis, she left him long enough to stay the flow of blood from J. T.'s deepest gashes, then went back to the boy.

She worked as fast as she could on Curtis, suturing the claw marks as gently as possible.

Redstone's killer found himself on the edge of town, not remembering how he got there. The stabbing pains in his head tormented him. He had to get relief. Looking around, he saw that he was in front of widower Wiley Haddon's house. Cold water on his head would at least give some relief. Hurrying alongside the house, he made his way to the well in the back-yard. He dropped to his knees in the grass and put his head under the spout of the water pump as he worked the lever feverishly.

He splashed water over his head and face, relishing the small degree of relief it brought. When his arm grew tired from pumping, he switched to the other arm and kept the cold water pouring over his head.

Finally, he fell prostrate on the ground, breathing hard. In only minutes the full force of the pain was back, throbbing like a hammer inside his skull. The lights were flashing in the corners of his eyes, and his head seemed filled with a foggy substance.

Lying there, his mind swung down the dark halls of his life....

Suddenly his mother was standing over him as he lay on the ground, her hands on her hips and a vicious scowl on her face. Her fierce blue eyes seemed to bore into his as she railed, "You've been bad, again! Why can't you be a good boy? What kind of punishment shall I put on you this time?"

Blinking against the wispy fog that seemed to hang over him, his attention was drawn beyond his mother's threatening form. Above her, he saw countless winged shadows sweeping across the sky like black vultures.

Following his line of sight, she looked up at them, then glared menacingly at him and said, "For being bad this time, boy, I'm gonna let those beasts up there come down and get you!"

He was about to scream when the sound of pounding hooves and tinkling harness brought him back to Wiley Haddon's backyard.

He sat up, gasping, and saw the husky, gray-haired Haddon pulling his wagon up behind his barn in the alley.

Wiley had not seen him yet.

The killer dashed to the front of the barn and slipped through the door before Haddon could get down from the wagon seat and open the large double doors at the back. He waited in the deep shadows, knowing that he was about to relieve the pain in his head.

The five ranchers had waited patiently in the front office while Breanna worked on J. T. and Curtis Yeager. When she appeared, they all rose to their feet, expectant looks on their faces.

"All done, gentlemen," she said with a weary smile. "Both of them are doing fine. They'll have a few small scars on their hands, arms, and faces—especially Curtis—but the worst scars will be on their chests."

"I'm just glad they're all right," said Leonard Rogers. "Not too many people have lived through a Half-Paw attack."

The others agreed.

"It would have been a different story if you hadn't come along when you did, Mr. Rogers," said Breanna.

"I'm mighty glad I did, ma'am. Can we take them home now?"

"I don't want to delay you, but I'll have to keep them here until Dr. Lowry returns. As the doctor who owns this practice, he'll want to look them over and make sure I did the job right. You can understand that."

"Sure, ma'am. We understand."

One of the ranchers said, "While we're waitin', could we go in and see J. T. and the boy?"

"I guess I can allow that," said Breanna. "But only for a few minutes. They need to rest."

Breanna watched the five ranchers file into the examining room and sat down at the desk. She sighed and rubbed her eyes. The work she had done on Half-Paw's victims had taxed her strength.

When a wagon pulled up to the hitch rail outside, Breanna looked through the window to see Dr. Lowry climbing down from the seat.

"How's your invalid patient, Doctor?" Breanna asked as he came through the door.

"Doing as well as can be expected," he replied, setting his

ANGEL OF MERCY

medical bag on the desk. "Any excitement here?"

"I'm afraid so. You know rancher J. T. Yeager?"

"Yes."

"Well, he and his son were attacked by Half-Paw while you were gone. Some of their rancher friends brought them in."

"Bad?"

"Not terribly serious. We can tell you the story later. I cleaned them up and did the suturing. I knew you would want to check my work before they went home. Their friends are back there with them now."

The ranchers were sent back to the front office while Dr. Lowry examined father and son. When he had looked them over carefully with Breanna at his side, he smiled at her and said, "You should have been a doctor, Breanna. You do excellent work. There's no way I could improve on this."

"Thank you, Doctor."

"And thank *you*, Mrs. Brockman," said J. T. "Right, Son?"

"Yes, Pa," said Curtis. "She's a good doctor! Thank you, ma'am."

Breanna leaned over and kissed the boy's brow. "You're welcome, Curtis."

"You two can go home now," said Lowry, "but I want to give some instructions to your friends, first."

"While you're doing that, Doctor," said Breanna, "I'll run over to the clothing store and get these two a couple of shirts. They can't wear the ones they wore in here."

"I hadn't even thought of that, Breanna. I guess I was so impressed with the way you bandaged them up that shirts never came to my mind."

J. T. chuckled. "I hadn't thought about it either." Reaching toward his hip pocket, he said, "Let me give you some money, Mrs. Brockman."

182

"I'll go ahead and get the shirts; we can settle up later," Breanna replied. "Besides, by the time you pay Dr. Lowry for services rendered here, you might not have enough money left to buy shirts!"

Lowry shook his head and said, "This girl is something else!"

As Breanna headed for the door, J. T. said, "But ma'am, you haven't asked us about our shirt sizes."

"I have a husband and a nephew, Mr. Yeager," she said over her shoulder. "Let's see how close I come."

As she stepped into the office, she said to the ranchers, "Gentlemen, Dr. Lowry is about to release your friends, but he wants to give you some instructions first. You can go on back."

They watched her disappear through the front door, then entered the examining room.

"Doc," said Rogers, "the lady said you wanted to give us some instructions before we take these two fellas home?"

"Yes. You need to keep in mind that J. T. and Curtis must not be jarred as they ride. Too hard a jolt could pull their stitches loose. Curtis has the most damage, as you can see. One of you should hold him in your arms in the bed of the wagon so you can absorb the jolts for him."

"That's close to what we did when we brought them here, Doc," said Rogers.

"All right," Lowry said, nodding. "And I would suggest that three of you sit in the wagon bed side by side and let J. T. lie across your legs. It won't be very comfortable for him, but it will cushion the normal jolts that come with riding in a wagon."

Breanna returned, and the shirt sizes were perfect. When J. T. tried to pay her, she said, "The shirts are a gift from me, Mr. Yeager."

"Ma'am," he protested, "I can't let you do this. Please take the money."

Smiling, she said, "Tell you what. How about you give the money to Curtis for being such a brave boy while I worked on him today?"

A smile spread over the boy's face. "Now, Pa, I think this is the smartest nurse in the world! You should listen to her!"

J. T. chuckled. "All right, Son. It will be as the lady has said."

Breanna kissed Curtis's forehead again and told him to take care of himself.

As the men were putting father and son in the wagon bed, Dr. Lowry stood looking on with Breanna by his side. Once Lowry was satisfied the patients were as protected and comfortable as possible, he said, "J. T., I'll be out to the ranch to check on you and Curtis in two or three days. I'll change the bandages then."

As the wagon pulled away, both father and son waved to Breanna and thanked her once more for her care.

"I think you made a couple of friends there, Breanna," Lowry said.

She smiled. "It's people like them who make this job worth it."

As they were returning to the office, they saw Woody Jones coming toward them on the boardwalk, waving a yellow envelope.

He handed the envelope to Breanna and said, "It's from acting Chief U.S. Marshal Solomon Duvall in Denver, Mrs. Brockman."

"Oh?" she said, ripping open the envelope. "This must mean John is in pursuit of some outlaws somewhere."

Lowry and Jones waited in silence while Breanna read the telegram.

To Lowry, she said, "John indeed is on the trail of some outlaws and can't be reached. He doesn't know about the change in my schedule, but Chief Duvall assures me that John will be given my wire as soon as he returns."

"I sure hope he gets back before your birthday," said Lowry.

"Yes, Doctor. Me, too."

To Woody, Breanna said, "Thank you for bringing this to me."

"My pleasure, ma'am. I'll see you both later."

As doctor and nurse turned to enter the office, Lowry said, "Well, Breanna, it's almost time to lock up and call it a day."

Breanna's eye caught sight of a wagon veering toward them and said, "Not yet, I'm afraid, Doctor. Looks like we have some more business."

Lowry watched as the driver pulled rein and said, "Doc, I've got Wiley in the back! He's been stabbed!"

Doctor and nurse stepped up to the side of the wagon as George Waters, Wiley Haddon's next door neighbor, climbed down from the seat.

Haddon looked up at Lowry, his beefy features pallid, and said, "Pitchfork, Doc. He got me with one of my pitchforks."

"Don't try to talk right now, Wiley. George and I will get you inside."

People on the street looked on as Breanna preceded the two men while they carried Wiley Haddon into the office.

When the bleeding man was on the examining table, Breanna went to work, cutting away his shirt.

"George," Lowry said, "go get the marshal. He needs to hear what you and Wiley have to say."

While Lowry and Breanna worked on the punctures in Wiley's upper back and shoulders, the silver-haired man tried to tell them what had happened, but Lowry said, "Wiley, let us get you stitched up first. By that time, Mike Halloran will be here. That way, you won't have to tell it twice."

"Okay, Doc," said Wiley. "I'm sure it was that dirty maniac."

"Just one question, then you'll have to lie quiet. Did you get a look at his face?"

"No. It was too dark in the barn. When he—"

"Don't explain it now. I was just hoping since this attack came in daylight, you might have seen who it was."

Doctor and nurse were getting a good start on their patient when George Waters returned to tell them the marshal was in a meeting with some of his night patrolmen and would be at the doctor's office within a half hour.

There were an even dozen punctures in Wiley's body. None had gone deep enough to do serious damage. Lowry and Breanna were finishing up when Marshal Mike Halloran came in.

Lowry told Halloran the extent of Wiley's wounds, and Halloran asked if Wiley would be able to talk to him.

"I think he's up to it, Marshal."

Breanna was cleaning up the examining table and the surrounding area.

"I sure am," said Wiley.

"All right, Wiley," Doctor Lowry said, "but if you get too tired, you'll have to stop and tell the rest of it later."

"Whatever you say, Doc." Wiley looked up at Halloran. "I'm sure it was the maniac, Mike."

"I don't doubt it, but why aren't you dead?"

"Let me start at the beginning."

"I'm all ears."

Breanna stopped what she was doing and moved up on the side of the table opposite the men.

Wiley told his listeners how he came home in his wagon and pulled up behind the barn in the alley. He had the double doors barred from the inside, so he had to go to the front of the barn and enter through a smaller door. When he stepped inside the barn, intending to lift the bar from the double doors, he suddenly felt sharp pain in his back and realized he had been stabbed. It was quite dark in that part of the barn. He could hear his assailant breathing hard. He managed to twist himself free of the tines and turned to face the man. It was too dark to see his face or to make out his size.

He swung at the man but was slammed on the jaw with the handle of the pitchfork. He staggered from the blow, then the man seized him with powerful hands and slammed him face-down on the barn floor. The jolt stunned him. He felt the tines stab him again. The fork was pulled free, and the man stabbed him a third time.

As Wiley was passing out, he thought he heard a big dog growling and barking. When he came to, the fork was embedded in his upper shoulders, and he was facedown on the barn floor. The tines were not in deep, so he was able to work the fork free.

It took him quite some time to crawl out of the barn and into George's yard. When he was able to climb onto the back porch, he kicked the door until George came to see who was making the noise.

"Thank the Lord for that dog," said Breanna.

"For sure," said Wiley. "Several of the neighbors have big dogs, so I have no idea which one it was, or I'd buy him a big steak."

"I hope he took a good bite out of the killer," said Breanna.

"So do I," said Mike Halloran, the muscles in his jaw flexing in anger. "If I get my hands on him, I'm gonna gnash on him myself!"

13

THE TERROR OF THE NIGHTMARE grew as he tossed and turned in fitful sleep. The dream had him reliving a moment when he was four years old...

He had knocked his bowl of breakfast oats on the floor while holding his favorite stuffed animal in one arm. It was a black and white dog his grandparents had given him when he was two years old.

His mother was in another part of the house, but she heard the bowl crash to the floor and came stomping into the kitchen, her face scarlet with rage.

His terror held him powerless to move or say a word as he stared into the blazing eyes of his mother. She cursed him for knocking the bowl to the floor and railed, "I've told you a thousand times not to bring that stinking dog to the table! Now look what you've done!"

She snatched the stuffed dog from his trembling grasp and ripped off one of the forelegs, throwing it on the floor.

He found his voice, and tears filled his eyes as he sobbed, "Please, Mommy, don't kill my doggie! Please!"

She twisted the head off, sending stuffing flying through

the air. The small boy covered his eyes, not wanting to see what she was doing to his beloved toy. When she tossed the head at him, hitting his hands, he opened his eyes to see her ripping off the other legs and tearing the stuffing out of the body.

"Please don't, Mommy!" he sobbed. "Please!"

Suddenly she dropped what was left of the dog and seized his wrist, dragging him toward the outside door and the shed....

He awoke in a spasm of terror and sat up in the bed, cold sweat covering his face. He tried to still his ragged breathing and mopped his face with his palms. The loathing he felt for his mother flowed through him like the rushing waters of the Crystal River.

Choking on the words, he said, "I...hate...you! I...hate you!"

Suddenly he was ripping his pillow apart, throwing ragged strips of pillowcase and feathers everywhere. It was as if the pillow had become his mother. "Tear my doggie up, will you!" he hissed. "I'll tear *you* up!"

On Thursday morning, Breanna awakened to a downpour outside. There was surprisingly little lightning and thunder, but the rain was coming down hard.

Some mornings, Breanna had eaten breakfast in the dining room downstairs with Frieda Schultz and the other tenants of the boardinghouse. At other times, she had eaten some small tidbit in her room, making her own coffee on the small stove.

This morning, she was unusually hungry. When her hair

was brushed and styled, and she was dressed for the day, she went downstairs to the dining room.

Frieda was placing food on the table while a few of the tenants—mostly elderly people—were just sitting down.

"Good morning, everybody!" said Breanna.

The tenants greeted her in return, then the portly landlady said in her highly accented English, "Ah, Breanna, dear, you will eat with us this morning! We are glad to have you!"

As they ate together, the tenants told Breanna they had enjoyed her presence in Redstone.

By the time the meal was over, the rain had stopped. Breanna was about to leave the table and head for work when Frieda said, "Breanna, dear, everyone in town is sad you will be leaving on Tuesday. Many have said it to me."

Breanna smiled. "I'm glad folks feel that way, Frieda."

"And I do, too," she said. "Even when it rains, your sweet smile gives us sunshine."

The others at the table spoke their agreement.

"Dr. Lowry has already rented a room here for Martha Waverly," said Frieda. "Do you know anything about her?"

"Only what little Dr. Lowry has told me. Martha is forty-five years old and a widow. She lost her husband in the Civil War. She has been a certified medical nurse since she was twenty-one. That's all I know."

"And she is still coming in on the Sunday afternoon stagecoach?"

"Yes."

"I know you wanted to go home on Saturday," Frieda said. "It was awfully nice of you to stay and give the new nurse a day of your time to help her learn about the office."

"Well, if it was me coming in to start anew like that, I certainly would appreciate the outgoing nurse doing the same."

Frieda took Breanna's hand and patted it. "This world needs more people like you, Breanna."

Dr. Lowry and Breanna were quite busy the first part of the morning. When things slowed down midmorning, Lowry left the office to make a call on Wiley Haddon at home to make sure his wounds were not showing infection.

On his way back to the office, Lowry pulled his buggy to a halt in front of the Western Union office, stepped down into the mud, and paused on the boardwalk to scrape it off his boots. He greeted two couples as they passed by, then crossed the boardwalk and entered the Western Union office.

Woody Jones was tapping out Morse code on the telegraph key. Doc Lowry smiled as the little man looked up at him from the desk and made a sign with his hand that he would be with him momentarily.

As soon as Woody finished sending the message, he left the desk. "Yes, Doc? What can I do for you?"

"I was passing by," said Lowry, "and thought I'd stop and see if Breanna has received any word from her husband. I know sometimes you can't get away from the office for long stretches of time. She doesn't say a lot about it, but I know she's edgy about her husband out trailing outlaws."

Woody shook his head. "Sorry, Doc. Nothing has come."

"All right. Thanks. See you later, Woody."

Breanna was at the desk when Pastor Eldon Severson came in with his wife, Karen.

"Well, hello!" said Breanna. "I don't have you down for an appointment. Is one of you not feeling well?"

192

"We're fine, honey," said Karen. "Do you have a few minutes? We came by to talk to you."

"How about right now?" Breanna closed the file she was working on and said, "Please, sit down."

The Seversons exchanged smiles, then the pastor said, "Breanna, the news of Martha Waverly's scheduled arrival on Sunday and your scheduled departure on Tuesday has spread all over town. We hate to see you go, but we know you must. However, before that happens, there's a little something that Karen and I and our people want to do."

"Yes, Pastor?"

"We want to schedule a special 'going away' time for you on Sunday night after the service. You've been faithful to the services since you've been here, but we wanted to make sure you were planning to be with us on Sunday night."

"Of course," said Breanna, deeply touched by the kind gesture. "I don't know what to say. But thank you for honoring me in this way."

"You've been a real blessing to us," said Karen. "We just want to show you our appreciation."

The sound of pounding hooves and the rattle of a buggy harness came close to the building. Breanna looked past them through the window and said, "It's Dr. Lowry. I so much want him to hear you preach, Pastor. I'm going to invite him for Sunday night."

"Probably be the best time to get him under the preaching," said the pastor. "He thinks so much of you. He might just come for your sake."

Lowry entered, glanced at the Seversons, and said, "Hello, Pastor...Karen. Something wrong?"

Severson stood up. "No. We just came by to talk to Breanna. The church is going to have a little 'going away' time for her after the Sunday evening service, and we wanted to tell her about it. She's been such a blessing to us. We felt she should be honored in this way before she leaves."

"Well, that's wonderful!" said Lowry. "She certainly deserves it."

"Doctor," said Breanna, "I'd like to ask you a favor."

"Name it."

"Would you come to the service Sunday evening and be a part of my 'going away' time?"

"Why, ah…why, yes. Yes, of course. I'd be delighted. Thank you for inviting me."

The Seversons smiled at each other, then the preacher said, "We'd love to have you, Doctor."

"I'll look forward to it," Lowry said.

Friday and Saturday were busy days at the doctor's office, even more than usual as patients whom Breanna had cared for since coming to Redstone stopped by to tell her good-bye.

On Saturday morning, Dr. Lowry was gone for better than an hour to the Yeager ranch to check on J. T. and Curtis. When he returned to the office, he found a small crowd of people telling Breanna good-bye and wishing her well.

On Saturday night, Breanna blew out the lantern in her room and glanced out the window. By the light of the street lamp, she saw one of the patrol bands walking past the boardinghouse. "Dear Lord," she breathed, "please let them catch that madman before someone else has to die."

She returned to the bed and slipped beneath the covers, then began praying. "Lord, You know my heart is heavy about John. Your eyes are on him right now, wherever he is. I ask, as always, that You keep him safe in the hollow of Your hand.

Pursuing outlaws is no easy task, and the man who wears a badge always has his life on the line. Please keep my darling John from all harm and danger and take him home safely in time for my birthday."

Weary from the long day's work, Breanna fell asleep praying for her loved ones, her pastor, and her friends in Denver.

Breanna enjoyed the morning service at church and felt loved and appreciated when Pastor Severson announced the special time to be held in her honor after the service that evening. The vocal response from the people to the announcement warmed her heart.

One of the church families invited Breanna for Sunday dinner, along with the pastor and his wife.

That afternoon, Breanna answered a knock at her door in the boardinghouse.

"Oh, Doctor!" she said. "Did I misunderstand? I thought you said three-forty-five."

"I did," said Lowry, smiling. "But I'd like to get to the stage office in plenty of time just in case the stage is early. It happens sometimes."

"Of course. Certainly you want to be there when Martha arrives. I'm ready now."

They walked down the stairs together, and when they moved out the door, she said, "Oh! You brought the wagon this time. You picked me up in the buggy."

Lowry chuckled. "I figured that Martha will have a whole lot more luggage than you did since she's moving here permanently. The buggy might not hold it."

"Oh yes, of course. I hadn't thought of that."

Lowry helped Breanna climb onto the wagon seat, then

rounded the wagon and climbed up.

As they drove up Main Street toward the Wells Fargo office, Breanna said, "I sure hope Martha works out for you, Doctor."

"Me, too. Her credentials are excellent, and she comes highly recommended. I just hope an Eastern girl can be happy in the West."

Breanna chuckled. "It'll take some getting used to, I'm sure."

As they drew near Wells Fargo, they saw the stagecoach coming from the north end of town.

"Looks like you timed it perfectly, Doctor," said Breanna. "Sure enough, the stage is a bit early."

While the driver and shotgunner were descending from the box, a man stepped out of the coach and turned to help two older women out, then an attractive brunette in her mid-forties.

Lowry and Breanna moved up to the younger woman, smiling.

"Martha?" said Lowry.

A smile broke across the brunette's face. "Yes."

"I'm McClay Lowry."

Martha extended her hand. "I'm so happy to meet you, Doctor." Her dark brown eyes went to Breanna. "And this is Mrs. Lowry, I presume?"

"Ah, no," said Lowry. "Mrs. Lowry died a short time ago. This—"

"Oh, I'm so sorry. I didn't know."

"No fault of yours," said the doctor. "This is Breanna Brockman, the nurse who has been working for me temporarily, pending your arrival."

Breanna smiled at Martha while thoughts about the Redstone killer circled in her mind. Since Martha knew nothing of Thelma's death, it was apparent that Dr. Lowry had not told her about the murders. Breanna hoped she would be able to handle it when she found out.

"You have quite a bit of luggage, I presume," said Lowry to his new nurse.

"Yes." Martha pointed to the top of the stage. "Those two trunks you see up there in the rack and four suitcases in the boot."

"I'll get the driver and the shotgunner to help me load them in my wagon."

As Lowry moved toward the stage crew, who were now unloading the luggage, Breanna said, "Martha, I hope you will be happy here."

Martha looked around at the mountains, drew a deep breath, and said, "I know I will. These Rockies enthrall me. And this area right here, with the river and all, is such a beautiful place."

"That it is. Just beautiful."

"Where are you from, Breanna?"

"Kansas, originally. But my home is now in Denver."

"I see," said Martha, glancing at Breanna's left hand. "And it is *Mrs.* Brockman."

"Yes," Breanna replied, her eyes straying across the street. "My husband is—"

Her words were cut off as she focused on Bart Gibson sitting on the seat of a wagon parked directly across from the stage station. When her gaze met his, he looked away.

Martha followed Breanna's line of sight. "Something wrong?"

"Oh. Ah, no. What was I saying?"

"Something about your husband."

"Yes. I...I was about to tell you that my husband is the chief United States marshal over this part of the country. His office is in Denver."

Bart Gibson drove the wagon away but not without giving Breanna a hard look.

Martha commented that it must be exciting to be married to the top federal lawman of the territory.

Breanna agreed that it was, and was answering some other questions about her life when Dr. Lowry came and told them the luggage was loaded.

As they drove away, Lowry explained to Martha that he had a room for her at the same boardinghouse where Breanna had been staying. Breanna told Martha she would love it and told her what a dear landlady Frieda Schultz was.

McClay Lowry kept his promise and sat beside Breanna in the church service that evening. Breanna let him look on her open Bible during the sermon. From time to time she looked at the doctor from the corner of her eye to see how he was reacting. Severson was a straight-from-the-shoulder preacher and made it clear from Scripture that all men were sinners in need of salvation, and that Jesus Christ was the only way to heaven and the only escape from the wrath of God and an eternity in the lake of fire. The message was preached with underlying love and compassion and with tears.

When he was on these points, Lowry showed a little nervousness but seemed to stay with the message without shutting his mind to it. Breanna thanked God in her heart for such a loving preacher, whose desire to see souls saved was so apparent.

At one point during the sermon, Breanna's eyes strayed to the section across the aisle. She saw Marcie Halloran sitting by herself, engrossed in what Severson was saying. In the row of seats just in front of Marcie was Biff Matthews.

Breanna had not seen Matthews in the services before. She was glad to see Biff sitting under the gospel, but when he turned and looked at her with his strange smile, she felt a chill dance down her backbone.

As she let her eyes stray over what part of the congregation she could see without turning around, she noted several faces she had not seen in the church before. Possibly some had come to be a part of the 'going away' time after the service. If so, she was honored. But even more, she was glad they were hearing the gospel.

When the invitation was given, several adults and young people walked the aisle to open their hearts to Jesus.

There was a brief time between the close of the service and the special time to honor Breanna. While some of the church people were talking to Dr. Lowry, Breanna crossed the aisle to speak to Marcie Halloran.

A couple of ladies were in conversation with Marcie, and Breanna waited till they moved away then approached her. "Hello, Marcie," she said.

"Hello, yourself. I sure wish you were going to stay in town longer, Breanna. We've hardly been able to get acquainted. Just those few times in the general store and that one little talk we were able to have on the street that day."

"I really would like to get to know you better," said Breanna. "Maybe someday you can come to Denver."

"I'd like that."

"Sure is good to see you here tonight. I wish Mike would have come with you."

"Well, I'm expecting him any minute."

"Really?"

"Mm-hmm." Marcie looked toward the back of the auditorium. "He had to take the place of one of the patrolmen for a

199

while, but he said he'd be here for this special time in your honor."

"Oh, I'm so glad."

Members of the church came by to welcome Marcie and to tell Breanna how much they appreciated the time she had spent in Redstone. Soon the pastor called for everyone to go into the fellowship hall. While they were filing in, Mike Halloran showed up.

When everyone was seated in the fellowship hall, Pastor Severson stood before them and made a brief explanation as to why they were gathered there. His words concerning Breanna were warm and touching, and he told her he hoped she could come back for a visit sometime and bring her husband with her.

Breanna noticed that Biff Matthews sat nearby, and from time to time he sent her a glance and one of his strange smiles.

Prayer was offered for the refreshments the church ladies had prepared, and while people were eating, a continuous line of church members filed by to tell Breanna good-bye.

When it was over, Dr. Lowry and the Hallorans were about to leave together. The Hallorans took a moment to speak to Breanna; then the doctor voiced his own words of gratitude for Breanna's excellent work, adding that he would see her at the office in the morning.

A few of the ladies were cleaning up the tables with the help of their husbands when Karen Severson came to Breanna and said, "My husband said for us to meet him at the front door. We'll take you home." She laughed. "That is, your home away from home."

When the Seversons and Breanna stepped outside, they saw one of the patrol bands standing in front of the building. They were there to escort people home who were on foot.

Moments later, the Severson buggy pulled up in front of the boardinghouse. When the pastor helped Breanna down from the buggy, she said, "Pastor, I can walk to the door by myself."

"Oh, no, you can't. Karen and I are going to escort you to the door just like always."

The trio walked to the porch of the boardinghouse, which was well lighted with lanterns, as usual.

Breanna's purse hung on her shoulder by a long strap. She reached into it and removed the key, inserting it into the keyhole. Before she took hold of the doorknob, Karen said, "Honey, we'll be at the stage station to see you off on Tuesday."

"That's very kind of you," said Breanna. "You people have a very special place in my heart."

"We feel the same way about you," said the pastor. "Good night, Breanna."

"Good night, Pastor. And thank you again for my special good-bye party tonight."

She embraced Karen, then opened the door and took a step across the threshold.

The Seversons waited till Breanna had closed the door and locked it before stepping off the porch. She heard them descending the porch steps and smiled to herself as she climbed the stairs.

She used the same skeleton key to unlock her door and stepped inside. She immediately locked the door again and dropped the key back in her purse.

The room was dark except for the soft light of a street lamp that came through the front windows. Breanna removed her hat and placed it on the dresser, then felt for the matches she kept close to the lantern.

She heard a slight creak of the floorboard and the sound of

cloth brushing cloth, but before she could turn around, she was seized from behind by powerful hands. She started to scream, but a hand clamped over her mouth. Struggling against the man was useless. He had her locked in a viselike grip, and she couldn't move.

Waves of hot breath pulsed against the back of her neck and terror froze her blood. She heard a screaming in her mind.

14

IN SPITE OF THE MAN'S GREAT STRENGTH, Breanna writhed against his steely grasp. But she was helplessly locked in his rough embrace. A prayer for help flashed through her mind but was cut off as he said in a hoarse whisper, "Fighting me won't help you, Breanna-a-a! I have you now, and you're going with me!"

She felt her feet leave the floor, and a wave of horror washed over her as he carried her across the room to the door. The screaming in her mind grew louder as he hissed, "You can make it easy on yourself, if you wish, or you can make it hard. If you scream when I take my hand away from your mouth, I'll break your neck and be gone before anyone can come. They'll find nothing but a warm corpse. Understand?"

She mewed softly, nodding.

"I mean it!" he said in his hoarse whisper. "You close your eyes and keep them that way! If you try to see my face, you die that instant! Understand?"

She squeezed her eyes shut and nodded, making the mewing sound again.

His powerful hand slipped from her mouth, and the temptation to scream was strong within her, but he had killed others without mercy, and he would do the same to her.

203

When he used his own skeleton key to unlock the door, Breanna realized her purse was still strapped over her shoulder. It was squeezed up tight against her, and she could feel the bulge of her small Bible pressing against her ribs.

The door opened, and he carried her out into the hall. There were no sounds coming from any of the rooms. Everyone was in bed asleep. Again, the scream inside her reverberated through the corridors of her mind. She heard him close the door.

He carried her downstairs and paused at the front door for a moment, then hurried across the porch and down the steps, turning toward the rear of the house.

When he stopped again, Breanna heard a horse nicker as she felt herself being placed in the bed of a wagon.

"So far, you've done fine," her abductor whispered. "You'll live a little longer by cooperating."

She kept her eyes closed while he bound her hands and feet with a thin rope, then used a bandanna as a blindfold. He hurt her when he cinched the knot on the blindfold, and she ejected a tiny whine.

He stuffed a bitter-tasting cloth in her mouth and used another bandanna as a gag. Then he spread a heavy tarp over her and climbed onto the seat.

His words came back to her: *"You'll live a little longer by cooperating."* She moved her lips against the gag, saying, "Oh, dear Lord, please deliver me! Only You can keep him from killing me!"

Her mind went to John. The Lord could use John to deliver her. Yes, John would take care of him in a hurry. The man was insane, and no doubt much stronger than the average man, but John had never met a man he couldn't handle. If John were here, he would tear the man apart with his bare hands.

Feeling every bump and jolt as she lay in the wagon bed, Breanna thought of the time she was in Hay Springs, Nebraska, before she and John were married. She hadn't even known he was in town.

A big brute of a man had accosted her on the boardwalk and pinned her against a storefront. He was chewing on a lighted cigar and blowing the smoke in her face. Then John stepped up behind the man, jerked him away from her, and pounded him to the ground. When he had him down, John stuffed the cigar down his throat, burning tip first.

Oh, Lord, she thought, *if only John were here now!*

While the wagon rolled along, Breanna thought of the other victims who had fallen prey to this maniac. Marshal Halloran could find no pattern to the killings and had pronounced them random. Yet, his abduction of her seemed to have some kind of scheme. He was taking her somewhere to kill her. Why? He could have done it easily in her room at the boardinghouse.

Was he going to torture her—kill her a little at a time?

Panic claimed Breanna Brockman. Her blood seemed to turn to ice and her arms and legs felt leaden. She bit down hard on the saliva-soaked cloth in her mouth.

Suddenly the road beneath the wagon became bumpier, jolting her hard against the bottom of the wagon bed. She could tell they were out of town, for there was no more echo of pounding hooves reverberating between the buildings, and the sound of the Crystal River was exceptionally loud.

She agonized with God, praying in her heart for His mighty hand of deliverance.

Soon she became aware of the wagon tilting upward. They were climbing into the mountains. The Crystal was louder than ever. *We're on a road that follows the river.*

Breanna's thoughts were racing. *Who is he? Biff Matthews?* Those probing eyes on her. And that frightening smile. The times he stood across the street by the general store and stared at her through the office window. And then he had the audacity to show up at church tonight!

Is that Biff up there on the wagon seat? Or Bart Gibson?

Bart. He was nursing a grudge against her. His hard looks had frightened her many times. And then on Wednesday, Bart had come into the office and asked if Dr. Lowry was there. She was saved when Leonard Rogers and the other ranchers had come in, carrying J. T. Yeager and Curtis.

This afternoon when she was talking to Martha Waverly at the stage station, Bart had been sitting in his wagon across the street, glaring at her.

Was she lying in the back of his wagon right now?

Biff Matthews. Bart Gibson. Which one?

The wagon was tilting upward even more. *We must be going high into the mountains.*

"Dear Jesus," Breanna prayed, mouthing the words, "You know I'm ready to die. I belong to You. I know I'm going to heaven when I die. But I want to live my life out as John's wife and continue to serve You on earth. As Your child, I am asking You to spare my life!"

Suddenly the wagon leveled off, then tilted downward. As the wagon made its descent, the river's roar became more pronounced. A minute or so later, Breanna realized she was being taken into a canyon. Its rock walls were sending back the echo of the river's thundering roar.

Abruptly the wagon leveled again. The canyon couldn't be very deep. When the wagon came to a halt, Breanna could tell she was very close to the river. She estimated they had traveled about an hour since pulling out of Redstone.

She heard her captor climb out of the wagon and then the sounds of footsteps on a boardwalk. *No boardwalk up here. A porch!*

She heard a door open, followed by more hollow-sounding footsteps. The sound stopped abruptly; then the tarp was pulled off her, and she was lifted by strong arms and carried inside.

The killer's hot, foul breath touched her face as he carried her across the floor, sending a shudder of revulsion through her.

For some reason, he had brought her to a cabin to kill her. Whatever he had planned, whether it was torture first, or sudden death, this was where he was going to do it.

Breanna kicked her bound legs and resisted him with every ounce of strength in her body. He just stood there, holding her in his powerful arms until she spent herself and then sagged against him.

When she was quiet, he bent over and laid her on the floor, whispering, "I know it's natural to fight me, Breanna, but quite useless. Don't…make…me…angry! If you do, you'll be sorry, believe me! But no matter how much you are suffering, I will not kill you until it's time." He paused, then added, "But when it's time, woman, you *will* die!"

He left her on the floor and moved a few steps away.

Breanna heard the strike of a match and the sound of a chimney being placed on the base of a kerosene lamp. At the very bottom of her blindfold, she could make out a thin thread of light.

All was quiet for a long moment; then the man walked past her, breathing hard. He went to what seemed to be the rear of the cabin, stopped, and made some noises she couldn't identify. Had he opened a wooden chest of some kind? Or was it a cupboard?

Suddenly she heard what sounded like the rattle of a heavy chain. A pulse began to pound in her temples. He was going to chain her inside the cabin!

The killer stood at the wooden box near the back door of the cabin and glanced at the terrified woman on the floor a few feet away. He smiled to himself, then hoisted the rest of the chain from the box and let it drop to the floor.

Breanna jerked from the sudden loud noise.

He dragged the twenty-foot length of chain to where Breanna lay helpless and trembling and let the ends fall with a clatter. The rumble of the river was constant behind the cabin.

He laughed hoarsely and leaned over her, whispering, "You will be quite secure here, Breanna-a-a."

She made a whining sound and shook her head.

"What's that? You want to know why I'm going to chain you here?"

She nodded.

"Oh, you'll find out presently. Mysteries are thrilling, though, aren't they?"

He went back to the large wooden box near the back door and took out a hammer, a pair of two-inch bolts, an iron clamp, and a flat rock. He saw that Breanna had an ear cocked in his direction, and he called to her in his wheezy whisper, "Don't despair, nursie. I'll be right back. Your lonesomeness is coming, but not for a little while yet."

The killer looked around and set his gaze on the four posts supporting the cabin's roof. The kitchen and living area were one large room. There was a hallway on the far side of the kitchen which led to the two bedrooms, one on each side of the hall.

He dragged the chain to the post closest to Breanna and wrapped one end of it around the base. He removed the washers and nuts from the bolts, then slipped the bolt through the last link of the chain. He pushed it through another link a few inches from the post, pressing the head tight against the washer.

Placing the second washer nut on the bolt, he twisted it down tight. Then, bracing the bolt against the flat rock, he used the hammer to strike repeatedly at the threaded end until it became a crude rivet head. Nothing but a metal-cutting tool like the one he carried in the wagon could ever free it.

The loud banging had totally unnerved Breanna, and her hands were trembling violently.

"Just fixing it so you can't get away, Breanna-a-a. There's really nothing to be afraid of till it comes time for you to die." He let that sink in, then said, "I'm going to untie your ankles now. Don't move."

When he had released her ankles from the rope, he placed the iron clamp on her left ankle, ran the chain through a heavy metal ring that was part of the clamp and riveted it in place with the hammer as he had the other end of the chain at the post.

"Now, listen to me, nursie," he whispered. "I've chained you to a post. The chain is just long enough for you to go out the back door to the privy. It's right by the back porch. You are in the kitchen area and will not be able to reach the front door. There's hardtack and water on the cupboard."

Breanna wondered how long he planned to leave her there before he killed her.

She heard him kneel down in front of her.

"All right, Breanna-a-a," he whispered, "I'm going to untie your hands and remove the gag. You hold still."

As he was working on the knot on her wrists, he felt a sharp pain shoot through his head and let out a tiny whine, which made Breanna perk up her ears. He let go of the knot and pressed his hands to his temples.

Not now! he thought. *I don't want to kill her yet!*

Breanna could hear him breathing strangely and recognized a reaction to pain. The man was hurting. She remembered reading in her medical studies that psychopaths often had severe headaches. Dr. Lowry had agreed when she brought it up. She recalled his words: *"With some psychopaths, this is the only time they kill. Studies have shown that the headaches actually do subside after they have done something violent, especially if they have killed someone."*

Breanna listened to her captor's labored breathing, which was now accompanied by low moans. Again she prayed for deliverance from the madman.

The killer concentrated on the pain and willed it away. When it eased some, he went back to untying the knot. It was a good thing there had been no lights flashing at the corners of his eyes. He must hurry and finish here.

Tossing aside the rope that had bound her wrists, the killer untied Breanna's gag and said, "You can spit the cloth out."

She licked her dry lips and swallowed hard, but there was little moisture left in her mouth. Working up what saliva she could, she said, "Why are you doing this?"

He ignored her question and rose to his feet and went to the lantern.

Breanna heard him blow out the light, then walk into the parlor area. He set the lantern on a table near the door, then came back to her. "There is only one lantern in this part of the cabin. I just put it out of your reach. You'll spend your nights in the dark."

"What do you mean *nights?* How long are you going to leave me here?"

He did not reply.

She knew it was useless to ask him anything, but she had to anyway. "What have I ever done to you? Is this some kind of punishment for wrongdoing? Why have I been singled out to be locked up in this cabin? And why do you want to kill me?"

"I'm going to take off the blindfold now." His strong fingers unloosed the knot in an instant. He let the bandanna fall to the floor.

Breanna stared into almost total darkness. She rubbed her eyes gently, blinked several times, and looked up at the vague form standing over her. His upper body was in deep shadow. There was no way to make out the shape of his form, let alone the features of his face. Even what she could see of his lower body was only enough to tell her that he had two legs.

"I asked how long you're going to leave me here," she pressed him.

The killer laughed hoarsely. "Until it's time for you to die."

"And why have you set a certain time for me to die? Something that I did?"

There was a long silence. Then he whispered, "I must go."

"Why are you disguising your voice?"

"I have my reasons for keeping my identity from you right now."

He headed for the door.

"Why won't you tell me why I was chosen as a victim?" Breanna said.

He stopped, and though she could barely make out his form, she heard him turn around. Then came the sibilant reply, "It's not what you've done. It's who lives inside you."

"What? I don't understand."

He took a couple of steps toward her, making sure to stay in the shadows. "Your birthday is September thirtieth."

"Yes. What has that got to do with your plan to kill me? And what do you mean it's who lives inside me?"

A wicked tone came into his whisper. "Your birthday is six days from now. You have five full days to live. I am going to kill you on your birthday, and I'll be killing *her* at the same time!"

He wheeled about and headed for the door, then stopped and whispered, "Enjoy your five days, Breanna, because on Saturday, both of you die!"

15

MARTHA WAVERLY LAY IN HER BED, tossing and turning in an effort to fall asleep. She was tired from the long journey by rail and stagecoach but told herself the weariness should send her into slumber.

She sat up and looked around the room. There was a faint glow coming through the windows. Tomorrow was her first day on the job. Maybe this was her problem. Was she subconsciously on edge about beginning her new life in Redstone as Dr. McClay Lowry's nurse? As she pondered it, she realized that indeed she was a bit nervous. She was thankful to have Breanna there. Breanna would be able to help her a lot, even in just one day.

She laid back down and rolled onto her side, then thought of her clumsy mistake at the stage station when she assumed Breanna was the doctor's wife. Of course, it really was no fault of hers. Dr. Lowry had not mentioned his wife's death in their correspondence. When he corrected her about Breanna, he said Mrs. Lowry had died a short time ago. Martha wondered just how recently it had happened.

She rolled onto her other side and tried to concentrate on going to sleep. But sleep refused to come.

She sat up again and decided that some cool night air in

her lungs might do the trick. She padded across the room to the closet and took out one of her dresses. When she had dressed and put on her high-top shoes, she threw a shawl over her shoulders, slipped out into the hall, and headed for the stairs at the front of the building.

As she passed Breanna's door, she whispered, "I'm glad you're sleeping. Get a good night's rest. You've got a big job ahead of you tomorrow. It's 'teach Martha day.'"

The night air was indeed cool, and as she reached the street, Martha pulled the shawl up tightly around her neck. She could hear the Crystal's rushing current as the cool breeze kissed her face. She looked skyward and took in the beauty of the massive vault of black sky bedecked with twinkling stars.

The night air was stimulating. A few minutes' walk would certainly help her to sleep when she went back to bed.

As Martha approached the corner and the street lamp's soft yellow glow, her eye caught movement down the cross street. She squinted to bring the strangely shaped shadow into focus. By the time she was in the circle of light at the corner, she saw that the shadow had separated itself into four men who were coming her way.

One of the men called out, "Ma'am, may we help you?"

Immediately, they picked up their pace, and when they came near the glow of the street lamp, she could see that each man was carrying a rifle.

Puzzled, Martha waited till they drew up and said, "I was having a hard time getting to sleep, so I decided to take a walk. I think the night air will help."

The man who had called out to her said, "You must be Dr. Lowry's new nurse. We heard you were to arrive on the stage today."

"Why, yes. I'm Martha Waverly."

"My name's Barry James, ma'am. These men and I make up one of the night patrols. You really shouldn't be out alone like this with that maniac on the loose."

Martha's features paled. "Wh-what? What maniac?"

James looked around at the other men, then said to Martha, "Hasn't Dr. Lowry told you about the murders here of late? His own wife was murdered by that madman several days ago."

"Wh-why, n-no," she stammered. "He hasn't said anything about it. Please, tell me what's going on here."

At the cabin high up Crystal Canyon, the killer closed the door and locked it. One of the horses whinnied as he stepped off the porch and headed for the wagon.

Suddenly, pain erupted at the base of his skull, sending streamers of fire lancing through his brain and showering his vision with bits of white light. The pounding in his head became a rock-hard fist beating on the inside of his skull.

A moan escaped his lips as he leaned against the wagon. Whether he opened or closed his eyes, he saw the strange jagged lines that were becoming more and more a part of his headaches.

He knew his condition was growing worse. The headaches had begun to increase in intensity near the end of June. He was even beginning to have spells in the daytime now, like the other day at Wiley Haddon's place. But they had been few and far between until now.

The killer pondered his ultimate fate, knowing the end would come no matter what he did, no matter how many people he killed. He was beyond any possibility of hope or help.

The time would come when he would have one of his headaches, and it wouldn't go away no matter what he did.

His body shook from head to toe as he leaned against the wagon. The headache was so fierce that it seemed like blood was boiling in his brain. He could hear it inside his head above the roar of the river.

The river. It would give him some relief.

He knew that killing the Brockman woman would bring the greatest relief, but he would deny himself for now and wait for the ecstasy on Saturday when he would finally rid himself of his mother by killing Breanna.

He staggered toward the bank of the river and fell to his knees. Crawling to the water's edge, he repeatedly dipped his head in the cold current.

After a few minutes, the cold water dulled the pain and drove away the stabbing lights in his eyes. His nerves were quieting too. When he was finally able to rise to his feet, he made his way back to the wagon and started to climb up to the seat but paused and looked back at the cabin.

She had asked why she was chosen as a victim. Maybe it would be good if he told her, so that his mother would get the message. He wanted his mother to suffer, knowing that on her birthday he would kill her again. And this time for good.

Breanna was sitting with her back to the post, head braced against it, praying for deliverance. Her heart thundered in her breast when she heard the key rattle in the door and saw the vague outline of a man standing in the door frame.

Moving inside but keeping himself in deep shadow, the killer said in his rough whisper, "So you want to know about the woman who lives inside you, eh?"

Breanna's throat was so constricted she couldn't speak. She made a little grunting sound.

"What's that? I can't hear you!"

Breanna managed to clear away some of the tightness. In a squeaky voice, she said, "I...just don't understand what you mean. And...I don't know what it has to do with my birthday."

"You look very much like my mother. She was a mean and wicked woman. When I was a boy, she beat on me all the time. Sometimes she beat on me till I was bleeding. She even hit me on the head till blood came out of my ears. And many times she destroyed things that were mine. I hate her!"

Breanna could almost feel the hatred as a tangible thing.

"When I was a boy, I wanted to kill her! But she was so strong, I was afraid to try. So I used to kill animals in the forest and pretend it was her I was killing. But I finally grew up, Breanna-a-a. When I knew I was stronger than her, I decided to kill her on her birthday. She came into the world on September thirtieth, so I figured the best day for her to depart the world would be the same.

"But she came back, Breanna-a-a. Oh, for many years after I killed her, she came back in my dreams, or should I say, nightmares. That was bad enough, but now she has come back inside *you!* She looks at me through your eyes, which are exactly the same color as hers! And your hair is exactly the same color as hers!"

Breanna swallowed hard. "Please. Listen to me. Your mother hasn't come back. She is not inside me. You must understand this. I—"

"Shut up, Mother! Shut up! I know it's you inside her, trying to get back at me for killing you! Well, it isn't going to work! Both of you will die on Saturday! I don't know how you did it, Mother—how you found a woman who looks so much like you. And what's more, a woman who has the same birthday as you. How did you do it, Mother?"

The killer laughed at Breanna's silence. "See? You won't talk to me now, will you? Figured out your scheme, didn't I? Came back to torment me by bringing little nursie here to Redstone and hiding inside her body, didn't you? Well, come Saturday, I'll be rid of both of you, *forever!*"

"Please…" Breanna said, praying in her heart for wisdom. "Please listen to me. I—"

"What is it now, Mother? Don't like it because I'm going to kill you again, do you. Well, I didn't like all those beatings either!"

"Please," Breanna said again. "This is Breanna speaking. Will you listen to me?"

There was a moment of silence. Then the killer said, "How do I know which one of you is speaking?"

Breanna ignored his question. "Tell me…how long has your mother been dead?"

"Twenty-six years."

"Would a dead person know who is president of the United States?"

"Well, I guess not."

"The president of the United States is Ulysses Simpson Grant. Now, does that tell you it's Breanna speaking?"

The silence stretched on; then finally the killer said, "All right."

"Good. May I say something to you now?"

"Yes."

"You need help, whoever you are. I'm a nurse, so you are aware that I know something about your problem. The strain your mother evidently put on you as a child, not to mention the beatings to your head, have done damage to your brain. You may not know that Dr. Lowry studied this kind of thing in medical school. If you will cut me loose and take me back to town, I will get him to help you."

The killer's ragged breathing sounded loud in the room.

"If you would rather, I could take you to Denver with me when I go on Tuesday. I am personally acquainted with doctors there who are trained to deal with your kind of problem."

His voice came back in a hiss. "I don't need your help! It's too late for me, anyhow. I just want one thing. I want my mother dead forever! And I'll take care of that on Saturday. But it must wait till Saturday."

Steeling herself for his answer, Breanna said, "Are you the one who's been killing people in Redstone since July?"

"I most certainly am."

"Can you tell me why?"

"I kill because it makes my headaches go away."

"Oh, please! Won't you let me help you?"

"It's too late," he said flatly.

"No, it's not. Let me take you to Dr. Lowry. If he doesn't think he can help you, I'll take you to Den—"

"No!" he said, cutting across her words, "I've been battling a headache since I brought you here. If it gets too bad, I'll have to kill you tonight to get relief. I don't want to do that. You and Mother have to die on Saturday. I must leave right now."

"I know you can be helped," Breanna said, "but you'll have to let me take you to Dr. Lowry. When your headache goes away, will you come back, let me loose, and go with me to the doctor?"

"No doctor. Ever." There was a slur of weariness in his hoarse whisper. "I'll be back to check on you every night until Saturday."

He paused at the door. "It won't do you any good to

scream. The cabin is in a hidden canyon off the beaten path. It's seldom that anyone comes around here. And even if somebody did, they couldn't hear you for the roar of the river."

Breanna didn't reply.

He started out the door, then said, "You still don't know who I am, do you?"

"No."

He let out an evil chuckle. "I'll let you see my face just before I kill you on your birthday."

With that, he stepped onto the porch and locked the door behind him. The pains were beginning to attack his head again. But he made his way to the wagon and climbed in, taking the reins. He guided the horses back to the narrow trail and headed toward the Redstone road on a long descent.

An hour later, the killer drove his wagon onto Main Street in Redstone. He was almost to the corner where he would turn to go home when he saw one of the four-man patrol teams passing under a street lamp at the end of the next block. He snapped the reins and quickly turned the corner. There was no way they could have recognized him from that distance.

Breanna rolled onto her knees and took hold of the post to pull herself to a standing position. She looked toward the cupboard, straining to see by what little starlight came through the windows. The madman had said there was water on the cupboard.

As she moved in that direction, the chain tugged at her ankle. She thanked the Lord that the killer had left her high-button shoes on when he chained her up. Without the shoe on her left foot, her ankle would have chafed in a hurry.

Holding part of the chain in her hand to give herself freedom of movement, she went to the cupboard. Her fingers found the water bucket and dipper, which hung on its side.

When she had taken her fill of water, she headed for the back door. Her fingers soon told her that it was secured with a sliding bolt. She slid back the bolt and opened the door. The loud rush of the river met her ears.

She looked up at the starry sky for a long moment, letting her gaze fall to the broad, foamy surface of the Crystal. The river was a ghostly motion in the near darkness.

After watching the river for a few moments, Breanna once again raised her eyes skyward. "Heavenly Father, I'm really in deep trouble. You know the intentions of that madman. If You don't deliver me, I will die on my birthday. This chain has me. There is absolutely no way I can escape on my own."

She wiped away the tears that had slid down her cheek and looked around to gauge her surroundings. She could see the shadowed wall of the canyon on the opposite side of the river. The wall couldn't be more than fifty feet high. She had guessed correctly. The canyon was relatively shallow.

The night air was cold, and a chill washed over her.

She turned and went back inside, dragging the chain. After sliding the bolt, she strained her eyes in the darkness to see if there was a chair within reach. She couldn't see one. There was no kitchen table either. Her captor must have moved the furniture to another part of the cabin.

Suddenly her eyes fell on a small dark object on the floor. She bent down and grasped it, crying out, "My purse! Thank You, Lord. It's got my Bible in it. I can draw strength from Your Word. I'll quote some passages for help tonight, but come morning, I'll be able to read it."

She put her back to the post and slowly slid down to a sitting position on the floor. She took the Bible out of her purse, held it close to her heart, and began quoting passages concerning God's watchful care over His children.

Tears flowed freely as passage after passage came from her lips. The Word was precious to her heart and brought a sweet calm.

Weary of mind and body, Breanna lay down on the hard floor and prayed until she had spent her strength. Lying there in the dark, with the sound of the river in her ears, she thought of John and wept, wanting more than anything to be with him.

16

A FLOOD OF GOLDEN SUNLIGHT streamed into Martha Waverly's room as she brushed her hair and dressed. Her mind switched back and forth between her new job and the story she had been told by the patrolmen. She wondered why Dr. Lowry had not informed her of the danger in Redstone.

She left her room to go down to breakfast and glanced at Breanna's door. Breanna was probably already downstairs.

Frieda Schultz and a few of her boarders were at the table when Martha entered the dining room.

"Well, good morning," said Frieda, shoving her chair back and rising to her feet. "Sit down here next to me. I will bring a fresh pot of coffee from the kitchen. But first, let me introduce you to these people."

While introductions were made, Martha noted that Breanna was not among the boarders. Having greeted them each with a warm smile, she turned to Frieda and said, "Breanna hasn't been down yet, has she?"

"No. Sometimes she does not eat breakfast with us. She eats something in her room."

"Oh. All right."

When Martha had finished breakfast, she climbed the stairs to get her purse before leaving for work. She paused at

Breanna's door and raised a hand to knock, then decided not to disturb her.

Dr. McClay Lowry pulled his buggy up in front of the office and saw Martha Waverly coming up the street toward him. Alighting from the buggy, he unlocked the front door just as Martha drew up.

"Good morning," he said with a smile. "Ready for your first day?"

Martha did not return the smile. As she moved inside ahead of him, Lowry said, "Is something wrong?"

Martha laid her purse on the desk and turned to face him. "Dr. Lowry, when you corresponded with me, why didn't you tell me about the killer on the loose in Redstone?"

A distressed look came over the doctor's face, and he couldn't quite meet her eyes for a moment. "So you've been told about him."

"Yes. Shouldn't I have been informed that by coming here my life would be in danger? Shouldn't I have been given the option of choosing to come in spite of the danger or choosing to find work elsewhere?"

Nodding, he said, "Yes, you should have had the option. I was wrong to keep it from you. I was just hoping that by the time you got here, the killer would have been caught and the danger removed. I'm sorry. I...I did the same thing to Breanna. And she rightfully asked the same question. I had planned to tell you about it when you arrived yesterday, and...well, it just slipped my mind. No excuse. I should have remembered to do it. If...if you want to go back home, I'll pay your way and give you a month's salary."

Martha did not reply for a moment, then she said, "Doctor,

I know now that your wife was murdered by that maniac. I certainly sympathize with what you're going through. As you know, my husband was killed in the war. I know what it's like to have your mate snatched away from you and leave your life shattered."

Tears sprang to the doctor's eyes.

"I will stay and work for you, Dr. Lowry, because I believe it's the right thing for me to do in spite of the fact that you withheld vital information that would have influenced my decision."

Lowry released a shaky breath and said, "Martha, you are very kind. I'm truly sorry for not advising you of the situation here. Please accept my apology."

A tiny smile tugged at the corners of her mouth. "I accept your apology, Doctor. I won't say that I'm not going to be afraid until the killer is caught. But I will do my best to perform my duties properly."

"Thank you," Lowry said.

"Well, Doctor, where do we begin?"

Lowry glanced at the clock on the wall, then looked toward the door. "I was going to have Breanna go over our general procedures first thing." He stepped to the door and looked down the street. "Hmm. She should be here by now. It isn't like her to be late."

"I'm sure she'll be along any minute."

"Of course. Well, let me begin by showing you the files. I think we have a pretty good system. By the way, I have to make a house call in about twenty minutes. When Breanna gets here, she can take up where I left off."

When fifteen minutes had passed, Lowry said, "You just go ahead and look around, both here and in the examining room, which is right behind that door. When Breanna gets here, tell her how far we got, and she can take you from there. As you saw in the appointment book, the first appointment isn't until ten o'clock. I should be back long before then. Should you have an emergency, do the best you can with it."

With that, Lowry picked up his medical bag and hurried out the door.

Martha glanced down the street, hoping to see Breanna, then went about the office, familiarizing herself with it as best she could.

A half hour passed before she entered the back room and began looking it over, familiarizing herself with the medicine cabinet and supply cupboard. After another half hour, she was on her way back to the front office when she heard someone enter.

"Oh, it's you, Doctor. Everything go all right?"

"Yes. I was checking on an elderly woman with arthritis and heart trouble, but she's doing well." He looked toward the back room. "Breanna back there?"

"No, sir. She hasn't come in yet."

Deep lines penciled themselves across his brow. "Martha, this is really strange. Something must be wrong. I'll—"

Suddenly they heard the piteous wail of a small child. A young woman charged through the door, carrying her two-year-old son, whose right hand was wrapped in a white cloth. "Doctor! Howie's fingers got slammed in our cellar door. I think one or two may be broken!"

"All right, Lorene, take him in the backroom." Then to Martha, "Would you go to the boardinghouse and see about Breanna while I take care of Howie?"

"Of course, Doctor."

Moments later, Martha bounded up the stairs at the boardinghouse and knocked on Breanna's door. When there was no answer, she knocked again.

Still no answer. She hurried down the stairs and knocked on the door of Frieda Schultz's apartment.

Frieda looked surprised to see her, and said, "What is it, Martha?"

"Have you seen Breanna this morning, Frieda?"

"No. She is not at work?"

"No. I just knocked on her door, but there was no response. Dr. Lowry asked me to come and see if I could find her. Will you open her door in case she's sick and can't get out of bed?"

"Of course, my dear. Come with me."

When the two women entered Breanna's room they found everything neat and in order, and the bed was made up.

Rubbing her chin, Martha looked at the bed and said, "Either the bed was not slept in last night, or Breanna made it up this morning and went somewhere quite early."

"No way to know," commented Frieda. "I do not know where else to tell you to look."

"I'll talk to Dr. Lowry about that, Frieda. Thank you."

When Martha returned to the doctor's office, he was at the desk, reading a patient's record. "So what about Breanna?" he said.

"Doctor, she's not there. The landlady hasn't seen her at all this morning. Her room is in order, and the bed is made up. There's no way to tell if it was slept in last night."

A look of deep concern came into Lowry's eyes. "I'm going to let Marshal Halloran know about this," he said. "You do the best you can here until I get back."

"Yes, sir. Doctor...?"

"Mmm-hm?"

"What about little Howie?"

"He's fine. No broken bones."

"Oh, good."

Mike and Marcie Halloran were standing by the desk when Lowry entered the marshal's office. "Mike, I'm afraid something's happened to Breanna! She didn't show up at the office, and no one's seen her at the boardinghouse. I had Martha go over there."

"Were there any signs of a struggle?" Halloran asked.

"No. If someone has done something to her, it didn't happen in the room. And her bed was made up, like maybe she hadn't slept in it. Something's definitely wrong."

"Doc," Mike said, "Breanna would certainly have advised you if she knew she was going to be late to work, wouldn't she?"

"Of course. She didn't say anything about it at church last night. I'm worried."

"Mike, you might go to Pastor Severson's house," Marcie suggested. "She's pretty close to them. Maybe for some reason she needed to see them."

"All right," the marshal said. "I'll go there first."

"I have to get back to the office," said Lowry, "Will you let me know if you find her? And…and if you don't."

"I sure will."

Karen Severson shook her head. "We haven't seen her since we took her home last night after church, Marshal. Have you checked at the boardinghouse?"

"That's been done, ma'am. No one has seen her this morning, not even Mrs. Schultz. There's no sign of a struggle in her room, and her bed is made up."

"So you don't know if she slept in it last night?"

"That's right."

"Eldon is in his office over at the church. Let's go tell him."

When the pastor was told about Breanna's disappearance, he looked at the marshal. "What are you going to do, Mike?"

"I'm going to search the town first. I'll get as many men to help me as I can."

"Well, here's your first volunteer. Let's go."

By nine forty-five, there were a dozen men gathered at the marshal's office to join the search.

By noon, everyone in town knew that Breanna Brockman was missing. Every business and house in Redstone had been visited and every person on the street questioned.

When all sources had been exhausted, Marshal Halloran gathered his small group of men in front of the doctor's office and said, "Gentlemen, the next thing is to recruit as many men as possible, saddle up, and begin searching in every direction from town."

"I know you need to talk to Dr. Lowry," spoke up Pastor Severson. "While you're doing that, we'll spread out and start recruiting."

"Thanks," said Halloran. "I'll meet all of you at my office within an hour."

As the group dispersed, Dr. Lowry came out of the office.

"Didn't find her, I assume," he said.

"No, sir. We've combed the town. Nobody has seen her since the Seversons took her home last night."

"Mike," Lowry said, "we're going to find her dead, sure as anything. That killer has struck again. He's probably killed her and put her body someplace where it'll never be found."

Halloran sighed. "Well, if he did, he's changed his pattern. With all his other victims, we found them where he'd killed them. Or right close by. Of course that doesn't mean he couldn't do the unexpected and change the pattern."

"What now?"

"We're recruiting as many men as possible to search in every direction from town. We'll do it on horseback so we can cover as much ground as possible before dark."

"What about Breanna's husband? Should you wire him?"

"I'll hold off until we've had a chance to search today. If we find her alive, it'll spare him a lot of worry. If we find her...dead, I'll wire him immediately."

"I'm going with you."

"Doc, I appreciate that, but it's best if you stay here."

"Well, one more man could make a difference. I should be in on the search."

"But look at it this way," said Halloran. "Say one of the search groups finds her alive but seriously injured. They'd bring her to town in a hurry, expecting you to be here."

"I hadn't thought of that. All right. I'll stay right here in the office."

By the time Halloran went home and explained to Marcie what he was doing and returned to his office, there were almost a hundred men gathered, ready to search for the nurse who had so endeared herself to the people of Redstone.

Included in the group were Biff Matthews, Clark Bentley, and Bart Gibson.

Marshal Halloran took Bart Gibson aside and said, "I'm a little surprised to see you in on this."

"Why's that, Marshal?"

"Well, from what I've heard, you seem to carry a grudge

toward Breanna over that eye of yours…like maybe you blame her for the loss of your sight."

A crooked grin curled Gibson's lips. "Aw, no, Marshal. I'm not carrying a grudge, believe me. She's a nice lady and a good nurse. I'm in on the search because I'm concerned about her."

Halloran divided the large gathering into groups of four and gave each group a territory to cover, instructing them that if they found Breanna alive to bring her to Dr. Lowry's office immediately then hunt up the rest of the searchers to advise them.

If they found her body, they would also let the other searchers know as soon as possible.

After a restless night of very little sleep on the hard floor, Breanna slowly got to her feet and rubbed her sore muscles. The sun was rising over the canyon wall across the river, sending its brilliant rays through the cabin windows.

Yawning, she laid a steadying hand against the post and looked around the cabin. Sure enough, she could see the kitchen table at the end of the narrow hall near the front bedroom. The chairs that went with it were in the parlor area near the cabin's front door.

"Thanks a lot, mister," she muttered.

Yawning again, she picked up the chain and went to the cupboard. When she had taken her fill of hardtack and water, she dragged the chain to the back door and stepped out on the porch, taking in her surroundings.

The canyon ran north and south. It looked like the shallow end of a much deeper canyon farther up the river. There were towering mountains to the north, and jagged peaks on the east and west sides, just beyond the canyon walls. To the south, the Crystal followed a winding valley. She could see more high peaks in the distance, including 14,100-foot Snowmass Mountain.

The river roared constantly as its foamy waters rushed to lower country.

Breanna noted the sun's position in the sky. It had to be eight o'clock by now. Dr. Lowry would certainly check with Frieda Schultz to see about her. When they found the room unoccupied, the doctor would advise Marshal Halloran that she was missing, and they would send out a search party.

"Lord," she said, her voice fluttering, "only You can lead them to me."

Her mind went to her beloved husband. Would they wire John when they saw that she had disappeared?

"If You wanted to do it that way, Lord, it would be all right with me. If John is back in Denver, and he gets a wire today that I'm missing, he'll be in Redstone by tomorrow afternoon. You could lead him to me by sometime Wednesday. That's three days before—Oh! here I am, trying to tell You how to do Your business. Do it Your way, dear God, but please don't let that beast take my life, whoever he is."

Breanna picked up her Bible and sat down on the floor with her back against the post. Opening her Bible, she said, "Lord, I need strength from Your precious Word. Guide me to the passages I should read."

Hours passed while Breanna read, wept, and prayed. In early afternoon she laid down on the floor and soon fell asleep.

At first, she wasn't sure what had awakened her. She sat up, blinking, and looked around the cabin. Then it came again.

Thunder.

The brilliant sunlight that had filled the cabin was gone.

She glanced out the kitchen window and saw dark clouds. Out the parlor windows and beyond the thick-trunked pines that stood in front of the cabin were more heavy clouds. Lightning flashed higher up, followed by the rumble of thunder.

Breanna rose to her feet and dragged the chain to the cupboard, where she stood looking out the window. The wind was picking up, swaying the giant trees that lined the Crystal.

And then the storm hit with fury. Rain came down in sheets and lightning continually slashed the sky, followed by the boom of thunder.

The storm had blown eastward by the time Marshal Mike Halloran and his search parties returned from their search and gathered in the muddy street in front of his office. The western sky was clear, and the sun's dying light spread over the ragged peaks.

Every man was soaked through to the skin. No one had taken a slicker when they had ridden out to search for Breanna.

"Gentlemen," said the marshal, "I appreciate your effort today. I'm going to ask you to help me search again tomorrow."

"You can count on me, Marshal," spoke up Clark Bentley. "I've got to head for home now. What time do we start in the morning?"

"Sunup."

The other men spoke up, assuring Halloran they would join the search at sunrise.

As they were riding away, Halloran saw Dr. Lowry hurrying his direction.

He pulled rein as the doctor drew up to him.

"We didn't find anything, Doc," the marshal said. "No trace of her alive…or dead."

"Now what?"

"We'll search again tomorrow, starting at sunrise."

"Good. Anybody tell you about the shoot-out?"

"Shoot-out? No. I haven't really talked to anyone in town since we got back."

"Happened down there in front of the hardware store. Two absolute strangers rode into town about noon from opposite directions. Seems both of them were gunfighters. When each found out who the other guy was, they decided to lift themselves a notch on the gunfighter's roster. So they braced each other in the middle of the street. The winner rode on out of town while the gunsmoke was still drifting in the air. The loser is lying in my shed out back. I'll have to bury him tomorrow."

Halloran shook his head, thinking of Rusty Atwood, the brother-in-law he had never met. "So downright foolish—men getting themselves killed for something so useless. These gunfighters die in the dust of the street in some obscure town, and half the time, nobody even knows what name to put on the grave marker."

"You're right, Mike. It is foolish. And you're right on the other part too. Nobody knew who the winner was, and I have no idea what the loser's name was. He'll just go into an unmarked grave."

Halloran took a deep breath. "Hope the same thing doesn't happen to Breanna."

"Excuse me?"

"I hope she doesn't go into an unmarked grave. I hope she doesn't go into a grave at all. We've just got to find her alive, Doc."

Lowry shook his head. "Yes. I can't let myself think any other way, Mike. Such a dear lady."

"Well, Doc, I've got to go to the telegraph office and send a wire to Chief U.S. Marshal John Brockman. He has to be told that Breanna is missing. See you later."

Woody Jones was at the telegraph key, clicking out the familiar Morse code when the marshal entered. He waved at Halloran, signaling that he would be with him shortly.

When Woody came to the counter, his eyes mirrored the sadness he saw in Halloran's. "I heard, Marshal. No Mrs. Brockman."

"I'm sick about this, Woody. We'll take up the search again in the morning."

"Yes. That's what some of your men told me. You've just got to find her, Marshal. And I mean alive and well."

Halloran sighed. "That's what I'm praying for."

Woody looked surprised. "I didn't know you were a prayin' man, Marshal."

Halloran's face tinted. "Well, I...ah...I haven't been. But I'm doing some tall praying now. I want that lady to be all right."

"Me, too," said the little man. "Somethin' I can do for you?"

"Yes. I've got to send a wire to Breanna's husband."

Woody shoved paper, pen, and ink toward the marshal.

When Mike Halloran walked out of the Western Union office a few minutes later, he thought of how the message would affect Brockman. A sick feeling settled in the pit of his stomach.

17

AFTER SENDING THE TELEGRAM, Marshal Halloran rode home, put his horse in the small corral behind the house, and entered the back door. He could see that supper was cooking on the stove and the table was set, but Marcie wasn't there.

"I'm home, Marcie!" He moved toward the front of the house, then went to the main bedroom.

Just before he reached the door, Marcie came out. Her eyes were swollen and bloodshot.

"Honey, what's the matter? What are you crying about?"

She moved into his arms and laid her head on his chest. "What about Breanna, Mike?"

"We didn't find her. But we're going out again in the morning."

"Oh, I hope she's all right."

"Me, too." He eased back to look into her teary eyes. "Is this what you're crying about?"

"No. I mean...I care about Breanna, but that's not what's had me crying."

"Well, what is it?"

"Did anyone tell you about the shoot-out today?"

"Yes. Doc told me."

"That's what's got me upset."

"I don't understand. Doc said nobody knows who either shooter was. Why are you upset?"

"It made me think of Rusty."

"Oh. Sure. He came to my mind too. You're wondering if he's lying in a grave in some Boot Hill somewhere."

Marcie nodded and broke into sobs.

"I'm sorry, honey," Mike said, pulling her tight against him. "I know you've always loved Rusty very much. If there was any way I could trace him to see whether he's dead or alive, I'd gladly do it."

"I know, I know. It's so awful, Mike. I'll probably never lay eyes on him again."

In Denver, former Chief U.S. Marshal Solomon Duvall was eating supper when he heard a knock at the door.

"Hello, Wally," Duvall said, surprised to see a Western Union messenger standing on his porch.

"Evenin', chief. I have a wire here that came for Chief Brockman, but since he's out of town and you're fillin' in for him, I figured I should bring it to you."

"Thanks, Wally. I appreciate your bringing it to me."

When the messenger had gone, Duvall returned to the kitchen and sat down at the table. He took another bite of food and opened the envelope. He almost choked when he read the message. Immediately he got up from the table, grabbed his hat, and bolted out the door.

"John, I wish you were here," the silver-haired Duvall mumbled as he hurried down the street. But John Brockman was on the trail of Virgil Mills and Rick Denison. There was no way to reach him.

Duvall moved swiftly up the steps of Sheriff Curt Langan's

front porch and knocked on the door. There were muffled footsteps inside; then the door opened.

"Howdy, Chief," said Langan. "Why…you look upset! What's wrong?"

Shaking the telegram in his hand, Duvall said, "Curt, this came a few minutes ago from Mike Halloran, the marshal of Redstone. It's for John. Something's happened to Breanna. She's missing."

"What? Breanna…missing? What do you mean?"

"Halloran says there's a psychopathic killer on the loose in Redstone. He's already murdered a few people, and all of a sudden, Breanna is nowhere to be found. Halloran says he hopes that Breanna's disappearance is due to something other than the killer, but he's afraid she's fallen into his hands. He has several teams of men who are helping him search for her. He says he would welcome John's presence."

Langan rubbed the back of his neck. "What a time for John to be chasing outlaws."

Stefanie Langan came into the hall and moved up behind her husband. "Hello, Chief Duvall. Curt, why don't you invite him in?"

"I really can't stay, Stefanie," said Duvall. "I've got to keep moving."

She ran her gaze between the two men. "What's wrong?"

"It's Breanna, honey," said Curt. "Chief Duvall just received a telegram from the town marshal at Redstone that was intended for John. She's disappeared."

"Disappeared?" gasped Stefanie. "What do you mean?"

"I'll let you explain it to her, Curt," said Duvall. "I need to go and tell Dottie and Matt about it. Then I've got to let Pastor Bayless know."

"I'll tell you what," said Curt, while Stefanie stood patiently waiting to hear what had happened to Breanna, "I'll go get Pastor Bayless and bring him to the Carroll house. Dottie, especially, is going to need him."

"Thanks, Curt."

Matt and Dottie Carroll and their children were stunned to learn of Breanna's disappearance and of the probability that she might be in the hands of a psychopathic killer. While Matt was trying to comfort Dottie, Pastor Bayless and his wife, Kathy, arrived with Curt Langan. Moments later, Stefanie Langan and her children showed up. Matt released Dottie to the women, who put their arms around her as she wept.

Pastor Bayless asked everyone to gather in a circle. They prayed, asking God to let Breanna be found alive and unharmed and that the Lord would bring John home very soon so that he might know the situation and be able to head for Redstone.

When they had prayed all around the circle, Pastor Bayless said he would contact all the members of the church and get a prayer chain started.

Breanna was standing on the back porch, holding what slack there was in the chain. She had eaten her supper of hardtack and water and was standing up in order to rest her body from the hard floor.

The sky had cleared completely after the rain, and the stars were twinkling overhead like lights in a fairy palace. The sound of the turbulent river never let up in the chilly, damp darkness.

Though the rainstorm had only lasted a few hours, Breanna could tell that the Crystal had risen above its normal depth.

239

She took a step back and leaned against the door frame. She thought of John and wondered if he was on his way to find her. Certainly Marshal Halloran had wired him by now. Of course, if John was trailing outlaws somewhere, they wouldn't be able to contact him.

"Lord," she said, lifting her eyes toward the night sky, "I'm trusting You to—"

Her words were interrupted by a rattling at the front door of the cabin. Her heart lurched as she spun around, trying to see through the murky gloom. She could barely make out the shadowy figure of a man coming through the door.

"Lord, he's back," she whispered. "Help me."

Breanna tried to remain calm, but tension filled her. Unconsciously, she was squeezing the chain so hard that her knuckles were white.

The shadow seemed to float toward her. His whispery voice grated on her nerves as he said, "Come in and close the door, Breanna-a-a. Sit down on the floor."

The stiffness in her legs and back had not completely gone away, but she obeyed and pressed her back against the post.

"Now, you sit still while I tie your hands and blindfold you."

After her hands were bound behind her back and the blindfold was in place, Breanna heard him go to the front of the parlor and strike a match. She could tell by looking through the tiny space where the blindfold touched her cheeks that he was carrying the lighted lantern to the kitchen.

"I brought you some more hardtack," he whispered. "Looks like you need some more water, too."

He walked past her and went out the back door. Breanna found herself wishing he would fall into the river and be carried downstream.

Soon he returned, and she could hear him muttering to

himself as he walked past her again and placed the full bucket on the cupboard, then moved to where she sat and stood over her, breathing raggedly.

"One less day to live, Mother. Monday's about gone. This time when I kill you, you'll stay dead." He leaned over and checked the bolts that held the chain to the post and to Breanna's ankle, then straightened up.

"Your mother is not here," Breanna said levelly. "Nobody comes back from the dead and lives inside someone else. If you kill me, you will not be killing your mother for the second time."

Abruptly, a strong hand gripped Breanna's jaws, squeezing so hard it made her wince.

"Don't you lie to me, Breanna-a-a! I know she's in there! And you're going to die with her!"

He shook her head roughly. "I know she's in there! I've seen her looking at me through your eyes!"

When he let go, there was pain in the muscles of Breanna's neck.

"I'm leaving now," he said curtly, "but I'll be back tomorrow to see that you have hardtack and water."

Pointing her face up toward his, she said, "I don't understand you."

"What do you mean?"

"If you're planning to kill me, why do you care if I have food and water?"

The madman laughed. "Don't you know?"

"I wouldn't ask if I did."

Bending low enough to breathe hotly on her face, he said, "I want you to be active and alert when I stab you to death, just like I did Mother, and will do again on Saturday! Happy birthday to both of you!"

He picked up the lantern, carried it back into the parlor, and blew it out. Breanna heard him set it down; then he returned in the darkness and took off her blindfold and untied her hands.

"Until tomorrow night," he said hoarsely and left the cabin, locking the front door behind him.

Breanna ignored the lingering pain in her neck and thought about the Scriptures she had read that day. "Dear Lord," she prayed, "help me to cling to Your Word and to Your mighty hand."

It was raining on Tuesday morning as Marshal Halloran organized the four-man teams in his search party, mapping out where each team would ride. All of them were clad in slickers this time. They were about to head out when they heard a familiar voice. "Marshal! Hey, Marshal!"

Woody Jones ran up to the marshal's horse and pulled a yellow envelope from inside his slicker. "This just came from the actin' chief U.S. marshal in Denver. Chief Brockman is out of town."

"Thank you, Woody." Angling the telegram to protect it as much as possible from the falling rain, Halloran read it quickly, then looked up at his men. "Yesterday evening when we got back, I sent a wire to Breanna's husband in Denver. The man who was chief U.S. marshal before him is filling in for him while Brockman is away from the office, chasing down a couple of outlaws. The acting chief's name is Solomon Duvall. They don't have any idea when Brockman will return but will advise him of Breanna's disappearance when he does. Duvall thanks us for keeping up the search."

"Marshal," said one of the men, "I just hope we'll find the

lady alive and well before her husband gets back to Denver."

"We all do," said another voice.

Halloran slipped the telegram into a shirt pocket inside his slicker then lifted his voice so all could hear. "Let's go out there and find her, men!"

When the four-man teams had ridden away to search in their designated areas, the marshal and three lumberjacks rode due north out of Redstone, following the west bank of the Crystal River.

Above the roar of the river and the pounding rain, Conrad Wiseman said, "Marshal, if that madman got to Mrs. Brockman and killed her, what do you think he would do with the body?"

"I doubt he'd go to the trouble of digging a grave," responded Halloran. "And I'm not too sure he would want to put it where she wouldn't be found. When he killed the others, it seems he wanted their bodies to be found. This situation has me baffled."

"I wonder why he would pick out Mrs. Brockman," said Paul Trevick.

Clark Bentley spoke up. "Maybe she unknowingly did something to irritate him."

"I doubt that," said Halloran. "If Breanna is indeed a victim of the killer, she was probably in the wrong place at the wrong time, like all his other victims."

The rain continued to pour down as Halloran and his three companions rode the riverbank, searching every clump of bushes, every low spot at the edge of the bank and the deeply shadowed forested areas along the way. From time to time they would catch sight of another team doing the same on the other bank of the river.

By early afternoon, the rain had stopped and the clouds

overhead were breaking up. Little shafts of sunlight seeped through, touching the earth and the foamy surface of the river with changing spots of color.

The foursome had just returned to the river after searching in a large area thick with birch, aspen, and pine when Paul Trevick pointed to the opposite bank of the river and said, "Marshal! Look over there! Doesn't that look like a body snagged in the brush on the other bank? See it? Just under the surface."

"That's a body for sure," said Bentley.

"Sure is," said Halloran. "Can't tell whether it's a man or a woman."

"I haven't seen our other team over there for quite a while," said Wiseman. "If they were in sight, we could signal them about the body. How are we gonna get to it without going back to the bridge in town?"

"We can't," said the marshal. "No way we can cross it. The river's too swift, and it's at least a couple feet deeper than usual. We'll have to ride back to town so we can cross the bridge."

Almost an hour and a half had passed by the time the team arrived on the east bank of the Crystal where they had seen the body. By that time, most of the clouds had drifted away, and the sun was shining brightly.

The men dismounted and made their way single file down the rugged bank toward the water's edge. Halloran was in the lead. When he reached the rushing water, he said loudly over his shoulder, "It's not Breanna! It's a man!"

They went to work, shoulder to shoulder, and finally were able to pull the corpse out of the water and onto the bank.

"These claw marks are clear enough," said Halloran. "Half-Paw got him somewhere upstream. By the looks of him, I'd say he's been dead three or four days. Any of you fellas recognize him?"

Two of the lumberjacks shook their heads.

Paul Trevick rubbed his jaw while studying the dead man's face. "I think this man is from Carbondale, Marshal. I'm almost positive I've seen him there in town."

"Well, I guess we'd better take him up there and see if we can find anybody who knows him," said Halloran.

"If you want, Marshal," said Clark Bentley, "I'll take him to Carbondale on my horse, and you three can go on searching for Mrs. Brockman."

The other three looked at him oddly.

"Oh," said Bentley. "I forgot. The Halloran rule. Four men on a team and always together because one of the men on a team could be the killer."

"That's the rule," said Halloran. "We'll take this dead man to Carbondale together. However, Clark, since you volunteered, you can carry him on your horse with you."

Breanna stood on the back porch, watching the lowering sun. She estimated that the morning's rain had raised the river a few more inches on its banks.

Suddenly her eye caught movement among the trees on the far side of the river. At first she thought it was a pair of deer or elk, but seconds later, she saw two men emerge from the timber into the sunlight and walk to the water's edge. Both had rifles in one hand and canteens in the other.

Breanna's heart thundered in her breast as she waved and shouted, "Over here! Hey! Over here! See me? I'm over here across the river!"

The river's roar drowned out her voice.

The men knelt down and began filling their canteens.

"Oh, please look over here!"

She picked up the chain and dragged it into the cabin, looking around for some object that she could wave from the porch to catch their eye. The killer had not so much as left a towel in the kitchen. She had gone through every drawer and found them empty.

Wait a minute! There were some tin plates in the cupboard. A tin plate might draw their attention! She went to the cupboard and took a tin plate from a shelf. As she turned to head for the door, she caught sight of the two men through the kitchen window. They were corking their canteens and looking directly at the cabin.

"Yes!" she cried, waving the plate at them through the window. "See? See the plate? I'm over here! Please see me!"

They were talking to each other while looking at the cabin but apparently had not seen her.

Panic claimed her as she picked up the chain and went as fast as she could to the back door. When she reached the porch, the two men were walking toward the trees. "Wa-a-a-it!" she cried, waving the plate. "Come ba-a-a-ack! Don't go!"

Breanna's voice trailed off as the men disappeared into the shadows. *So close,* she thought, her heart sinking within her. *So close.*

She shuffled back inside the cabin and tossed the plate toward the cupboard. It sailed through the air, striking the cupboard, then clattered to the floor.

Breanna went back to the post and slid down to her normal sitting position and buried her face in her hands.

"Oh, John!" she sobbed. "I need you so desperately! John! Please come to me!"

When her weeping had subsided, Breanna said, "Lord, please forgive my little faith. I'm sorry I panicked. It's just that…well, if those hunters had seen me signaling to them, they would have found a way to come across the river and see what I was signaling about. They could have shot the chain and set me free. They could have—Oh, there I go again. Trying to tell You how to answer my prayers.

"Please forgive me, Lord. I'm trusting You to deliver me. Sometimes—as You know—my faith gets pretty thin. Increase my faith. Oh, help me, Lord. I don't want to fail You in this time of testing."

Breanna had eaten her supper of hardtack and water and was standing at the kitchen window, looking at the starry sky, when she heard the rattle of a wagon and the snort and blow of a horse.

Her knees grew weak.

"He's back, Lord," she said in a shaky whisper and turned around, bracing herself against the cupboard.

The night was dark, and when the killer opened the front door, he was barely more than a shadow.

Moving inside, he paused, apparently able to tell that she was not seated on the floor at the post, and his sibilant words cut through the darkness, "Breanna-a-a! Where are you?"

She rattled the chain purposely. "Here. In the kitchen."

"I want you sitting down at the post. Do it! Now!"

She made her way in the dark to the post, dropped the chain with a thud, and sat down on the floor.

The killer's hot breath was on Breanna's face as he tied the blindfold in place. When that was done, he tied her hands behind her back.

She heard him go to the parlor, light the lantern, and walk to the kitchen. There was a metallic *scrunch* as he stepped on the tin plate.

He picked it up. "What's this plate doing on the floor, Breanna-a-a?"

She turned her face his direction but did not answer.

His breathing became labored, and she was startled when he bent over and whispered coarsely in her ear, "Why did you put this tin plate on the floor? What were you hoping to gain by that?"

She was trying to think of a way to pacify him without lying when suddenly he clutched her throat, cutting off her air.

"Answer me, woman! Answer me!"

Breanna could only make a gagging sound.

"All right," he said, letting go of her. "Speak."

"I...I tossed the plate toward the cupboard from the back door. It ended up on the floor. I'm a little bit upset, you know. I...I just didn't bother to pick it up."

"What were you doing with it, anyhow?" he demanded. "You don't need the plate to eat your hardtack."

Breanna could see that he was going to press her till she satisfied his curiosity.

"All right, I'll tell you." Her voice sounded hollow, as if piped through a long tunnel. "I saw two hunters across the river, and I used the plate to wave at them to get their attention. I'm sorry to say it didn't work."

A burst of profanity came from him in a tight, garbled voice, and he slapped her savagely across the face.

Breanna's head rebounded from the blow, and he slapped her again. She saw stars behind the blindfold.

"Don't you ever try a thing like that again!" he hissed. "You hear me?"

He grabbed her jaw and gripped it with strong fingers. "You hear me?" he repeated.

"Yes," she choked out. "I hear you. But what do you expect?"

The vise tightened. "What do you mean?"

"Do you just expect me to lie down and die? I want to live. It is only natural that I try to find a way to escape. You are an intelligent man. Isn't that what you would do if you were in my position?"

He stood up and went back to the kitchen. Breanna could hear him placing more hardtack on the cupboard. Without a word, he took the bucket out the back door and returned shortly, then took the lantern to its place by the front door and blew out the flame.

He did not say another word as he moved through the darkness, untied her hands, and removed the blindfold. Seconds later, he went out the front door and locked it. Breanna could hear the *clip-clop* of horses' hooves as he drove away.

18

THE SETTING SUN PAINTED THE SKY a deep vermilion as outlaws Rick Denison and Virgil Mills guided their weary horses up a gradual slope in the eastern foothills of the Rockies. When they topped the slope, both men hipped around in their saddles to look behind them.

"No lawmen in sight," said Mills, chuckling. "So far, there ain't been a posse on our trail since we left Denver."

"Well, I can't believe they ain't comin' after us, Virg," said Denison. "When that smart aleck chief U.S. marshal found out somebody had killed his pal, Rusty Atwood, he had to have known it was us. You can bet your boots on that. There's gotta be a posse of some kind tryin' to track us down."

Squaring himself in the saddle and looking ahead, Mills said, "We'll just keep on pushin' for New Mexico. I'd say another coupla days will have us over Raton Pass."

"That'll be good," said Denison, taking one last look at their back trail. "We could've made New Mexico sooner if we hadn't weaved back and forth between the plains and these foothills all the way from Denver, but at least nobody's found our trail yet." He turned forward and clucked at his horse.

As they started down the gentle slope ahead of them, Mills pointed to a deep ravine off to the side of the trail.

"How about we camp down there?"

"Suits me. Looks like a small brook runnin' through it."

Soon they were at the bottom of the ravine, which was dotted with brush and a sprinkling of old stunted trees, gnarled and twisted by decades of wind.

They watered their horses at the brook, then tethered them on its bank where there was plenty of grass.

As they sat down to a cold meal of beef jerky, hardtack, and water, Mills said, "What I wouldn't give for some hot food."

"Yeah, me, too," said Denison. "But if we built a fire here, we'd be wavin' a flag at our pursuers if they're back there somewhere." He put a slab of beef jerky between his teeth, tore off a piece, and began chewing. After a few seconds, he shoved the wad of jerky to the side of his mouth and said, "I don't mind havin' to rough it like this. Killin' Atwood was worth it."

Denison swallowed the jerky, smacked his lips, and said, "Even though we won't gain any recognition for killin' the famous gunslinger, we still have the satisfaction of knowin' we put him six feet in the ground."

Mills snickered. "Yeah. That is a good feelin'."

When their stomachs were full, Denison yawned, scratched his ribs, and said, "Well, ol' pal. I'm ready for the sack."

"Me, too."

Both outlaws slid into their bedrolls.

Mills glanced at the horses, barely able to make them out in the dim light of the stars. They were busy munching the rich grass on the bank of the stream. By the time he got comfortable with his hat over his face, Rick Denison was snoring.

At dawn, a thin fog hovered in the ravine. Virgil Mills was the first to awaken. He lifted the hat from his face and glanced at his friend, who was still snoring.

Mills yawned and stretched, then rolled onto his side and closed his eyes. He lay there for a few seconds, then opened his eyes.

Something was wrong.

Mills rubbed his eyes and focused on the spot where they had tethered their horses.

He jerked up to a sitting position, rubbed his eyes again to make sure.

No horses!

He reached over and shook Denison. "Rick! Wake up! The horses are gone!"

While Denison was gaining his senses, Mills got free of his bedroll.

"How could they have gotten loose?" said Denison. He threw back his blanket and got to his feet. Glancing all around, he said. "We had 'em tethered solid!"

Suddenly a deep, resonant voice from behind them said, "Right, boys. I let them loose."

The outlaws whirled about to find themselves looking down the black muzzle of John Brockman's Colt .45 Peacemaker.

"You!" gusted Denison.

John smiled. "Mm-hmm. Me. Now you boys get on your feet and drop those gunbelts. You're under arrest."

Denison's eyes showed a hint of rebellion.

"Don't try something foolish," said Brockman. "If you're thinking of taking a chance because you'd rather die by a bullet than a rope, let me explain something."

Denison narrowed his eyes. "Don't tell me Atwood's still alive."

"I *will* tell you he's still alive because it's the truth. You didn't kill him."

The outlaws exchanged glances, surprise evident in their eyes.

"Rusty's still alive, and the doctor says he'll live," said John. "So instead of taking you back to face a judge and jury for murder, for which you absolutely would hang, I'm taking you back to face charges of *attempted* murder. Eyewitnesses saw you shoot Rusty and will testify at your trial. You'll both go to prison for at least forty years on the attempted murder charge. But just think! If you get the minimum sentence, you'll only be in your sixties when you get out."

Denison and Mills exchanged dismal glances.

"If that doesn't sound too good, boys," said John, "you can make your try for freedom right now, but I warn you, I can shoot as straight as I can draw fast. So do what I tell you and drop those gunbelts or make your play. Choice is yours."

Moments later, Denison and Mills found themselves disarmed and their hands cuffed behind their backs. They watched while the tall man in black went behind a nearby clump of bushes and led their horses to them along with his own horse. Helping both men into their saddles, he mounted Ebony and said, "Okay guys. Let's go to Denver."

As they headed north, John's mind went to Breanna. For a couple of days he'd had a distinct feeling that she was in danger. In his heart, he prayed for his precious wife once more, asking God that if his feelings were right, and Breanna was in danger, to protect her and remove the danger.

On Wednesday morning, Breanna stood at the kitchen window, watching the violent rainstorm that had awakened her only moments before.

Multiple lightning bolts chased each other across the dark sky. The blasts of thunder that followed shook the cabin and rattled the window. Between the raindrops that ran down the window pane, Breanna saw a small herd of deer come out of the forest on the opposite bank of the raging river. They seemed almost to be apparitions as they moved slowly down the bank and soon vanished from view.

Breanna's line of sight dropped to the Crystal. The heavy rains were taking their toll on the river's level. It was dangerously close to its banks.

She ran her gaze to the canyon wall on the other side and peered as far upriver as she could see. The canyon was relatively narrow. If the river should swell very far over its banks…

As she walked back toward the post, she was keenly aware that the clamp on her ankle was making it sore in spite of some protection by the leather of her shoe.

Bracing her back against the post, she slid down to her usual sitting position, picked up her Bible, and started reading where she had left off in the Psalms.

As the hours passed, Breanna read her Bible, prayed, and talked to John as if he could hear her.

It was still raining hard that night when the killer came to the cabin. He bound and blindfolded Breanna as usual, getting her wet while the rain water dripped off his hat and slicker. Finding plenty of water in the bucket, he replenished her hardtack supply, extinguished the lantern, then removed the rope and blindfold.

Breanna watched her captor go to the door and open it, then pause and turn toward her in the gloom. The cold wind drove sheets of rain into the cabin around him as he laughed and reminded her that only two days remained. He was still laughing when he closed the door and locked it.

Breanna's teeth began to chatter uncontrollably, and goose bumps crawled on her flesh. She shivered and tucked her hands between her knees for warmth. The killer's laugh echoed through her head, and suddenly fear came swooping like a great dark bird into her mind, enfolding her in its powerful black wings.

She bent her head forward until it touched her knees. Crying out to God, she begged for deliverance from the heartless maniac's clutches. She wept for a long time, and when the weeping finally stopped, she was spent, both physically and emotionally.

After quoting some of the verses from the psalms she had read that day, she stretched out on the floor and finally fell asleep.

The sky was clear, and a brilliant sun shone down on Thursday morning as Chief U.S. Marshal John Brockman drew up in front of the Denver County Sheriff's Office and jail with his prisoners in tow.

Rick Denison and Virgil Mills sat glumly astride their mounts with their hands cuffed behind their backs.

"All right, boys," said John. "End of the line."

He helped them dismount and moved behind as he said, "Right through the front door."

Breanna was still very heavy on John's mind. He was eager to find out if she had come home. It was only two days till her birthday.

Deputy Sheriff Steve Ridgway was at his desk when the door opened and the two handcuffed men came in with Brockman on their heels. He laid down the papers in his hand and rose to his feet. A smile spread over his handsome young face as he said, "You never fail, do you, Chief? Did you ever go after outlaws and not get them?"

"Couple of times, Steve."

"Really?"

"Mm-hmm. Both times, those men I was trailing were already dead by the time I caught up to them. One had been mauled to death by a black bear, and the other one had been tracked and killed by another outlaw who had it in for him."

"Oh. It was like that, huh?"

"Mm-hmm. I'll relieve Mr. Denison and Mr. Mills here of their handcuffs, and I'll let you lock them up. Is the sheriff around?"

"Right here, John," came the voice of Sheriff Curt Langan as he entered the office from the cell block. "I see you caught up with the guys who shot down Rusty Atwood."

"Mm-hmm. I told them you have real nice accommodations here."

"I'm sure they'll think they're real nice by the time they've spent a few decades down at the Territorial Prison in Canon City. Steve, take our guests back and show them their suites."

"Be my pleasure," said Ridgway. "This way, boys."

As the deputy and the prisoners headed for the door, John turned to the sheriff and said, "Curt, do you know if Breanna has come home yet from Redstone?"

Langan flicked a glance at the three men as they were filing through the door. "Ah...no, she hasn't."

"But she was going to be home three or four days before her birthday," said John. "This is Thursday. I thought sure she'd be home by now."

John looked closely at Curt's face. "Something's wrong concerning Breanna. What is it?"

When the door clicked shut, Langan said, "John, Chief Duvall got a telegram that was meant for you from Redstone's town marshal."

"Mike Halloran?"

"Uh…yeah."

"Well?"

"John, they've got a psychopathic killer on the loose up there in Redstone. He's already murdered several people. Halloran's been doing everything he can to catch him, but so far, hasn't been able to do it. And…well, Breanna disappeared Sunday night. Several teams of townsmen are searching for her, but so far they haven't turned up a trace. Halloran fears—"

"That the psychopath has killed Breanna."

Langan nodded. He took hold of John's arm. "But it might be something totally unrelated to the maniac, John. Since they haven't found a…body, they're hoping she's disappeared for some other reason, and that they'll find her well and unharmed."

"Curt, I've had a strange feeling for the past four days that Breanna might be in some kind of danger. I've prayed for her in a special way. Now I know what I've been feeling is real and came from the Holy Spirit."

"Pastor Bayless has had a twenty-four-hour prayer chain going among the church members ever since the wire came, John."

"I'm glad for that." The tall man rubbed his brow, and his hand trembled slightly. "Curt, I'm going over to the depot and book myself on tomorrow morning's train to Grand Junction. I'll rent a horse in Glenwood Springs and ride for Redstone. I can get there faster on horseback than by stagecoach."

"I'll go to Redstone with you."

"I appreciate that, but you're needed here."

"But I can help search for her. I'll—"

"From what you said, I think they've got enough men to search. Thank you for your willingness to help, but like I said, you're needed here. I'll see you later."

"We'll be praying," Curt called after him.

"That means more than anything," John said and started out the door. He paused and looked back. "These two horses out here belong to Denison and Mills."

"I'll take care of them."

John nodded and hurried to Ebony. He swung aboard and galloped through the streets of Denver to Union Station.

With a ticket on the morning train in his pocket, he rode to the federal building and went inside.

Deputy Marshal Billy Martin was alone at the desk. He looked up and smiled when he saw his boss. "Welcome back, Chief!"

"Thanks, Billy," said Brockman. "Denison and Mills are in Langan's jail. Will you alert Judge Johnson for me? I'm leaving town again."

"Sure will, sir. I assume Sheriff Langan told you about the...the situation on Mrs. Brockman."

At that moment the door to Brockman's office came open, and Solomon Duvall emerged, having heard John's voice.

"Yes, he did, Billy. That's what I meant when I said I was leaving town again."

"You're going to Redstone, John?" said Duvall.

"On the train in the morning." John moved toward the older man. "I'd ride all night if it would get me there any faster, but it wouldn't."

"John, I'm so sorry about this. But don't you give up. I've been praying along with everybody else in the prayer chain. The Lord has His mighty hand on that sweet girl."

Tears misted John's iron-gray eyes. "Yes. I'm trusting Him to take care of her. I'll wire you with any new information after I get to Redstone."

"Please do, John," said the silver-haired man. "The wire from Halloran said for you to let him know when you're coming."

"I'll send the wire for you, Chief," volunteered Billy.

"All right. I appreciate that. I'm going over to the hospital to see how Rusty Atwood's doing, and I need to go see Pastor Bayless and then go talk to Dr. Goodwin. In addition to that, I need to spend a little time with Breanna's sister and family. It'll help, Billy, if you'll send the wire for me. Tell Halloran I'm booked on the train in the morning, and that I'll come from Glenwood Springs on horseback. I should be in Redstone between one and two o'clock."

"Got it," said Martin. "I'll see that the wire gets right out, sir."

Moments later, Brockman dismounted in front of the hospital and dashed through the front door. Madge Landis looked up from her desk. "Oh, Chief Brockman, you're back. Did you catch those outlaws?"

"Yes. Is Rusty Atwood still in the same room?"

"Yes, sir. And he's doing much better."

Just as he rounded the corner, he bumped into orderly Dirk Jacobs. Both men grabbed each other to keep from falling.

When they had regained their balance, Dirk said, "Glad to see you back, Chief. Did you catch—"

"Yes. They're in jail, waiting for trial."

"I'm sure sorry about Miss Breanna, sir. I sure hope it will turn out all right."

"She's in God's hands, Dirk."

"Yes, sir."

"See you later," said Brockman, rushing down the hall.

Dr. Lyle Goodwin emerged from one of the rooms, and his face brightened when he saw Brockman.

The tall man came to a quick stop. "Hello, Doctor. I was going to stop by your office in a little while. I just got in with the outlaws I was tracking. Curt Langan told me about the wire Chief Duvall received from Redstone's marshal. I'm booked on the Grand Junction train in the morning. I'll be in Redstone by early afternoon."

"John, I'm so sorry about this. Bless Breanna's heart. I just have to believe she's all right. Martha and I are praying for her."

"Keep it up, Doctor." John patted his arm. "I have to believe it, too."

"John!" came the familiar voice of Dr. Matthew Carroll. "I'm glad you're back!"

John turned to look at Breanna's brother-in-law. "Thanks, Doctor."

"I assume you're heading over the mountains."

"On the Grand Junction train in the morning."

"You have time to come by the house, then? Dottie's really upset. It'll help if she can talk to you."

"Sure. I was planning on going by the house."

"John," said Goodwin, "I have to get back to the office. Please know that Martha and I will keep praying."

"Thank you, Dr. Goodwin. God bless you."

"You, too, John. Please let us know when you find her."

As Goodwin walked away, Matt Carroll turned back to John. "I know I can speak for Dottie. Will you have supper with us?"

"Sure. My appetite's not real sharp right now, but I think I could eat some of Dottie's cooking."

"Great! I'm going home a little early today. I'll tell her you'll be coming. Six-thirty all right?"

"Yes, I'll be there. I'm here to see Rusty. Madge says he's doing better."

"Sure is. He'll be out of the hospital in another week."

"That's great. Anyway, after I spend some time with Rusty, I've got another stop to make. I need to go home, too, and make sure the other horses are all right."

"Your neighbors are looking after them, aren't they?"

"Yes, but I just want to make sure all's well before I head over the mountains, and I don't want to get the Moores out of bed. Anyway, I should be able to make it to your house by six."

"That'll be fine. Dottie and the kids will be glad to know you're back, and that you're going to Redstone to see about Breanna." His voice caught. She's...she's so dear to our hearts."

John swallowed the lump that had risen in his throat. "Just keep praying, Matt. See you this evening."

"We'll look forward to it," said Carroll and started to walk away.

"Oh! Wait!" John reached into his pants pocket. "If you release Rusty from the hospital before I get back, he'll need a place to stay." Peeling off several bills from a wad under a money clip, John handed them to Carroll. "Give this to Rusty and tell him to stay in the Westerner on me."

Matt shook his head in wonderment. "John, you never cease to amaze me. You're the most generous man I know."

John stuffed the bills in his hand. "God's been good to me, Matt. It's a joy to share His blessings with people who need it."

"So you're not going to tell Rusty about this money when you go in there to see him?"

"No. You give it to him when you release him."

"Will do," said Matt, and walked away.

Rusty was sitting up in the bed, reading a Bible, when John entered the room. A smile spread over his face when he saw the man in black coming through the door.

"Chief! I'm so glad to see you!"

261

"Same here, Rusty," said Brockman. "They tell me you're doing well."

"Yes, praise the Lord."

"Sitting up, taking nourishment, and reading God's Book. Can't beat that."

"God's been so good to me," said Rusty. "So, did you catch those two?"

"Yes. They'll get at least forty years for attempted murder."

Rusty nodded and closed the Bible. "Your pastor has been in to see me every day. Gave me this new Bible the second time he came. My other one is still in my saddlebags at the stable."

"That's Pastor Bayless. He's got a heart as big as all out-doors."

"Chief...I...ah...I was really saddened to hear that your dear wife is missing."

John nodded silently.

"I've been praying for her."

"I appreciate that. I'm heading for Redstone in the morning."

"I know you'll be occupied with finding Mrs. Brockman, but if you get a minute to go by and see Marcie—"

"I'll make time for that, Rusty."

Rusty wiped away the tears that were spilling down his cheeks. "Tell Sis I love her, Chief, and that I'll be coming to see them as soon as I'm able to travel."

"Will do."

"Would you tell them something else for me?"

"Sure."

"Be sure to tell them it was *you* who made it so I could never draw a gun with my right arm again and that it was *you* who led me to the Lord, which really made the change in my life."

"I'll do as you ask, Rusty."

"I want Marcie and Mike to be saved, Chief. Work on them, will you?"

"I will."

"Thank you, Chief. And I'll be praying for you as you go to find your wife. And I'll keep on praying for her."

"Thanks, pal," said John, gripping Rusty's hand. "You get well, you hear?"

"I'll do my best."

After leaving the hospital, John Brockman went to the parsonage and talked to Pastor and Mrs. Bayless. He thanked the preacher for the prayer chain, and together they had prayer before John moved on.

John's next stop was his place in the country. He found Breanna's horse and the two buggy horses doing fine and stopped to thank his neighbor for taking care of them. He explained that he would leave Ebony at the stables in town while he went to Redstone.

That evening, John had a sweet and tender time with the Carrolls. None of them had much appetite, but they all ate a little. Dottie, James, and Molly Kate felt better about Breanna's plight, knowing that John was going to Redstone to make his own search.

They had prayer together, asking God to bring Breanna back to them alive and unharmed.

19

ALL DAY LONG ON THURSDAY, western Colorado was under a heavy downpour until just before sundown. Slowly the clouds broke up, and the last rays of the setting sun fanned out across the western sky ever so slowly as if in parting reluctance.

Breanna observed that the boiling river was now over its banks by two to three feet and threatening to rise higher as the water from the high country charged headlong into the narrow canyon.

She judged the distance between the bank of the Crystal and the back of the cabin to be about thirty feet. The swift water was now closer than that.

Finally, the sun's golden rays faded, and twilight rapidly followed. Its gray shades accentuated the forlorn loneliness Breanna felt as she thought of John, of Dottie, of Matt and the children, and of her many friends in Denver. Would she ever see them on earth again?

The roar of the Crystal was deafening as its violent waters crashed against canyon walls in an unending roar. The white foam was a full three feet or more beyond the bank.

"Lord," she said, "I'll drown if the river keeps rising like this." *Better than dying at the hands of that insane killer,* she thought as she went inside the cabin and returned to the post.

She sat down on the floor and picked up her Bible. There was still enough light left to see the print. Thumbing the pages gently, she said, "Lord Jesus, I need Your guidance. I need You to give me strength and encouragement from Your Word."

Suddenly Breanna was overwhelmed with despair. She broke down and wept. After a minute or two, she was wiping the tears away when her gaze lowered to the page where the Bible had fallen open. She read:

> And when he was entered into a ship, his disciples followed him. And, behold, there arose a great tempest in the sea, insomuch that the ship was covered with the waves: but he was asleep. And his disciples came to him, and awoke him, saying, Lord, save us; we perish.
>
> And he saith unto them, Why are ye fearful, O ye of little faith? Then he arose, and rebuked the winds and the sea; and there was a great calm.
>
> But the men marveled, saying, What manner of man is this, that even the winds and the sea obey him!

Breanna pressed the Bible against her cheek. Closing her eyes, she could hear a Voice in her mind, saying, *"Why are ye fearful, O ye of little faith?"*

Suddenly it was like the Lord Jesus was right there in the cabin with her, even as He had been in the ship with the disciples, and said, "Breanna, dear, why are you so fearful? Don't you know that I am just as capable of saving your life in these circumstances as I was to save the disciples in theirs?"

Breanna trembled. "Oh, Lord, I don't mean to be afraid, but that insane man means to kill me! There's just one day left. And the river...You can see how high it's getting. I keep asking myself, will it be the madman or the river that kills me?

Please…help me. Help me to trust You to deliver me!"

Again, He seemed to say, *"Why are ye so fearful, O ye of little faith?"*

Over and over, those words captured her, reverberating through her mind.

"I know, Lord. I know. I am of such little faith. Please forgive me. I—"

Now only two words penetrated her thoughts: *"Little faith. Little faith. Little faith."*

Breanna's tears continued to flow as she replied, "Yes, I know, Lord. I'm sorry my faith has been so small. Please help me to trust You."

The still small voice came in her heart again. This time, speaking only one word: *"Faith."*

The word echoed over and over again.

Breanna thought of Scriptures that dealt with faith: "By grace are ye *saved* through faith." "Being *justified* by faith." "The *righteousness* which is of faith." "The just shall *live* by faith." "We *walk* by faith, not by sight."

With those words fresh in her mind, she could hear the Lord say, "Breanna…what is faith?"

Immediately she remembered the great *faith* chapter of the Bible. Hebrews eleven. "Why, Lord," she said aloud, "You gave Your own definition of *faith* in the very first verse of Hebrews eleven. 'Now faith is the substance of things hoped for, the evidence of things not seen.'"

The Voice said, "Breanna, think on these words, especially the last three."

Breanna quickly turned to the passage, and though the light was almost gone, she could see well enough to let her attention focus on the last three words of Hebrews 11:1… *things not seen.*

"Oh, of course, Lord! Of course! I can't *see* how I'll survive if the river washes this cabin away with me chained to it. I can't *see* how I'll escape the killer. I can't *see* a way out of this horrible predicament I'm in. But You still want me to believe that You are going to deliver me."

The Voice which spoke to her heart and mind seemed to say, "Yes, My daughter. I want you to trust Me and believe that I will do it even though you cannot see how."

Breanna read verse 6: "But without faith it is impossible to please him: for he that cometh to God must believe that he is, and that he is a rewarder of them that diligently seek him."

She read the verse aloud several times, then with constricted throat, said, "Oh, Lord, I indeed want to please You! I...I want to believe You for my rescue, no matter what You have to do to accomplish it. But my faith is weak. Please. Give me the faith to believe You for it."

To mind came Romans 10:17: "So then faith cometh by hearing, and hearing by the word of God."

"Yes, Lord!" Breanna exclaimed. "You will give me the faith I ask for through Your Word!"

Breanna was still quoting Hebrews 11:1 when she rose to her feet and felt her way in the dark to the cupboard. The chain rattled with her every movement.

The river roared in her ears as she stood in front of the window at the cupboard and ate her meal of hardtack and water. The moon was rising over the canyon wall, sending its silvery light on the racing, white-foamed waters of the Crystal River. Again, thoughts of drowning came to her mind.

"No, Breanna!" she audibly corrected herself. "You mustn't worry about the river. You must keep your mind on the One whom the disciples spoke of when they said, 'What manner of man is this, that even the winds and the sea obey him!'"

She finished her dull meal, then dragged the chain back to the post and and sat down.

She laid her head back, closed her eyes, and let her mind go over what she could recall of Hebrews chapter eleven. She thought of the great Old Testament saints who were written about there—Abel, Enoch, Noah, Abraham, Sarah, Isaac, Jacob, Moses—and so many others. All of them saw great and mighty things happen in their lives by faith.

The moon was beginning to send its silvery light through the kitchen window, but Breanna knew it wouldn't be strong enough to clearly illuminate the words on the pages of her Bible. She would read the chapter tomorrow morning.

Breanna's thoughts were interrupted when the front door of the cabin opened.

Her heart leaped in her breast, and immediate panic rose in her. *No!* she thought. *I mustn't be afraid. Jesus is here in the cabin with me, just like He was with the disciples in the ship.*

The killer blended with the night like a dark ghost as he moved to where Breanna sat on the floor. His voice was a smoky whisper; "I'm back, Breanna-a-a!" He laughed. "I see you're still here!"

"Does that surprise you?"

"You know the answer to that. When I put the clamp on you, I meant for it to stay there."

Barely able to make him out, Breanna studied the nearly shapeless form of him as he bent over and slid a sack across the floor into the kitchen. "More hardtack," he whispered. "I'll let you take it to the kitchen tonight; the moonlight might show more of me than I want."

"Guess it might," she said, still trying to see something of his size or build. But his outline was too vague, even against the small bit of moonlight reflecting off the trees at the front of the cabin.

Chuckling, he said, "Can't make me out, eh?"

Breanna's mouth snapped shut.

"Didn't think I could tell what you were doing, did you?"

She didn't reply.

"You really want to know who I am, don't you, Breanna-a-a?"

Still, she didn't reply.

He laughed hoarsely. "Well, you'll know Saturday, just before I kill you!" He laughed again. "It's really strange, Breanna-a-a. With Mother living inside you, I'm surprised you haven't been able to convince her to tell you who I am."

"Then that ought to be enough to convince you that your mother is *not* inside me," Breanna said crisply.

"Oh, but you don't know Mother very well, do you? She's mean as a teased rattler, Breanna-a-a. She is fully aware that you want to know, and she'll let you suffer in your ignorance. Isn't that right, Mother, you mean old woman!"

After a long silence, he whispered, "See, Breanna? I told you she's mean! Won't even speak to her own son! Well, I'll get her to reveal her presence inside you on Saturday? I'm going to use a long-bladed knife so it will be sure to reach Mother."

The killer looked toward the kitchen. "How's your water supply?"

"I have enough."

"Good. I'll be going then." He moved toward the front door. "One more night, Breanna-a-a. One more night."

He laughed fiendishly. "It will be so wonderful when you are gone forever, Mother! You will no longer be in the world to invade my dreams and turn them into nightmares! You won't be able to look at me through little nursie's eyes, either! Both of you will be gone forever!" With that, he was gone.

Breanna swallowed hard and thought of the last three words in Hebrews eleven: *things not seen.*

"Oh, God, help me," she breathed. "Help me to believe You for deliverance from this horrid predicament. I cannot see any way of escape. This chain holds me captive. That madman has me at his mercy, and come Saturday, there will be no mercy. I cannot see any way out. I know you understand my fear, Lord Jesus, even as Your disciples were so afraid that day in the ship. Help me."

Breanna thought of the killer's face, always guarded beyond her view by shadows. If only she could see the man's face and know for sure who he was!

Then it struck her. The killer's face was like the things of faith...*not seen.*

The Lord had allowed her to be in this life-threatening situation, which by mortal standards was absolutely hopeless, to teach her to trust Him more. Her entire plight was involved in *things not seen.*

She ran her tongue around inside her dry mouth. She needed water, and her body needed to be off the floor for a little while before she lay down for the night. She rose to her feet, picked up the usual length of chain, and dragged it into the kitchen. Moonlight filled the room with a faint silver hue. She dipped water from the bucket and took her fill.

Dragging the chain, she went to the back door and stepped out on the porch, filling her lungs with the fresh night air. After her session with the maniac in the confines of the cabin, it felt good.

She looked northward up the canyon and thought of the many streams among the peaks above timberline that fed the Crystal. She set her gaze once more on the river in front of her, and it seemed the water was even higher above the bank than earlier. Suddenly something moved in her peripheral vision. When she turned to focus on it, she realized she was looking at a huge male cougar. He was standing at the river's swollen edge, and at the same instant that she saw him, his head came around and he spotted her.

His powerful muscles tensed, and he bared his teeth in a deep-throated roar. The pale moonlight showed Breanna the glint of his yellow eyes as he sprang from the spot and headed toward her. There was a slight limp to his gait, but he was clearly intent on her.

Breanna whirled and rushed through the door, swinging it hard to close it. She felt the door hit the length of chain that still lay over the sill, and its rebound slipped the latch handle from her grasp.

As if sensing the human creature's fear, the fierce beast opened his jaws wide, exposing his glistening yellow-white incisors, and roared. The sound sent chills down Breanna's spine as she seized the length of chain and yanked it toward her and lost her balance and fell.

Breanna groped her way up the door frame to a standing position and managed to jerk the full length of the chain inside. With trembling hands, she slammed the door and slid the bolt home just as the big cat hit the door with his full weight, making a loud *thump*. He landed on the porch floor with a threatening growl, then hit the door again.

Breanna sucked hard for breath and backed away from the door till she bumped into the post to which she was chained.

As the cougar clawed savagely at the door, the latch clattered as if it would give way.

While cold sweat ran down her face, and her eyes stayed fixed on the ever-weakening door, Breanna prayed with a trilling voice, "Please, Lord! Please! Protect me! He's going to come through that door!"

As suddenly as it had started, the roaring and clawing stopped.

Breanna waited breathlessly, but the cougar didn't renew his attack. Rather, Breanna could hear him breathing laboriously. Seconds later, she heard him leave the porch.

"Oh, thank You, Lord!" she gasped, dry-mouthed. "Thank You!" Drawing a shaky breath, she said in a tremulous whisper, "Thank You, Lord Jesus. Thank You. What manner of Man is this, that even the beasts of the mountains obey Him!"

Moving on watery knees, Breanna dragged the chain into the kitchen and went to the cupboard. Cautiously, she inched up to the corner of the window. The cougar was standing at the edge of the swollen river, looking back toward the cabin. His tail swayed back and forth.

She ran a trembling palm over her eyes and said, "Lord Jesus, truly I have seen Your mighty hand on me tonight!"

The cougar looked up and down the river as if deciding what to do next, then turned and looked directly at the cabin again. As if he realized he had been cheated of a kill, he threw his head back and ejected an angry roar.

Breanna ran her tongue over dry lips. "Go away, kitty. Go away. Please go away."

The cougar turned and headed downstream. Breanna noticed his limp. It was his right forepaw that gave him trouble. The moon gave her enough light to see that part of it was missing.

It was Half-Paw!

She shuddered as she thought of the people who had been mauled by the man-hating mountain lion. She stood at the window for several minutes, looking at the last spot where she had seen Half-Paw, but he did not return.

Slowly, Breanna turned and went to the post. She lay down next to it on the floor, and said softly, "Oh, John, this has been such a frightful ordeal. I need you, darling. I need your strong arms around me. John, have you gotten back to Denver yet? Do you know about my disappearance from Redstone?"

Breanna made herself as comfortable as possible on the floor, and after some time, fell asleep while talking to the Lord.

20

WHEN TWILIGHT WAS FALLING over Redstone on Thursday evening, Marshal Mike Halloran and his three partners were riding abreast as they drew near town. The roaring Crystal River was spilling over its banks as they followed it southward.

Paul Trevick glanced at Halloran. "Marshal, I know you feel terrible about this, but all we can do is keep trying. Mrs. Brockman has to be *somewhere.*"

"Yeah," sighed Halloran. "Somewhere. But where?"

"Well, we have to face it, Marshal," said Conrad Wiseman, "the killer could have carried her body somewhere up in those mountains and thrown it in some narrow crevice where nobody would ever find it."

"I know, but it simply isn't his style. I just can't shake this feeling that she's either still alive and being held captive by him for reasons unknown, or if she's dead, he'll want us to see what he did to her. He'll make the body appear so we'll know of his accomplishment."

"You still planning on holding that meeting this evening, Marshal?" asked Clark Bentley.

They were entering Redstone on Main Street.

"Have to," said Halloran "I think some of the men in the

search parties are wearying of it, and I've got to keep them in the saddle. We can't let up. We've got to keep looking till we find her."

Up ahead, they could see horses and riders gathered in front of the marshal's office, and two more teams were coming in from the south side of town.

"Reason I asked, Marshal," said Bentley, "is that I can't make it to the meeting. I want you to know, though, that I'm with you all the way. I'll plan on riding out with you at sunup in the morning."

"Good enough, Clark," said Halloran. "We'll see you then."

The marshal and his partners drew up to the group, who were looking as whipped as Halloran felt.

"Nothing, fellas?" said Halloran.

There was a chorus of negative answers.

It was the same when the other two teams drew up. They had not found a trace of Breanna Brockman.

"As I told you this morning, men," said Halloran, "if we didn't find her today, I wanted to meet with all of you at the church after supper. This still all right, Pastor?"

"Sure," replied Eldon Severson. "Seven-thirty?"

"Right. Seven-thirty. Now, you boys all go home and eat yourselves a good supper. See you at the church at seven-thirty."

Marcie was at the door to greet her husband with a hug and kiss as he came through the door.

Mike held her in his arms and sighed. "We didn't find a thing, honey."

"You're still having the meeting tonight?"

"Yeah. Have to. At seven-thirty."

"Well, get washed up, sweetheart," she said, squeezing him around his slender waist. "I've got fried chicken for you with all the trimmings."

"Hey! Sounds mighty good!" he said, trying to lift himself from the doldrums.

Marcie was putting the last of the steaming plates and bowls on the table while Mike washed up at a small table by the cupboard.

"Do you think any of the men will quit on you?" she asked while he was drying his face.

"I can't be sure till I meet with them, but I know they have to get back to their jobs soon. I'm just hoping they'll stay with me a few more days. Something's got to turn up, Marcie. It just has to. I can't write Breanna off as a lost case."

Marcie smiled at him across the table. "You still feel that she's alive, don't you?"

"Yes. Maybe it's just wishful thinking, but I do. There haven't been any more killings, or even someone reporting any disturbances since Breanna disappeared. It's like maybe the killer's got her locked up somewhere and is occupying himself with his captive."

Marcie's features paled. "Oh, Mike, you don't think he'd be torturing her, do you?"

Mike sighed. "With that maniac, honey, it's hard to say. He's such a—"

His words were interrupted by a knock at the front door.

"I'll get it, honey," he said, and left the kitchen.

There was a second knock as Mike neared the door. He opened it to find Woody Jones with a yellow envelope in his hand.

"Telegram from Chief U.S. Marshal Brockman in Denver, Marshal."

"Oh, thanks, Woody. I've been hoping I'd hear from him soon."

"No sign of Mrs. Brockman today, I take it, Marshal?"

Ah…no, Woody. Nothing."

"Well, bless her heart, I sure hope she's all right. I guess as long as her body hasn't been found, we can assume she's still alive, can't we?"

"I'm assuming it with all of my heart."

"Good. Then I'll keep doin' it, too. See you later, Marshal."

"Yes, Woody. And thanks, again."

Mike closed the door and ripped the envelope open. He read the message and hurried back to the kitchen.

"Mike, is that from Breanna's husband?"

"Yes. He's taking the Grand Junction train out of Denver in the morning. Says he'll rent a horse in Glenwood Springs and ride down here. Expects to be here between one and two o'clock."

Marcie nodded. "I…wish you had some good news to give him when he arrives."

"Yeah. So do I. Well, maybe tomorrow morning will bring that good news. I'll have to take somebody else along with Paul, Conrad, and Clark in the morning, so there'll still be four when I head back. I want to be here when Brockman arrives."

Marcie frowned and shook her head as she sat down at the table. "I just can't believe the killer would be one of those three men."

"I can't either, honey," Mike said, pulling out his own chair and sitting down. "But that maniac is somebody we all know and trust."

It was almost ten o'clock that night when Marcie looked up from her sewing table at the sound of a rider moving past the side of the house. She laid down her needle and thread and pulled off the thimble. Picking up the Colt .45 Mike had trained her to use, she made her way to the kitchen and looked out the window. She saw her husband dismount in the moonlight and lead his horse into the barn.

When she heard him mount the porch, she called through the door, "What's the password? If you don't know the password, you'd better leave because I'll shoot through the door!"

"The password is *Snowmass,*" came his reply.

Marcie opened the door to her smiling husband, who stepped in and said, "Good girl. Just in case that madman can adopt disguises, I want you to do exactly as you said if you don't get the password. Give a warning, and if whoever is on the porch doesn't leave, start shooting."

"I will," she assured him. "So how'd it go?"

"I'm glad to tell you that not one man is backing out yet. They all want to find Breanna as much as I do, even if it means having to ride farther each day as they search."

"Good."

"I told them about Brockman's wire, and everybody's glad he's coming." He paused. "Well, everybody except the killer, if he's among the searchers."

At first, Breanna wasn't sure what had made her suddenly sit up and open her eyes in the dark cabin.

And then it came again.

A loud, thundering noise at the back door.

This time, there was a bone-chilling growl.

Half-Paw! He was back!

There was a high-pitched snarl, and the sound of powerful

claws tearing at the door, shaking it, and making the hinges rattle.

Suddenly the cabin door splintered and swung open.

A bloodcurdling scream escaped Breanna's mouth as the man-killing cougar came through the door, setting his yellow eyes on her.

She backed away from the post as far as the chain would allow, her arms and legs tingling, and her pulse pounding in her temples. Half-Paw crouched, ready to spring at her.

Another scream came from deep within her as the cougar lunged with claws distended.

Instinctively, she tried to jump back further, but the clamp on her ankle bit into the leather of her high-top shoe, and she fell flat on her back.

The beast was on her in a flash, roaring and snarling as he ripped and tore at her flesh.

Suddenly Breanna sat up, the echo of her scream still in her ears.

The nightmare had shaken her like a leaf in the autumn wind, and she gasped for breath as she looked around the dark cabin. The moonlight was paler than when she had fallen asleep, but the roar of the river was still deafening as it echoed off the walls of the canyon.

Using the post to get to her feet, Breanna muttered, "Only a nightmare. But it sure was real."

She picked up the length of chain and walked to the water bucket and scooped up a dipperful of water. Drinking slowly, she emptied the dipper, hung it back on the side of the bucket, and looked out the window.

The moon shone silvery on the surface of the raging Crystal, but it had moved to the southern sky and was barely visible from Breanna's viewpoint. Her line of sight trailed to the spot where she had last seen Half-Paw. "Good kitty," she said. "You didn't really come back to get me. Just stay away, too, won't you?"

She moved back to her usual spot and laid down.

"John," she said softly. "I need you, darling. I need you."

At the Brockman place outside of Denver, John Brockman stirred in his bed and sat up. Looking around the moonlit room, he said, "Lord, that dream was all too real. It was like Breanna was calling to me."

He threw back the covers and swung his long legs over the edge of the bed. After a moment, he stood up and walked to one of the windows. The moon was in the southern sky now.

John padded across the room to the west window. Gazing at the starry sky, he said, "Breanna, darlin', I'm coming. You just hold on."

He began pacing back and forth. "Lord," he said, "the cry of her voice in my sleep was real. Breanna's in grave danger. I know it. Please, God, keep Your mighty hand on her."

He paused in his pacing and went to the west window again. "Lord, other than You, Breanna is my whole life. You brought us together through circumstances that could very easily have kept us apart *after* we had met and fallen in love. You know how many times we were blocked from getting married. Now that she is finally my wife, Lord, I don't want to lose her. You know where she is and what she's facing. Please protect her and let me find her alive and unharmed when I get to Redstone."

Some two hours later, after much more prayer, John slipped

back into bed. He slept lightly and awakened at dawn.

Three hours later, he boarded the train at Denver's Union Station, still praying, and trusting the Lord to take care of his precious wife.

When Breanna awakened, it was barely light outside. The roar of the river seemed louder, but even above its thunderous sound, she heard the wind coming down the canyon in a fierce howl.

Rising stiffly from the floor, she dragged the chain into the kitchen and looked out the window. What she saw took her breath. She estimated the river was now within fifteen feet of the cabin. And it was beginning to rain.

Bulging black thunderclouds hung low, bursting with water and rumbling sounds. The wind was slapping rain against the window as if to mock her.

A bolt of lightning struck close by, making her jump. Its white flare showed Breanna her own startled face reflected in the rain-specked window pane.

Breanna leaned close to the window and scanned the porch and the area around it. No Half-Paw. Dragging the chain to the door, she opened it cautiously and looked out. A shudder went down her spine when she saw the way the cougar had shredded the door with his claws. Thank the Lord the door was thick and strong.

She ran her gaze carefully over the area again and made her way to the privy in the driving rain. Returning moments later, she closed the door, slid the bolt, and went to the kitchen. She was dripping wet, but she would have to let herself dry off naturally since there were no towels.

She ate her meager breakfast of hardtack and water while

looking at the storm and the rising river through the window.

When she swallowed the last piece of hardtack, she said, "Lord, You are the great and almighty God of the universe. Only You can make tomorrow a happy birthday."

The storm grew worse and the rain came down in sheets.

Breanna picked up her Bible and returned to the kitchen. Opening the Bible to Hebrews chapter eleven, she laid it on the cupboard and slowly read through the entire chapter. As she came to each person listed, she considered how they got their names in there by trusting God in various ways and under different circumstances.

Her attention was drawn to verses 32 and 33:

> And what shall I more say? for the time would fail me to tell of Gideon, and of Barak, and of Samson, and of Jephthae; of David also, and Samuel, and of the prophets: Who, through faith subdued kingdoms, wrought righteousness, obtained promises, stopped the mouths of lions—

Breanna's jaw slacked. "Stopped the mouths of lions! Yes! Yes, Lord! Through faith they stopped the mouths of lions! You gave them the faith to believe You for deliverance from ravening lions. And when they exercised that faith, *You* stopped the lions from devouring them! Just like you did for me last night. Dear Lord, I'm asking You to keep that beast from coming back. Please stop his mouth against me by sending him high into the mountains somewhere."

Her eyes fell on verse 34:

> Quenched the violence of fire, escaped the edge of the sword—

"Oh, dear God," she said breathlessly, "I'm trusting You to

let me escape the edge of the sword in this situation. I can't see how You are going to do it, but by faith, which is the evidence of things not seen, I am believing You for deliverance from the river, the cougar, and the killer."

It was one forty-five on Friday afternoon when John Brockman rode into Redstone, his head bent against the wind and the driving rain. He hauled up in front of the marshal's office and dismounted.

Stepping under the partial protection of the canopy over the boardwalk, John tilted his hat to let the rain run off the brim, shook his slicker to rid it of excess moisture, and was about to reach for the doorknob when the door swung open and the man with the town marshal's star on his vest said, "Come in, Chief Brockman! I'm glad you're here."

Stepping into the office, Brockman shook Halloran's hand. "Marshal Halloran, it's good to meet you."

The town marshal was more than six feet tall, but Brockman towered over him.

"The pleasure is mine, sir," said Halloran. "You don't remember me, I'm sure, but we met once when you were only known as The Stranger."

Removing his slicker, Brockman said, "Where was that?"

"Santa Fe. 'Bout eight years ago. You kept a gang of bank robbers from getting away with the money, and—"

"Oh, sure!" said John. "I remember now. You were a deputy under Santa Fe's Marshal Ben Richman."

"Yes, sir."

"I thought your name rang a bell, but I couldn't place you. Happy to see you again. Now, what can you tell me about my wife?"

Halloran's features sagged. "We haven't found a trace of her, sir. I've got almost a hundred men out there on the search right now, in spite of the weather. We haven't let up since Monday, and we're not going to let up till we find her."

"I appreciate that," John said. "Marshal, Breanna said nothing at all to me about a killer being on the loose in this town before she left Denver to come here. Do you have any idea if Dr. Lowry had told her about him?"

"Ah...well, no. He hadn't. She was unaware of the situation when she came."

"I thought so. I'm wondering why Dr. Lowry didn't warn her before she got here."

"You'll have to take that up with him, sir."

"I will," said Brockman levelly. "Now. I'd like to hear the whole story on this killer, and I want the details about Breanna's disappearance."

John listened intently to every detail of the psychopathic killer's moves and who his victims were. He learned that Breanna's disappearance was after the special "going away" time in her honor on Sunday night. Halloran closed off by explaining that he had requested of the landlady at the boardinghouse that she not rent the room until John could see where Breanna had been staying.

"Good," said Brockman. "I'd like to take a look at the room. In fact, I'll just rent it while I'm here if the landlady will let me. Right now, I'd like to talk to Dr. Lowry."

Martha Waverly was at her desk when the door opened and the two lawmen entered, rain dripping from their hats and slickers.

"Hello, Martha," said Halloran. "This is Breanna's husband, Chief U.S. Marshal John Brockman."

Martha smiled weakly. "I am glad to meet you, Chief, but I wish it were under different circumstances. I'm so sorry about your dear wife."

"Thank you, ma'am," John said softly. "I would like to talk to Dr. Lowry if he's available."

"He's working in the back. I'll tell him you're here."

While they waited for Martha to return with the doctor, Brockman said, "Marshal, I didn't ask you back there in your office, but is there a man or men in Redstone that you suspect could be the killer?"

Halloran lifted his hat, scratched the back of his head, and replied, "Well, sir, there are some men who have crossed my mind, but only because they might have a bad temper, or even are just physically strong, which the killer definitely is, but not one of them has given me any reason to suspect him by his behavior."

Brockman nodded. "Of course, but just because the killer has shown great strength when he has murdered his victims doesn't necessarily mean he looks strong. Psychopathic killers are exceptionally strong. Even small men, who are not muscular, have proven to be very strong when they're killing their victims."

Halloran rubbed his chin. "I've heard that, sir, but I guess it's just natural for me to assume that our resident psychopath is a big man."

"Chief Brockman!" said Dr. McClay Lowry, entering the office with Martha on his heels.

While the two men were shaking hands, Lowry said, "I'm so sorry about what has happened to your wife. She is such a sweet person. This whole thing has me very upset."

"I appreciate that, Doctor," said John. "Marshal Halloran has filled me in on all of the details regarding the murders and

Breanna's disappearance. I understand you were with her at the church service on Sunday night."

"Yes."

"Did she seem nervous or upset in any way?"

"Not at all."

"So it wasn't like she had already been threatened or anything like that?"

"No, sir."

"And as far as you know, she wasn't afraid of anybody in town?"

Lowry rubbed his jaw. "Well, she had one patient who seemed to intimidate her a little."

"And who is this?"

"His name's Bart Gibson. He came into the office with a splinter in his eyeball. I wasn't here. He insisted that Breanna remove the splinter, though she told him she was not qualified. He pressured her so hard that she went ahead. He lost the sight in his eye, and he blamed her for it. When I explained that no matter who took the splinter out, he would have lost sight in the eye, he cooled down and apologized to Breanna. But—"

"But what?" asked Brockman.

"Well, she seemed to fear him even after the apology."

"You think he might be the killer?"

"No more than any other man in town," said Lowry. "Bart has been faithful to ride in a search party every day."

"You want to talk to Bart, Chief?" asked Halloran.

"Not at this point." Then to Lowry: "Doctor, I do have one question just for you."

Lowry blinked. "Of course."

"Why didn't you warn Breanna about this killer being on the loose when you engaged her to come and work for you?"

The doctor's face flushed. "She asked me the same question, sir. As did Martha when she came. With both nurses, I feared they wouldn't come if I did. And I was so confident that the madman would be caught even before Breanna came. I really needed her as now I really need Martha. I was wrong not to warn both of them. I apologized to Breanna and I've apologized to Martha. I now apologize to you, Chief Brockman, for not telling Breanna about the killer before I let her come here. I'm truly sorry."

"I accept your apology, Doctor," said John. "I'd like to think that if you had warned her, she wouldn't have come, and she wouldn't be missing right now. But I know my wife too well. Since she knew you were desperate for help until your new nurse arrived, she would have come in spite of the warning."

"I'm sure she would have," agreed Lowry. "She's that kind of woman."

"Just one other thing, Doctor."

"Yes?"

"I know about psychopathic killers in general, but I'm sure you know more than I do. Are they usually as cunning as this one? I mean, to live among the people of this town and not ever slip up and give one little clue that he's the one doing the killing. Could a psychopathic killer really be that sharp?"

"Oh, yes. They aren't always as cunning as this one, but they certainly can be."

"Be honest with me now and don't spare me. Do you think there is a remote chance Breanna is still alive?"

Lowry studied John's angular face for a few seconds. "I think she may very well be alive. The maniac may have her locked up somewhere."

"But from what the marshal tells me, the killer has not done this with any of the other victims. He's killed them on the spot and left their bodies so they could easily be found. Why would he change his pattern this time?"

Lowry pulled at an ear. "Psychopaths are very unpredictable. They often change or vary their patterns. This is not that unusual."

"I see. All right. You've given me some encouragement, Doctor. Thank you. And thank you for your time."

"You're most welcome," said Lowry. "I want you to know that I volunteered to be in a search party, but Marshal Mike asked me to stay here so that if Breanna should be found and need medical attention, I would be available."

John patted Lowry's shoulder. "I appreciate that you volunteered, Doctor, but I agree with Marshal Halloran. In case she needs you, I want you readily available. Thanks again."

21

As JOHN BROCKMAN and Mike Halloran walked back toward the marshal's office under the canopy covering the boardwalk, John said, "We haven't talked about what precautions you're taking to protect the people from the killer."

"I've organized patrol teams to stay on the streets in shifts all night long every night. I've also ordered the townspeople to stay off the streets after dark unless they are in large groups, like the people who attend the church. I've warned them to keep their doors and windows locked and to be very, very careful who they let into their homes. They are also to keep firearms handy should the killer break through a door or window, which he has been known to do. That's how Mrs. Lowry was killed. That maniac crashed through the door and took her by surprise."

They drew up to Halloran's office. As they stepped inside, shaking rain off their hats and slickers, John said, "Well, Mike, I guess you've done everything you can do to keep people safe."

"Yes, Chief Brockman, and if there's anything else I find I can do, I'll sure be on it in a hurry. But now what? Do you want to ride out with me and hook up with one of the search teams?"

"I'll do that in the morning since the day's getting older.

But there's something I'd like to do real soon if possible."

"Name it," said Halloran, heading for his desk.

"I'd like to meet Marcie."

Mike stopped in his tracks. "How do you know my wife's name? I haven't brought her up, and I've been with you every minute since you arrived."

John let a grin slant his mouth. "I know somebody who's related to her."

Mike's eyebrows arched. "You do? Who is it?"

"Rusty."

"Her brother? You know Rusty? Present tense?"

"Yes, sir."

"He…he's alive?"

"Sure is."

"Where is he?"

"In Denver. I saw him just yesterday. And he gave me a message to pass on to his sister when I got to Redstone."

Mike shook his head in wonderment. "Chief, this is really something! We need to go to the house right now and let you tell Marcie that Rusty's still alive! I've never met Rusty, but—"

"Yes, I know."

Halloran frowned. "How well do you know him?"

"Well enough."

"When did you meet him?"

"Couple of years ago. May of '69 to be exact."

"Where was it?"

"Los Alamos, New Mexico."

"How did you come to meet him?"

"Tell you what," said John, "so I don't have to tell this story twice, why don't we go to your house and let me tell it to you and Marcie at the same time?"

"Good idea! Let's go!"

290

Marcie Halloran had seen her husband and the man in the black slicker ride by the side of the house. She was waiting at the back door to let them in as they ran from the barn to the porch in the driving rain.

"This must be Chief Brockman!" she said.

"Yes, ma'am," said John, removing his hat. "I'm very happy to meet you, ma'am."

Marcie noticed the bright gleam in her husband's eye. "Mike, what is it? You look like the cat that swallowed the canary. I know! You found Breanna!"

Mike's head lowered. "No. Not yet. I wish we had. But—"

"Well, what brings you home this time of day? I figured once Chief Brockman arrived, you two would head out to search for Breanna."

"We had some talking to do, honey. And Chief Brockman wanted to meet Dr. Lowry. He had some questions to ask him. We'll be headlong into the search come morning unless the guys find her yet this afternoon."

"Oh, I hope they do! Mike, you started to tell me why you're here at this time of day."

"Well, when Chief Brockman and I got back to the office after he had talked with Dr. Lowry, he said he would like to meet Marcie. I hadn't told him your name."

Marcie swung her gaze to the towering Brockman. "How did you know my name?"

"Honey," cut in Mike, "before he answers that question, why don't we go sit down in the parlor?"

"Oh, of course. I'm sorry, Chief. Forgive my lack of hospitality."

"Nothing to forgive, ma'am," John said amiably.

When they were seated in the parlor John said, "The reason I know your name, Marcie—may I call you Marcie?"

"Of course."

"The reason I know your name is because I'm a friend of your brother's."

Marcie looked like she had seen a ghost. "My...my brother?"

"Mm-hmm. Rusty and I have known each other for better than two years."

"He's alive?" she squealed, tears filling her eyes. "Rusty's really alive?"

"Sure is. I was with him in Denver yesterday."

"Oh, I can't believe it! I've felt for some time that Rusty had been killed in one of his quick-draw shoot-outs, and was probably buried in some obscure, unmarked grave."

John smiled again. "Well, I've got some good news about his gunfighting. He hasn't been in a quick-draw since May of 1869."

Mike put his arm around Marcie, whose entire frame was trembling.

The Hallorans listened intently as Brockman told them how he had taken Rusty's challenge in Los Alamos, New Mexico, in May of 1869 and put a bullet in his arm instead of his heart, so that Rusty would live but never use his gun arm again.

Marcie wept for joy to hear this and to learn that Rusty had turned into a responsible citizen, and that he had come through Denver a few days earlier on his way to see them in Redstone.

John went on to tell them about the incident in front of the federal building with the two greenhorn gunslicks and of how they shot Rusty in the back outside the Westerner Hotel.

"Now, don't worry. Rusty's in the hands of the best physician and surgeon in the country, and Dr. Matthew Carroll assured me Rusty will be just fine."

Marcie was wiping tears away as Mike held her close with one arm. "Oh, I'm so glad to hear this, Chief Brockman! Thank you for coming here to tell me about Rusty! Thank you!"

"My pleasure, Marcie. Rusty asked me to be sure to see both of you and tell you about him. And he gave me a message for his sis."

"Really? What is it?"

"He said to tell you he loves you, and that as soon as he's able to travel, he'll be here to see you. He's eager to see his sister, and he's just as eager to meet his brother-in-law."

More tears spilled down Marcie's cheeks. "I'm so glad to hear this good news, Chief. Thank you for telling us, and thank you for sparing my brother at Los Alamos when you could have killed him."

John nodded. "I've done that a few other times, too. Every one of those men are now my friends. And something else I would like to tell you about Rusty."

Both waited expectantly for Brockman's next words.

"The reason he's turned out to be such a responsible citizen is that he became a born-again Christian right after I shot him in the arm. I had the joy of leading him to Christ."

Mike and Marcie exchanged glances, then looked back at Brockman.

"Ah…that's…great, Chief," said Mike.

"It sure is," Marcie said. "Must've made a real…difference in my big brother."

Brockman knew by their reaction that neither had become Christians since Rusty had last seen his sister. Pressing a smile on his lips, he said, "Do you understand what I mean when I say a born-again Christian?"

Again the Hallorans exchanged glances.

"Well, not exactly, sir," said Mike. "Pastor Eldon Severson and his wife have been in our home to explain that to us and, well…Breanna talked to us about it, too. Marcie was in the preaching service last Sunday night and learned some more about what you call being saved or born again. But neither one of us have gone any further with it."

"I don't want to shove anything down your throats," said Brockman, pulling a small Bible from his inside coat pocket, "but if you'd give me a few minutes to go over it with you and to answer any questions you might have, I'd sure appreciate it. In fact, Rusty would, too. He asked me to talk to you about it."

"Sure," said Mike.

"Of course," said Marcie.

Brockman read them several Scriptures concerning salvation, making sure they understood their need to be saved, and how it could be a reality in their lives. When he offered to help them call on the Lord, they both stiffened and said they needed to think on it some before taking the step.

John's experience in leading souls to Jesus told him it was best at that point not to press them further. *Wise as serpents and harmless as doves,* he reminded himself.

"All right," he said, "but will you promise me something?"

"What's that?" Mike asked.

"That you'll attend the services at the church. Breanna told me in one telegram that Pastor Severson is a very good preacher. Will you do that?"

"Sure we will, sir," said Mike.

"Yes," said Marcie.

"Good. Now, Mike, would you tell me how to find the home of the pastor? I'd like to meet him and his wife."

"Well, sir, right now Pastor Severson is out in one of the

search parties, looking for Breanna." He glanced at the clock on the mantel and added, "They'll be back to town in about an hour and a half."

"All right. Then how about pointing me to the boarding-house? I'd like to see Breanna's room and ask the landlady if I could rent it while I'm here."

"Sure," said the marshal. "I'll go with you and introduce you to her."

Before the two men were out the back door, Marcie looked up into Brockman's steel-gray eyes and said, "Chief, thank you again for telling us about Rusty. And thank you for caring about our eternal destiny."

"My pleasure, Marcie. I'll see you later."

After John had seen Breanna's room and her personal things and been told by Frieda Schultz that he could rent the room, they returned to the marshal's office.

The rain was letting up some.

As they sat down, John said, "Lawman's intuition, Mike. If you knew this Bart Gibson wasn't the killer, who would you suspect?"

Halloran leaned forward, putting his elbows on the desk. "Well, sir, Breanna brought up a man to me. Not that I hadn't thought of him, and I've even had some of the townspeople say they wondered about him. His name's Biff Matthews. But let me say right here that some folks have also shared their suspicions with me that Gibson could be the killer. Anyway, this Biff Matthews seemed to show up on Breanna's path just about every day, and from what she said, he always smiled at her in a way that gave her the creeps."

John felt his blood heat up. "Smiled at her. Is that all?"

"Yes, sir. That's all. It just seemed to Breanna that Biff was around her when it would have taken definite effort to be there."

"Well, Breanna's intuition is about as keen as it comes," said John. "If she felt something was wrong about this guy, there had to be something to it."

"I agree. But his actions have not warranted my grabbing him by the nape of the neck and arresting him."

"I can believe that. But I'd say he'd bear watching."

"Right. And I'm doing that. I have to say, though, that both of these men have faithfully ridden in the search teams since day one. I know that if one of them is the guilty man, he could be doing it to throw off any suspicion. The possibility of the killer taking part in the search parties is the reason I've had the men riding in fours, just like I've had the patrol teams made up of four men. I happen to think the madman *is* in both the search team and the patrol team to make himself look good. But at least, moving about in a four-man team, he's well enough outnumbered that he'd get caught for sure if he decided to try to take on three other men."

"Good thinking," said John. "From what Dr. Lowry said about the cunning and cleverness of psychopaths, I can appreciate what you've been up against."

"It's had my feet to the fire, sir. I feel so bad about not being able to stop that madman."

"Well, it's been my experience that sooner or later, even a clever psychopath will make a mistake. I think he's about due."

"I sure hope so."

"Let's talk about suspects some more. If you knew for sure that the killer wasn't Matthews or Gibson, are there others you have wondered about?"

Halloran rubbed his jaw, then shook his head. "No, sir. If

it's neither one of them, I'm fresh out of suspects."

"Keep in mind," said Brockman, "that he doesn't have to be a big man or even a young man. A psychopath gets his strength from the adrenaline produced by his insanity. From what I've read about psychopaths, even a very small man, or even an old man could have the strength to do what this killer has done."

Halloran blinked in astonishment. "I haven't thought of this possibility, Chief. From what you just said, the killer could be just about any man in this town."

"Mm-hmm. And when he *is* caught, Mike, it may surprise everyone in Redstone when they learn who he is."

Looking past Brockman through the front window, Halloran saw a wagon go by in a hurry. Rising from his chair, he said, "I think somebody's hurt, Chief."

Brockman left his chair and looked toward the street. "What do you mean?"

"A wagon just went by at a pretty good clip. There were two men in the back, leaning over someone who was lying down."

Halloran opened the door and looked up the street. "Yep. Just as I thought. They've stopped in front of Doc Lowry's office. Somebody's hurt, for sure. I've got to go see about it."

John ran toward the doctor's office with the marshal.

"I hope the killer didn't strike again," John said.

"Well, if he did, he missed killing his victim for the third time. I told you about the first two."

"Yes. Wiley Haddon and Len Drazek."

"Or it could be Half-Paw," said the marshal. "He's missed killing some of his victims, too."

"Half-Paw? Who's that?"

"Cougar. Part of his right forepaw is missing. He was killing

297

livestock in these parts for quite a while, then went to attacking humans. Bad one. Slick, too. We haven't been able to catch him."

"They can be mean," said John. "They don't usually go crazy killing humans unless some human has done them wrong."

"Yeah. It was probably some hunter or trapper who mangled his paw. That's probably why he's got it in for humans."

They drew up to the wagon to find Dr. Lowry guiding two men as they carried the victim into the office. The young man's clothing was in shreds, and there were deep claw marks on his face and chest. Lowry quickly led them to the back room, and Martha followed, closing the door.

Halloran knew all four men. He looked to the driver of the wagon and said, "Looks like Half-Paw got to Jerry, Abe."

Abe Rollins' face was pale. "He sure did, Marshal. You know Jerry and his dad live on the Crystal 'bout five miles north of town."

"Yes."

"Jack and I dropped by their place a little while ago, 'bout the time the rain was lettin' up. We were talkin' to Hank on his front porch when we heard the most awful roar come from back of the barn somewhere. Hank had his rifle with him on the porch. We ran back there, and when we came around the corner of the barn, Hank saw Half-Paw had his boy down, clawin' at him.

"Well, ol' Hank was 'fraid of hittin' Jerry if he tried to shoot Half-Paw, so he shot as close to him as was safe. It was enough to send that mountain lion a-runnin' into the woods."

"I sure hope Jerry's not hurt bad," said Halloran.

"Me, too." Abe swung his gaze to the tall man in black. "This Mrs. Brockman's husband? We heard he was comin' in today."

"Yes. John Brockman, shake hands with Abe Rollins."

"Mr. Brockman—I mean Marshal Brockman, sir, I sure hope your little wife turns up alive and well."

"Thank you, Mr. Rollins."

At that moment, the two men who had carried Jerry into the doctor's office came out.

"What's the verdict, Hank?" Abe asked.

"Doc says the lacerations are all superficial. He'll be all right."

"Well, great! I'm glad to hear that!"

The marshal introduced Hank and Jack to John Brockman, then the two lawmen headed back toward the office.

As they walked together, John said, "Something else I wanted to ask you, Mike."

"Sure."

"You've probably already taken care of this, but since there is the possibility that this madman has Breanna held captive somewhere, have all the buildings in town and in the area been searched?"

"Yes, sir. For about ten miles in every direction. And as we spread out further in our search each day, every building is searched thoroughly. We don't count a house, barn, shed, or privy as clear until its been searched."

"I figured so, but just wanted to make sure."

"Doesn't insult me when you ask such questions, Chief," said Mike. "I'm open to anything you might suggest. If you think of—"

A drumming of horses' hooves came to their ears, and Mike Halloran turned around to see two of his search teams riding in.

"Looks like the boys are coming in now, Chief. We'll meet at my office."

Both John and Mike listened as the teams reported they had found nothing. By the time all the others were in, with nothing positive to report, John expressed his appreciation to the men for what they were doing and told them he would be joining them in the morning.

The men told Halloran they would be there to ride out again, no matter what kind of weather. There was some talk as they rode away about the rising of the Crystal River and the possibility of flooding.

One man dismounted while Halloran was talking to his own team of searchers and approached the tall man in black.

"Chief Brockman," he said, extending his hand. "I'm Eldon Severson, pastor of the church here in town."

John reached for his hand and smiled. "I'm very happy to meet you, Pastor. Breanna told me in one of her wires that she really liked your preaching."

"I'm honored that she feels that way, sir," said Severson. "You have a wonderful wife. And—"

"Yes, pastor?"

Tears misted the preacher's eyes. "We're not giving up, Chief. The folks in our church are praying for Breanna. We're trusting the Lord to bring her back to us—Excuse me. We just feel like she's a part of us. I mean, we're trusting the Lord to bring her back to you, safe and sound."

"Me, too, Pastor. And I can't tell you what it means that you have taken her to your hearts as you have. Everybody in our church in Denver is praying like that, too. Do you happen to know my pastor, Robert Bayless?"

"No, but I've heard of him and of that great church. I'd sure like to meet him."

"Maybe someday you can," said John. "If not here on earth, then in glory."

"Yes, praise the Lord."

Looking over his shoulder, Brockman noted that Halloran was still talking to the men who had made up his team. Keeping his voice low, he said, "Pastor, I appreciate the interest you've shown in the spiritual welfare of the Hallorans."

Severson smiled. "We're not giving up on them, either. I know Breanna has witnessed to them. Did they tell you we'd been coming around now and then?"

"Yes. I gave them the gospel today and tried to draw the net, but they're still hesitant about receiving the Lord. However, they have a good attitude. I'm sure that if you stay with them, you'll win them."

"That's the plan."

The nearby conversation broke off, and Halloran headed toward the preacher and Brockman.

"Well, Pastor," Halloran said, "I guess I'd better take the chief, here, and feed him. I think Marcie's fixing something real good."

"I hear she's a splendid cook," said Severson. "Guess I'd better get home to my own cook. Gentlemen, I'll see you at daylight in the morning."

"Sure enough," said Halloran.

"Thanks for your prayers on Breanna's behalf, Pastor," said John.

Severson mounted his horse and looked at John. "We have a great big powerful God, Chief. I believe He is going to deliver Breanna right into your arms."

"Amen!" John said.

"Amen!" echoed Mike Halloran.

✦

The night was crisp and cool in the mountains.

Breanna stood at the cupboard, chewing the dry hardtack. Her water bucket was empty.

She set her eyes on the window but could see nothing outside. The sky was heavy with clouds, and the night was pitch-black. Although it had stopped raining late in the afternoon, the last time Breanna saw the river before darkness fell, it was no less than three feet from the back porch of the cabin and raging worse than ever. She could easily step out the door and fill her bucket, but she knew the water would be murky with foreign matter the river had picked up.

She was just finishing the last of the hardtack when she thought she heard hoofbeats and the rattle of a wagon. Turning away from the window, she pressed her back to the cupboard and waited.

She heard the door swing open and bang against the small table that held the lantern.

"Breanna-a-a!" came the killer's hoarse whisper. "Are you seated at the post?"

"No," she replied coldly. "I'm in the kitchen by the window."

He stepped further into the cabin. "I'm only staying a moment. I just wanted to make sure you and Mother are still here."

"Your mother never has been here," Breanna said, "but where do you think I would go with my ankle chained to the post?"

He laughed. "Well, I've worried some that the two of you would find a way to escape." He laughed again. "But how foolish of me to worry. Even the two of you together couldn't out-smart me."

"There aren't two of us," insisted Breanna. "There's just me."

The killer stomped to the edge of the kitchen, breathing wildly. "I know you're in there, Mother! You can't fool me! Don't cover for her, Breanna! The wicked woman is there, all right! Aren't you, Mother."

The only sound was the angry river, its rage magnified by the thundering echoes off the canyon walls.

"Okay, don't say anything! I know you're in there, Mother! And I'm looking forward to your moment of death tomorrow. I enjoyed killing you before, but the second and final time will be even better."

"Listen to me!" cried Breanna, unable to even make out his form in the pitch-black darkness. "People don't come back from the dead in spirit or in body! Your mother is not inside me! There is no reason to kill me!"

The angry man came closer and said "You will die tomor-row morning, Breanna-a-a! And when you die, she dies!"

With that, he whirled and headed for the front door. Before stepping outside, his hoarse whisper cut through the darkness. "Happy birthday, Mother! At least it will be happy for me! And happy birthday, Breanna-a-a! Tomorrow is going to be a wonderful day!"

The door slammed shut, and the lock clicked.

Breanna could barely hear him drive the wagon away for the roar of the river.

22

BREANNA MOVED TO HER REGULAR place at the post and sat down. The maniac's words came back to her: *"You will die tomorrow morning, Breanna-a-a! Tomorrow is going to be a wonderful day!"*

He had said more than once that she would get to see his face just before he killed her.

Trembling, she said, "Lord, You know I'm trying so hard not to doubt You. I've clung to passage after passage of Scripture. I can't see how You are going to deliver me, but my faith is in the same God who delivered Shadrach, Meshach, and Abednego from the fiery furnace. Even though they went into the furnace that was seven times hotter than normal, they came out unharmed without even the smell of fire on them. Only You could have delivered them.

"Dear God, only You could have stopped the mouths of the lions when Daniel was thrown in their den. And only You, Lord Jesus, could have saved the lives of those disciples in the boat when it filled with water, and the storm was about to take it to the bottom of the sea. I'm trusting You, Lord, to deliver me, though right now it looks impossible. You are the God of the impossible. My life is in Your mighty hands, and—"

Breanna's prayer was interrupted by the sharp sound of

wood ripping and water rushing. There was a loud thump, followed by one even louder. Something was happening at the rear of the cabin. Scrambling to her feet, she picked up the length of chain and groped her way to the back door. She threw the bolt and swung open the door.

The night was dark, but her eyes told her the privy was gone. The normal shape of it at the edge of the porch against the clouded sky was no longer there.

Suddenly, as if to join the river in its assault, stark blue-white bones of lightning slashed through the thick darkness of the heavy sky directly above the cabin. Its abrupt crack made Breanna jump back through the door.

A cannonade of thunder, like a bellow of rage, joined in, shuddering the air. And then the rain came in sheets like a waterfall.

Breanna closed the door and shot the bolt home. Stumbling her way to the post, she gripped it and slid down to the floor.

Her mind went back to that day at the hospital when Dwight Moreland accused her of bungling and letting his baby die at birth. When she was hurting so deeply because of it, sweet Mary Donelson had given her a squeeze and said, "Honey, I'm not telling you anything you don't know, but I'll say it anyhow. What you just experienced is one of the prices you have to pay for being a nurse."

She had replied that it got pretty rough at times.

And then came Matt's words: "But it's still worth it, isn't it?"

"Of course," Breanna had said.

She ran trembling fingers through her hair and drew a shaky breath. She was in this awful, harrowing predicament because she was a nurse. If she had not been a nurse, she would never have come to Redstone and fallen into the hands of a savage maniac who was planning to kill her tomorrow morning.

"How about now, Breanna?" she asked herself. "Is it worth it?"

She thought back over the years of her nursing career, of the hundreds of lives she had been able to save. And the great number of souls she had led to the Lord; precious souls whom she would never have won if she had not been a nurse.

"Yes, it has been worth it!" she said through tears. "Even if I never tend to another patient, it's been worth it! But I will take care of more patients! Lots of them! Because my God is going to deliver me out of this predicament!"

While the violent storm raged outside and the river clawed at the very foundation of the cabin, Breanna Baylor Brockman clung to her Lord, trusting Him to deliver her even though it seemed impossible.

In Redstone, John Brockman found sleep elusive. He got up and lit the lantern then paced from one end of the room to the other, stopping at times to pick up some item among Breanna's personal belongings.

Outside, lightning popped and thunder rolled and rain pounded on the roof.

At one point, John found himself facing the closet door. He opened it and looked at Breanna's dresses, skirts, and blouses. Taking a dress in hand, he pressed it to his face. The sweet smell of it brought his emotions to the surface. "Oh, God," he said, weeping, "please let me find her. Let me hold her in my arms once again and feel the warmth of her love. Only You can bring her back to me. Tomorrow is her birthday, Lord. Let it be a happy one."

Not far from where John Brockman was fervently praying for his wife, the killer was bent over the couch in his own parlor, holding his head in agony.

Through clenched teeth, he railed, "Mother, these headaches are all your fault! I never had one till you slammed my head in the shed door!"

As the blood pulsed through his temples, he cried out in pain. This was the worst he could remember. The ache and the stabbing throes had never been so bad.

"Kill!" he hissed. "Yes! I must kill! This pain is too terrible to wait for relief when I kill Mother and the Brockman woman in the morning! I must kill now...tonight!"

He staggered to the kitchen and opened a drawer of knives. He took out a butcher knife with a twelve-inch blade. Pausing to put on his slicker, he carefully slid the knife blade under his belt, buttoned the slicker, and plunged out into the stormy night.

The pain was getting worse as he drew near Main Street. Suddenly he saw one of the patrol teams coming his way. He hid behind a tree. Lightning spread fiery branches across the heavy sky, clearly showing the killer the features of the four men as they walked by slowly, rain pelting their faces and dripping from the brims of their hats.

The awful pain stabbed his head, and his stomach rolled. An acid burning rose in his chest. He hated those men. They were after *him!*

For an instant, he entertained the idea of rushing them from behind and stabbing all four of them in the back. But he had enough presence of mind to know his chances of success were nil. Four men were too many for even him to take on at one time.

He waited till they vanished into the night more than a

block away, then hurried on toward Main Street. He had not bothered to put on his hat and was glad. The cold rain that peppered his head eased the pain a little.

But the only way he was going to get total relief for this particular siege was to plunge the long blade of the butcher knife into human flesh.

Woody Jones was in his apartment above the Western Union office, sitting at his kitchen table. He could hear the rain beating down on the roof and pelting the windows and exterior walls.

Before him on the table was a photo album. The storm had brought back memories, and he had taken the album from an old trunk stored in a back room.

He looked at the faded photographs of his deceased wife and himself when they were young. As he focused on one particular picture he said, "Mattie, I miss you so terribly. Do you remember the day we had this picture taken? It was just a week before our wedding. Remember? The next night, one of those east Texas rainstorms caught us outside of town in my father's buggy. Just like what's going on outside right now. Remember?"

He pulled a bandanna from his hip pocket and dabbed at his eyes, then blew his nose. Lightning lashed the sky and thunder followed.

Woody looked up toward the ceiling and said, "Sure is rainin' hard, Mattie. But, sweetheart, where you are, there are no storms. It's peaceful and nice up there with Jesus, isn't it?

"Someday, honey, I'll be comin' up there to be with you. I'm sure lookin' forward to it. 'Course, you'll have to be second in line to hug me, cause I'm going to hug the precious Lord Jesus first. I know you understand that. I'm sure you've hugged Him thousands of times since you went home to glory.

"I'm wonderin', Mattie darlin', if that nice Mrs. Brockman has come where you are. She's been missin' now for almost a week. I know folks are prayin' just like I've been that she'll be all right, but I've been thinkin' that maybe the Lord decided to let her come on home. Main thing is, if that dirty killer got to her, that she didn't suffer."

A bolt of lightning flashed close by, and thunder shook the building. While it was rumbling, Woody thought he heard a knock at the door but couldn't be sure.

When the rumbling subsided, he bent an ear toward the door, and sure enough, there was somebody knocking.

"Who'd be out in the storm at this time of night?" Woody said as he shoved the chair back and headed for the door. "Certainly no one expects me to go downstairs and send a wire at this hour."

The knocking grew louder as Woody drew up to the door. He paused, remembering Marshal Mike Halloran's warning to everyone in town about opening their door to anyone at night. The marshal had pointed out that the killer was someone everybody knew.

Woody hesitated, but the pounding persisted.

He went back to the kitchen table and picked up the lantern. Going to the window next to the door, he pulled back the curtain and held the lantern close so he could see through the rain-spattered glass.

The wet face that greeted him was very familiar, a dear friend. He had several such friends in town and would trust them with his very life.

A smile broke across the little man's face as he threw the bolt and opened the door, saying, "Howdy, my friend! You look like you don't feel so good. What can I do for you?"

Saturday morning, September 30, 1871, came to the Colorado Rockies with a clear sky and brilliant sunshine.

Breanna had not fallen asleep until nearly dawn and was in deep slumber as the sun's rays touched the kitchen window. A sudden cracking sound invaded her sleep, and she sat up with a start. She blinked against the brightness and rubbed her eyes.

There was another loud sound that came from the rear of the cabin. Breanna used the post to raise her stiff body to a standing position, picked up the length of the chain, and made her way to the kitchen window.

She was just in time to see the back porch rip loose from the house. It was instantly swept away by the raging current.

Terror gripped Breanna's heart as she saw boiling waves crashing against the back of the cabin. Water was seeping beneath the door and spreading out on the floor.

The cabin shook, and Breanna had to grab onto the post to keep from falling. The entire structure was trembling and making squeaking noises from one end to the other.

"Lord, please, please! I need You to deliver me now! If you don't, I'll perish!"

She thought of the disciples who awakened Jesus and said, *"Master, carest thou not that we perish?"*

The Scripture came back to her mind:

And he arose, and rebuked the wind, and said unto the sea, Peace, be still. And the wind ceased, and there was a great calm. And he said unto them, Why are ye so fearful? how is it that ye have no faith? And they feared exceedingly, and said one to another, What manner of man is this, that even the wind and the sea obey him?

The river roared, and the cabin shuddered.

Hanging on to the post with all her might, Breanna closed her eyes and said, "Master of heaven, earth, and sky, I need You to speak to that river and make it calm! This cabin is about to come apart and be carried downstream! Help me!"

The sun was barely peeking over the mountains as Marshal Mike Halloran and Chief U.S. Marshal John Brockman left the Halloran home on horseback after a hearty breakfast.

"If you wish, Chief," said Halloran, "you can ride with my team today. I can spread some of the other fellas out and maybe come up with another four-man team."

"Be fine with me," said Brockman, glancing at Snowmass Mountain. "Has anybody looked up on top of that peak?"

Halloran looked that way. "Well, no. I hadn't thought about it, but the killer could have taken Breanna up there."

"Right."

"Then that's where we'll go first, Chief."

"Good. Can't leave a stone unturned, Mike."

"Yes, sir. Sorry I hadn't thought of it."

"You've had a lot on your mind. Don't worry about it. We'll soon know if she's up there."

As they turned onto Main Street, they saw a few of the riders already gathered in front of the marshal's office. More were gathering as they rode up.

Halloran looked at the men and said to Brockman, "We've got about half of them. The rest will be here in the next few minutes. Come on inside."

When they entered the office, John asked, "Mike, what time does the Western Union office open?"

"Woody always has it open by seven o'clock." Mike glanced at the clock on the wall. "It's almost seven now. Why?"

"I told my acting chief in Denver that I'd wire him after I got here and let him know the situation. I'd like to send the wire before we ride out."

"Sure. I'll go with you. Time we walk over there, it'll be seven o'clock. Let's go."

Moving back outside, Halloran told the men that he and Brockman would be back in a few minutes. He would give the day's assignments when all the men had arrived.

Walking at a brisk pace, Halloran and Brockman reached the Western Union office at seven o'clock on the dot. When they stepped up to the door, Halloran took hold of the knob but found the door locked.

"That's strange. Woody's always down here a few minutes early."

"Well, maybe he's running a little late this morning," said John.

"Since our time is short, maybe I'll run up and tap on his door."

"Okay. I'll wait here."

The marshal disappeared quickly around the corner of the building.

Brockman stepped to the same corner and looked past the building at the majestic Snowmass Mountain. "Breanna," he said, "I've got this strange feeling that you are somewhere in the mountains. Are you way up there?"

⚹

Mike Halloran bounded up the back stairs of the Western Union building and noticed even before he reached the landing at the top, that Woody's door was standing open a few inches. An uneasy feeling came over him.

When he stepped onto the landing, he eased open the door and called out, "Woody! You in there? It's Mike Halloran."

Touching the door with his fingertips, he pushed it open a little further. "Woody? Hey, pal, you up?"

Silence.

Taking a deep breath, Halloran shoved the door all the way open. A gasp escaped his throat when his eyes focused on the sight before him. "Chief Brockman!" he shouted over his shoulder, "come here!"

John rounded the back corner of the building on the run. When he saw Mike standing at the open door, he raced up the stairs.

As he topped the landing, Mike said, "The killer has been here."

Woody Jones's body lay on the floor in a pool of blood, next to the back wall of his apartment.

Both lawmen moved inside and stood over the body.

"He was stabbed," Halloran said.

John nodded and knelt down. "Looks like he lived long enough for his heart to pump out a lot of blood. And I'd say by the looks of it, he's been dead for five or six hours."

John ran his gaze from the place where Woody lay to a spot in the middle of the floor just inside the front door, where blood was pooled. "Looks like he was stabbed and left for dead over here near the door, Mike. See this blood? He left a trail. Must've crawled over here after the killer left."

"Sure enough," said Halloran, following the crimson trail across the wooden floor.

John's eyes suddenly went to red marks on the wall next to the body. "Look, here, Mike. Woody must have moistened his fingertips with his blood to make these marks on the wall."

Mike's eyebrows arched. "I see. Why would he do that? Wait a minute! He was trying to write on the wall! Sure! He was trying to write out a name! Identify the killer for us before he died!" His shoulders sagged. "Too bad he died before he could tell us, Chief."

Brockman cocked his head while studying the marks. "Wait a minute, Marshal Halloran. Woody did indeed identify the killer."

Halloran's brow furrowed. "With these marks?"

"They're more than marks. It's Morse code. See the dots and dashes?"

"Yes! Those are dots and dashes! But I can't read Morse code."

"I can. Now I know who the killer is."

"Well, tell me!"

Redstone's town marshal was stunned beyond words when John told him what the dots and dashes said.

Mike Halloran was still trying to find his voice when John said, "I told you he'd make a mistake sooner or later. They always do."

"What was his mistake, Chief?"

"He didn't make sure Woody was dead before he left the apartment. Now we've got him."

Halloran closed his eyes and nodded, then shook his head in disbelief before saying, "Chief, if Breanna is alive, I know where he's got her! He owns a cabin high up in Crystal Canyon!"

↑

The killer drove his wagon up the winding road, looking down at the Crystal River.

Muttering to himself, he said, "I hope the river hasn't taken the cabin with it. No, please, no! I don't want Mother and the Brockman woman to drown! No, no! I want to kill them myself! That river can't cheat me out of it!"

He snapped the reins and screamed at the horses to go faster. Soon, he came around the last bend, drove the wagon off the road, and down toward the river. He breathed a sigh of relief when he saw the cabin still standing, though the back side was being pummeled by the fierce waves, and the privy and porch were gone.

"Yes!" he cried. "Now, you wicked old woman, you will die forever!"

As he drew near the cabin, his heart was beating wildly with the exultant joy of the kill.

He pulled rein and stopped at the front porch. "Happy birthday, Mother! Oh, yes. And happy birthday to you, too, Breanna-a-a."

Just as he was climbing down from the wagon, the horses ejected screams and bolted. The killer fell to the ground and rolled over to curse the horses and watch the wagon bound away, fishtailing behind the terrified team.

A second later, his eyes bulged when he saw the yellow-eyed beast coming at him from the side of the cabin. A shriek of terror came from his lips as he fumbled to pull the 12-inch butcher knife from under his belt.

Half-Paw took three smooth gliding bounds toward him and leaped.

23

THE TUMULTUOUS RIVER was unleashing powerful waves against the rear of the creaking log structure. Breanna could feel the weight of the current shaking the whole cabin.

"Lord Jesus!" she cried. "The sea is about to drown me! You saved Your disciples that day! I need You to save me now!"

Suddenly she heard the shrill whinny of horses at the front of the cabin and the sound of pounding hooves growing fainter. In their place she heard the low growl of a cougar followed by a man's scream. The screams continued to slice the air even above the roar of the river.

"Half-Paw!" Breanna cried, clutching the post with both hands and staring toward the front of the cabin. The windows showed her nothing, but she knew the cougar's vicious attack was taking place near the door.

Suddenly the screaming stopped.

Seconds later, the air was filled with gunfire, and the cougar roared in pain. More shots were fired and the cougar's growls of anguish stopped.

Breanna kept her eyes on the front door, her breath coming in short gasps.

When the door crashed open, a tall, broad-shouldered figure stepped inside, smoking rifle in hand.

"John!" sobbed Breanna! "Oh, John!"

The cabin was rocking and reeling on its foundation as John Brockman dashed to Breanna, with Marshal Halloran on his heels.

"It's all right, sweetheart," he said, looking at the chain clamped to her ankle and fixed to the post. "We're going to get you out of here!"

The cabin lurched to one side.

"Cover your ears, honey!" John pressed the muzzle against a link about a foot from Breanna's ankle and squeezed the trigger. The rifle roared and the chain fell apart in two pieces.

Handing Halloran the rifle, John swept Breanna up into his arms. "It's all right, honey! We'll make it!"

The cabin swayed and lurched as it began to tear away from its foundation.

"Hurry, Chief!" shouted Halloran, holding the door open.

With Breanna held close to his chest, John bolted out the door. When his feet were on solid ground, he stopped, allowing her to take in the scene.

Breanna couldn't believe it. So intent was she on seeing the killer's face that she couldn't take her eyes off him to look at the cabin when it tore away from its foundation with a high-pitched screech and a loud roar.

On the ground before them lay the dead cougar, bullet holes in his head and body. Beneath the right forepaw—which was partially missing—lay the body of the man who had come to kill her. His face was clawed horribly, but not so much that she couldn't recognize Dr. McClay Lowry. A long-bladed butcher knife lay next to his lifeless hand.

Breanna made a gagging sound as John carried her to his horse and placed her in the saddle, then swung up behind her.

"How—?" she began.

"We'll explain later how we knew it was Lowry, and how we knew where to find you, sweetheart," John said, putting his arms around her.

Mike Halloran pulled up beside them on his horse. "I'll tell you this much now, Breanna. When we found out that Lowry was the killer, I knew where to come. I knew he had this remote cabin because he brought me here one time. I figured this was where he had you."

Breanna nodded, then glanced toward the raging river where she saw what was left of the cabin bobbing in the current and coming apart as it was swept downstream.

She looked back at Lowry and Half-Paw, and said, "Stopped the mouths of lions…escaped the edge of the sword…peace, be still. What manner of man is this?"

"What did you say, honey?"

Breanna twisted in the saddle and looked into John's eyes. "I'll explain later."

He kissed the tip of her nose. "You do that. Let's go home."

As they trotted to higher ground, Breanna looked skyward and said, "Thank You, Lord Jesus, for the evidence of things not seen."

"What was that, honey?" John said.

Reaching back to pat his cheek, Breanna said, "I'll explain that later, too!"

Angel of Mercy Series

Post-Civil War nurse Breanna Baylor uses her professional skill to bring healing to the body, and her faith in the Redeemer to bring comfort to thirsty souls, valiantly serving God on the dangerous frontier.

Mail Order Bride Series

Desperate men who settled the West resorted to unconventional measures in their quest for companionship, advertising for and marrying women they'd never even met! Read about a unique and adventurous period in the history of romance.

Hannah of Fort Bridger Series

Hannah Cooper's husband dies on the dusty Oregon Trail, leaving her in charge of five children and a general store in Fort Bridger. Dependence on God fortifies her against grueling challenges and bitter tragedies.

#1	*Under the Distant Sky*	ISBN 1-57673-033-6
#2	*Consider the Lilies*	ISBN 1-57673-049-2
#3	*No Place for Fear*	ISBN 1-57673-083-2
#4	*Pillow of Stone*	ISBN 1-57673-234-7
#5	*The Perfect Gift*	ISBN 1-57673-407-2
#6	*Touch of Compassion*	ISBN 1-57673-422-6
#7	*Beyond the Valley*	ISBN 1-57673-618-0
#8	*Damascus Journey*	ISBN 1-57673-630-X

An Exciting New Series
by Bestselling Fiction Authors

Let Freedom Ring
#1 in the Shadow of Liberty Series

It is January 1886 in Russia. Vladimir Petrovna, a Christian husband and father of three, faces bankruptcy, persecution for his beliefs, and despair. The solutions lie across a perilous sea.

ISBN 1-57673-756-X

The Secret Place
#2 in the Shadow of Liberty Series

Popular authors Al and JoAnna Lacy offer a compelling question: As two young people cope with love's longings on opposite shores, can they find the serenity of God's covering in *The Secret Place?*

ISBN 1-57673-800-0

A Prince Among Them
#3 in the Shadow of Liberty Series

A bitter enemy of Queen Victoria kidnaps her favorite great-grandson. Emigrants Jeremy and Cecelia Barlow book passage on the same ship to America, facing a complex dilemma that only all-knowing God can set right.

ISBN 1-57673-880-9

Undying Love
#4 in the Shadow of Liberty Series

19-year-old Stephan Varda flees his own guilt and his father's rage in Hungary, finding undying love from his heavenly Father—and a beautiful girl—across the ocean in America.

ISBN 1-57673-930-9